Too Many Secrets

Also by Lynn Osterkamp:

Too Near the Edge

Too Far Under

Stress? Find Your Balance (nonfiction)

How To Deal With Your Parents When They
Still Treat You Like a Child (nonfiction)

Too Many Secrets

a novel

by

Lynn Osterkamp

PMI Books

Boulder, Colorado

Copyright © 2013 by Lynn Osterkamp

ISBN: 978-1-933826-486

Published by
PMI Books
an imprint of
Preventive Measures, Inc.
254 Spruce St.
Boulder, CO 80302

Printed in the United States of America

For information regarding special discounts
for bulk purchases, visit our website at:

pmibooks.com 

"To abandon oneself to principles is really to die - and to die for an impossible love which is the contrary of love."

Albert Camus

Prologue
Boulder, Colorado
November 20

Rescuers abandon search for missing Boulder woman

The Boulder County Sheriff's Department ended the official search today for Sabrina Larson, a Boulder nurse missing for twelve days from The Rainbow Lakes Campground in the Indian Peaks Wilderness area. "We've suspended the search indefinitely until we get additional information," Valene Radde, a Sheriff's Department spokeswoman said today. "Detectives will take over the effort as a missing persons case. If new information becomes available, we will resume the search."

Larson went to the Rainbow Lakes campground on Monday, November 6 to celebrate her fortieth birthday as part of a group of six Boulder women, one of whom, Rivka Ravenstar, is a Wiccan high priestess and the owner of Wiccan Wilderness Journeys. Ravenstar said, "Sabrina wanted to celebrate the life passage of her fortieth birthday with a personal journey that would allow her to enter this new stage of life consciously with strength, compassion, honor, humility, and reverence. She asked me to guide her and our friends through a purifying spiritual ceremony and a wilderness journey. Part of the process involves spending quiet, reflective hours in the company of nature until our souls echo the earth's harmony. Sabrina has not returned from her exploration, but we have not given up hope."

Ravenstar reported that on Monday night the women participated in traditional Wiccan rituals of casting a circle, singing, dancing and sharing a community meal. Tuesday morning they each set off on a 24-hour silent expedition of prayer and meditation. They took only rain gear, water, a knife, and raw organic food bars—no cell phones or other electronic devices. The women were due to return to the campground at sunrise on Wednesday, November 8. When Larson had not returned by noon of that day, Ravenstar called the Boulder County Sheriff.

Although the weather in the Indian Peaks area was unseasonably warm on November 6th and 7th, it turned cold and snowy during the afternoon of November 8.

Since Larson was reported missing, teams of searchers from the Boulder County Sheriff's Department, the Rocky Mountain Rescue Group, Front Range Rescue Dogs, and other groups have combed the Indian Peaks Wilderness area in an extensive ground search. Despite snowfall and freezing temperatures last week, more than 100 professional rescue team members coordinated by the Sheriff's Office, complemented by nearly as many citizen and military volunteers continued to scour the vicinity without success. Also, a Denver Police Department helicopter flew repeatedly over the area with Forward Looking Infra-Red (FLIR) equipment, looking for any significant heat sources, like the heat generated by a human body, within the search area. Unfortunately, nothing that couldn't be attributed to another source, such as a rescue team member, was found.

Larson's friends and relatives are hopeful that she will be found alive. Her sister, Brandi Peyton, said, "Sabrina has a strong heart. She does what is right for her to be in control of her destiny. We have confidence that she will come back to us."

Larson is 5 feet 5 inches tall, weighs 125 pounds and has short blond hair and blue eyes. She was last seen wearing jeans, a dark green fleece jacket, and brown Merrell hiking boots.

Anyone with information regarding Larson's whereabouts is asked to call the Boulder County Sheriff's Office at 303-441-4444.

Chapter 1

December 11

Waves of nausea overwhelmed me as I rushed into Turley's Restaurant at noon that icy December day. A blast of hot air smelling of fish, burgers, onions and such sent me careening to the ladies room to avoid puking on the dining room floor. Amazingly, once I was inside the safety of the stall, I managed to avert the worst, containing my sickness to dry heaves. I hurried out to the sinks to make myself presentable for my lunch meeting with Bruce, the local dot-com millionaire who funds an experimental project that is a major part of my grief-therapy practice. I was a wreck. I'd had a miserable morning, I was late to a meeting with Bruce who prizes promptness, and my shaky queasiness exacerbated my anxiety about why Bruce had summoned me.

As I calmed my breathing and dabbed at my face with a wet paper towel, the ladies room door flew open, letting in a tall blond woman wearing designer jeans and a red ribbed turtleneck, topped with a necklace of multicolored glass beads. My best friend Elisa, looking stunning as always. We both jumped in surprise, then she darted over and enveloped me in a welcome hug. "Cleo? Honey, you look under the weather. Is the morning sickness getting worse?"

"Shhh," I said. "Let's not spread the news all over Boulder." I wasn't ready to tell the world about my pregnancy, since I was only three months along, and Pablo and I aren't married. So far Elisa and Pablo are the only ones who know.

Elisa pulled back, looking up and down the room. "Sorry for the blabbing, but you know me. Sometimes my mouth works faster than my brain. The good news is it looks like we're alone in here. Now let's fix you up a little," she said, straightening my sweater. She grabbed a comb out of her bag and worked some magic on my hair.

I felt better right away. Elisa is like a big sister to me. The kind of sister who knows how to do stuff you don't, but never makes fun of you. She just helps.

"You're a lifesaver," I said, "but I have to run. I'm already late for my lunch meeting with Bruce." I headed for the door.

Elisa waved me on. "Oh—you're meeting Bruce! Well hang in there, honey, and call me later with the scoop."

Back in the dining area, I scanned the room a couple of times. Didn't see Bruce. Deep breath. Maybe I'm not as late as I thought? But no, there he is sitting with a petite dark-haired woman in a booth next to a brick wall. Unexpected. Bruce is a brilliant guy who works all the time. Divorced. No social life. Who is this woman and why did he bring her?

I hustled over to their table and slid into the booth across from them, my mind on autopilot running through possible menu choices that my gut would be willing to tolerate. "Sorry to be late," I muttered, hoping my winning smile would distract from my tardiness. "Good to see you, Bruce."

"Hi, Cleo, I thought you forgot. This is my sister, Gayle. She needs your help."

Whew! A relief on that score. Good to know he hadn't summoned me to talk about problems with the funding for my Contact Project.

Gayle gave Bruce a poke. "Whoa, Bruce. This isn't a computer-programming job. It's personal. Let's take a few minutes before we dive in."

"Okay, let's order first, then talk," he said, burying his face in the menu.

As we perused our menus, Gayle's cell phone rang. She answered, and jumped up. "No," she said sharply into the phone. "That's not acceptable." She turned to us. "I have to take this," she said. "Be right back." She dashed toward the door, talking intently into the phone with her hand over her other ear to block the restaurant noise.

"Gayle's a real estate agent," Bruce explained. "Her phone is her life."

We sat quietly looking at our menus. Bruce isn't much of a talker. He's a techie. Brainy, but basically shy. Even though he's forty-five and a self-made multi-millionaire, his social skills aren't well developed. He's one of those guys who goes around looking at the floor or off into the distance so he doesn't have to make eye contact. Small talk is definitely not his forte.

Gayle darted back across the room to our booth. "Sorry," she said. "I'm ready to order if you two are."

I took a last look at the menu. Turley's trademark is its healthy food, and in addition to more traditional lunch and dinner entrees, they serve breakfast all day. Knowing I needed protein for the baby, I decided on a garden omelet with mushrooms, spinach, and tomato with toast on the side. Hoped I could get it down with the help of a ginger ale. Bruce ordered a buffalo burger with a side of fresh fruit, and Gayle ordered the sesame spinach salad with the dressing on the side.

"So like I was saying," Bruce began as the waitress left to turn our orders in, "Gayle needs some help from you."

I turned to her. "Would you like to tell me about it?"

She took a deep breath and launched in to her story. "You've probably heard about the woman who went missing from the Rainbow Lakes Campground in the Indian Peaks Wilderness area a few weeks ago."

"I did," I said. "Do you know her?"

Gayle looked down at the table silently for a couple of minutes, her shoulders slumped as if the weight of her problem was a burden too heavy to lift. When she finally looked up, tears streamed down her face. "She's my best friend, Sabrina—or maybe I should say she *was* my best friend. She's probably dead. But they can't find her and we don't know what happened to her and that's even worse." She wiped her face with a tissue, but her tears continued to flow.

Bruce put his arm around Gayle's shoulders and hugged her. More empathy than I would have expected from him, but then again until today I didn't even know he had a sister. All I know about Bruce is what he told me in his grief therapy sessions after his eighteen-year-old daughter died from a drug overdose. He's such a private person, he would have never come for grief counseling except that his business partner—who saw how paralyzed Bruce was after his daughter's death—insisted. Bruce's relationship with his daughter had been stormy for several years before she died, and his deep regrets that they hadn't made peace had intensified his grief.

Gayle continued wiping her face as she struggled to regain her composure. But I could see grief winning out. "Take your time," I said gently. "I know it's hard to talk about."

Her face crumpled. "I've cried so much in the past few weeks that I've made myself sick," she sobbed. "I'm totally devastated about Sabrina."

She closed her eyes, took a deep breath and collected herself. "Okay. I'm ready to tell you the story," she said quietly. "I was part of the group at the campground—there were six of us who've been friends for years. We each went off separately on our personal journeys and Sabrina never came back. We searched, the rescue groups searched, the dogs searched, the helicopter searched. But no one has found her. And now they're calling off the search." She closed her eyes and leaned back in her seat.

The waitress showed up with our lunch. I took a quick bite, which actually tasted good. Bruce spread mustard on his burger and bit in.

Gayle picked at her salad. "I was blown away when Bruce told me about your Contact Project—that he actually talked to his daughter Charlene after she died and how he resolved things with her," she said, her voice perking up a little. "At first I didn't believe him when he said you put him in your apparition chamber. It's so unlike Bruce to have anything to do with the paranormal. He debunks everything. When he told me he reached Charlene, and they forgave each other and said goodbye, I knew it was real for him."

Bruce put his burger down. "I don't debunk everything," he said.

"Ha!" Gayle said. "Remember when I played the DVD of that movie, *What the Bleep Do We Know?* for you last year? You went on and on about how it misrepresented science, that it was pseudoscience, and quantum mysticism. You weren't open to it at all, even though so many people liked it that it's made over $16 million."

Bruce scowled. "Gayle, the science was unsupported and incorrect. New Age hogwash. One of their so-called experts turned out to be a 35,000 year-old spirit from Atlantis." Bruce gave her a self-satisfied grin as he speared a chunk of pineapple with his fork and returned to eating.

She laughed and gave him another poke. "Bruce, I've told you before, you totally missed the point. The movie is supposed to blow your mind, not engage it in an analysis. It's about learning to become the creative force in your own life, instead of being a victim of circumstances. My friends and I have watched it over and over. We know group consciousness can change reality. If you looked up from your computer now and then, you'd see."

They were off the track here, but I hesitated to break into habitual brother-sister banter. Also, I figured Gayle needed a few minutes to relax before we talked more about her missing friend. I focused on my lunch, thankful I could eat without gagging.

Bruce ignored Gayle's jeers and turned to me. "Here's the thing, Cleo," he said. "Gayle needs to go into your apparition chamber and try to contact Sabrina to find out if she's dead or alive. She needs to know and the sooner the better."

Uh oh. As soon as Gayle said they didn't know whether or not Sabrina was dead, I should have guessed this was what Bruce wanted. But my apparition chamber is for grief-therapy clients who want to reach a loved one to resolve an issue, not for solving missing-person cases. I didn't want to refuse Bruce's request, but I had concerns about Gayle. "I understand that it's hard not knowing what happened to your friend," I said. "But the contact process may not make you feel any better."

Gayle looked straight into my eyes. "It's not about how I feel," she said intensely. "It's about how Sabrina's sister Brandi has taken over Sabrina's house and her son Ian. Sabrina would be furious. She expressly didn't want that to ever happen. If she's dead, everything is in trust for Ian, and I'm Ian's guardian. But Brandi jumped in as soon as Sabrina went missing, and right now she has control. So I need to know if Sabrina is dead or alive."

"I'm not sure the contact process can answer that question," I said. "You could try to reach her, but if you do, it wouldn't constitute legal proof of her death, and if you don't, that doesn't mean she's alive."

Bruce broke in. "Actually I'd already thought of that," he said. "I want you to do a thorough job. If Gayle can't reach Sabrina, then the other women who were up there should try. In fact, why not start by meeting with all of them and telling them about the process. Get some of that group consciousness going. I'll pay for your time—whatever it takes."

Before I had a chance to think about how else to voice my reservations, Bruce slid out of the booth, stood up, and picked up his coat. "I have to go. You two can go on from here. Gayle can keep me updated." He nodded at us and headed for the door.

"Oof!" Gayle said. "That's my brother. Makes his point, and ducks out before the discussion gets complicated. But I suppose you're used to his tactics."

I shrugged. I'd have to go along, at least for a while. Not only had Bruce been very generous in funding my Contact Project, all he'd asked of me was that I operate professionally and that he remain anonymous as a funder. So even though the timing wasn't ideal for me to get involved in a situation that smelled like trouble, I didn't see any other options. "No problem," I said. "Here's my card. Call me and we can set up a time to talk more."

Chapter 2

Back at my office for the afternoon, I was busy with grief-therapy clients until 5:00. Exhausted, I grabbed a ginger ale and flopped down on my couch to try to get some perspective on my miserable morning with my boyfriend, Pablo.

The morning's squabble had started at my kitchen table. I was focusing on the sunlight streaming through my kitchen window as I took deep breaths and tried to ignore the nausea the smell of Pablo's coffee brought on. I didn't want to turn into a whiny pregnant lady, so I didn't mention the nausea even though my stomach was rising into my throat. Then out of the blue he said, "Cleo, living in two places makes our lives so complicated. I feel like we're always negotiating about where we'll spend the night. I want to get this settled."

I gagged. I couldn't summon the energy for yet another Longmont vs. Boulder debate. I thought he might drop it if I didn't respond, so I just sipped my herbal tea and said nothing.

He spread some blackberry jam on his English muffin and waited, his intense brown eyes boring a hole in my forehead. I ignored his gaze, focused inward and stayed quiet. He continued staring as he finished his food and coffee, then got up and headed for the bathroom. "Fine," he said in a quiet strained voice, "I'm going for a shower. We can talk about it while you're taking me to the airport."

Not if I can help it, I thought. But of course I couldn't stop it.

Don't get me wrong, I give Pablo credit for trying to be supportive. We didn't plan this baby, but when I told him, he was as excited about it as I was, and wanted us to get married and live happily ever after in Longmont. But I wasn't ready to do that. I was ready to be a mom, but I had well-founded reservations about how happy Pablo and

I would be as a married couple, and I definitely didn't want to move to Longmont. Fighting about our future got so intense, we agreed to a moratorium on the marriage discussion until after the holidays. But we continued to haggle about where to hang out.

I love living in my grandparents' cozy old historic house nestled against the Boulder foothills. Its sloping hardwood floors, small closets and noisy plumbing are more charming than annoying, and memories of my grandparents and the happy childhood summers I spent with them fill every room. When I need comforting, I snuggle into this house. It hugs me and holds me safe like Grampa used to do before he died.

But Pablo doesn't really get my attachment. For him a house is just a place to live. He rents a generic two-bedroom ranch in Longmont. Only his artwork makes it interesting and he can easily move that to another place.

We'd compromised on spending some nights together—either in Boulder or Longmont—and some nights apart. That worked for me. I love him and I especially love spending nights together. Now Pablo was leaving for a weeklong training session in California and suddenly he wanted to settle our living arrangements.

§ § §

We took my car, but I let him drive hoping that would distract him from the conversation. It didn't. Once we were on the highway, the argument picked up for real.

"Cleo, we can't keep putting off making decisions. You don't even want to talk about it."

"True. But that's because every time we talk about it, we end up at the same place. I want to stay in Boulder in my grandparents' house. You want us to live together in Longmont."

Pablo sighed and rolled his eyes. "Look Cleo, I want to live with you. But not in Boulder, because I'm a detective with the Longmont Police Department. I've told you over and over that a huge part of what our department does involves working with the community. It's important that I live there. You know the surrounding communities think Boulderites are new-agey tofu eaters who are too rich and flakey to understand real life. Longmont residents won't take me seriously as part of their community if I live in Boulder."

Pablo pulled out to pass a long U-Haul truck. As we went by, I saw the phrase "America's moving adventure" on the side. No. I didn't want that adventure. I didn't want to move. Tears welled up. "I get that you want to live in Longmont, Pablo. But I love Boulder and I love my house and my office is right down the street. Nothing would be convenient for me if I lived in Longmont. Plus my house is really still Gramma's house."

Even though Gramma's Alzheimer's is at the point where she has to live in a sheltered assisted living home, I feel good that I'm keeping her house safe for her. I don't want to sell it and I definitely don't want to rent it to college students. I was sick of this argument. "Can't we just drop it until you get back?" I begged.

"You'll just have another reason to drop it then." Anger filled his voice. "But you're alone in that old house and it's winter and you're pregnant. I'll be gone all week." His voice softened. "What if something happens? What if you get snowed in? If you were in Longmont, all my family is nearby to help you."

Yikes! Now he wants me in Longmont even when he's not in town? And he wants his family to take care of me? I'm a thirty-seven year-old licensed therapist with a doctorate in psychology and a thriving private practice. Does he see me as weak, friendless, and incompetent? My sadness morphed into anger. "You don't need to worry," I said crossly. "I can take care of myself. I'm not going to get snowed in. And even if I did, I have friends I can call."

"Fine," he said crisply. "I give up, Cleo. You're impossible. I don't know why I try to have a reasonable discussion with you." He turned his full attention to the road without uttering another word until we got to the airport.

I stayed silent as well and kept my tears inside until I was back in the car driving away from our awkward goodbye hug. Then I let my tears flow freely as I drove. I knew I had decisions to make. But I felt stuck. I wanted all of us to have good lives—Pablo, the baby and me. But I had no idea how to work that out.

§ § §

While reliving my traumatic morning there on my office couch, darkness had closed in on me and I had almost dozed off. When my phone rang. I jolted awake, hoping it was Pablo calling to patch things up now that his plane had landed. I wanted to do that too. I wanted to hear a sweet loving voice from him to erase my memory of his anger. But when I grabbed the phone, it wasn't Pablo after all. It was Gayle wanting to set a time for a meeting.

Chapter 3

"Nothing about Sabrina's disappearance is what it seems. I can't even begin to tell Bruce and I probably shouldn't be telling you. But I have to tell someone." Gayle frowned and bit her lower lip. "This is all confidential, right?"

She was perched on the edge of the brown sofa in my office, leaning forward as if about to jump and run. When she called for this appointment yesterday, she insisted we needed to meet ASAP. Was she having second thoughts now that she was actually here?

I answered in a calm reassuring tone. "Yes, what we say here is confidential. Don't worry, I won't tell Bruce anything you don't want me to tell him."

Gayle fiddled with her purse and pulled out several crumpled papers. She glanced down at them, then up at me, then down again. "I brought a few notes so I'd remember the most important things to tell you," she said, her voice breaking. "I'm having some trouble lately keeping my thoughts organized."

"That's not surprising," I said softly. "Grief makes your thinking confused. It can be hard to concentrate and easy to forget things."

Tears dripped from Gayle's dark brown eyes. She grabbed a tissue from the box on the table and wiped her face. Then she shook her head. "I'm not here to cry. I'm here to talk." She took a deep breath and sat up straight, her shoulders down and back. "Okay. I'm going to jump right in. There's no way Sabrina just wandered off into the wilderness. She's capable and careful and used to taking care of herself." Gayle's voice rose several notches in intensity and volume and she clenched her fists. "Sabrina's a nurse for God's sake—a hospital nurse. She takes care of other people. She can certainly take care of herself. I'm sick and tired of hearing the so-called experts run on about how hikers make careless mistakes."

Anger at the searchers. Not surprising. Often a bereaved person looks for someone to blame. It's a way of displacing anxiety over being left and guilt over surviving, but it's not helpful in dealing with the loss. I diverted her focus to the reality of the situation. "Do you have a theory about what happened to Sabrina?"

Gayle squirmed around, but her posture was still ramrod straight. She looked me in the face with an unwavering gaze. "I've gone over and over that day in my mind and I do have some ideas. But I'd rather just go into your apparition chamber and try to reach her. If her spirit shows up, then I can ask her what really happened."

Here was a woman who knew what she wanted and was used to taking charge. I sighed. This was going to be tricky. People tend to think that talking to the dead is just a matter of connecting—like finding the phone number for a friend you've lost touch with—and then you can get all your questions answered. But it's actually a process that requires preparation. "I know that sounds like the quickest, easiest way to go," I said gently. "But the process is more complicated and less clear than you may think."

"It didn't sound very complicated when Bruce told me about it," she snapped back.

Uh, oh. That sounds like Bruce. Skip over the details, go right to the point. I'd have to set her straight. "Did he tell you he'd been coming for grief therapy for more than a month before he went in the apparition chamber, or that we'd spent several sessions preparing for his contact session, or that he didn't reach Charlene on his first try?"

She shook her head. "He may have. I was so blown away that he'd ever try something paranormal that I probably didn't take in all the details." Gayle leaned closer, still with the fixed glare. She spoke sharply. "Are you saying I have to wait months to try out this apparition chamber? That's not going to work for me. I need to get some resolution now."

We sat, eyeball to eyeball, until Gayle's phone rang. She grabbed it out of her purse. "Oops, I have to take this," she said. "I'll just be a minute."

While she talked to her real-estate customer, I considered my response to her request. Every client who'd gone into my apparition chamber had spent time dealing with the reality of the loss of the loved one before trying the contact process. I'd never had someone in the Contact Project trying to find out whether someone was dead or alive. I wanted to be careful. If Gayle went in and did contact Sabrina, the sudden realization of the reality of the death could hit her brutally.

Gayle ended her call and looked inquiringly at me. "So how soon can I do it?" she asked.

I took a deep breath to calm myself before I spoke. "I'm not saying you have to wait months, but I am saying you can't do it today." Gayle clenched her jaw and flicked her gaze upward.

I continued determinedly. "I know that's not what you want to hear. You want to find out right away whether Sabrina's alive or dead. But to have the best chance of the contact process working for you, we need to spend some time preparing for your session before you start."

"What kind of preparation?"

"Part of it is getting clear about your expectations. The main purpose of the contact process is to work through grief and make peace with the person who died. In your case, you're thinking she may still be alive. You said that nothing about her disappearance is what it seems. Can you talk more about that?"

Gayle sighed and cast her eyes down toward her papers, which rustled in her shaky hands. "We didn't go there just to celebrate Sabrina's fortieth birthday," she said. "There was so much more going on. The six of us had a lot to work out."

Suddenly she lost it. Burst into tears. "Moxie had turned into a nightmare," she sobbed. "Sabrina was determined to change that."

I didn't try to stop her crying. Tears are good stress reducers. She wept deeply for a few seconds, then grabbed a couple of tissues and mopped her face. "Sorry," she said, "Everything sets me off these days."

"You don't need to apologize," I said. "Who's Moxie?"

She looked at her notes again, then launched into what sounded like a prepared speech. "Moxie is our women's group—the six of us.

Sabrina and I started it seven years ago. When we first met we were both single moms in our early thirties. Our kids were almost the same age. Her Ian was eight and my Nicole was seven-and-a-half. We shared so much, our stories were so similar that we bonded right away. It was almost like we knew what each other was thinking and feeling." She gazed wistfully off into that faraway time.

I waited silently, giving her time to return to the present.

After a minute or so, she turned back to me and continued. "We got the idea for Moxie—of course we didn't call it that then—at the same instant. Like a bolt of lightning hit us with the message that we needed to do this. We needed to bring other women like us to-gether—divorced single moms who were moving forward on our own, getting no help from our kids' dads. We were strong, could support each other." She stopped, as if waiting for a reaction.

Instead I responded with a prompt to keep her story on track. "So you've all known each other for seven years?"

"Yes." Now that she was explaining what she apparently came to talk about, Gayle was much more collected. "Once we got the idea for the group, we each brought in two others. Sabrina got Lark and Diana. I found Paige and Hana. So then we were six. We decided six was the perfect number. We had chosen carefully, found women who were compatible on every level. After divorce, we all wanted a new start. We wanted strong single friends."

"And you named your group Moxie. Is there a story behind that?"

"We called ourselves Moxie because it means grit, gumption, and guts—contradicts the stereotypical traits of women. We saw ourselves as bold, determined, audacious, willing to take risks, and as shameless advocates for single moms."

Sounded like my kind of women. "You must have had some great times over the years."

"It was fun in the beginning. We met weekly for potluck dinners, and hired teenagers to entertain our kids so we could enjoy dinner in peace. We made it special for the kids with pizza, games, movies, ice cream, stuff like that. We all looked forward to Wednesday nights. We talked about everything, shared it all. Our ex's, men we dated, our jobs—whatever came up. And we supported each other as we managed as single moms. We made agreements about confidentiality. What is said in the group and what happens in the group stays in the group.

Her face crumpled as she broke down again. "But now I wish we'd never started Moxie," she sobbed. "And I can't keep that confidentiality agreement anymore. Because I think something Moxie set in motion ended up killing Sabrina."

Chapter 4

A cold wave of foreboding swept over me as I tidied up my office after Gayle left. She'd insisted that I meet with all the members of Moxie as soon as she could set that up. I'd swallowed my misgivings and agreed. But now I realized I was headed down a familiar slippery slope. Clients in my Contact Project had already involved me in two messy murder investigations this year that ended up in life-threatening situations for me and other people I care about. Why would I want to do that again? Especially when I had my baby to think about. How could I risk putting him or her in danger? Plus it's Pablo's baby too, and he had warned me many times that a grief therapist has no business getting involved in crime investigations.

But I was so indebted to Bruce. How could I refuse to help his sister? He funds my Contact Project and he had said he wanted me to meet with all the women. He'd even said he would pay for my time.

I sagged into the tan leather armchair in my counseling room, staring into a dark corner.

"Yo, Cleo. Looks like you hit some punchy waves."

There, perched on the counter next to the microwave, was the first dead person I had ever talked to—Tyler, a blond blue-eyed surfer dude spirit who's been visiting me from time to time over the past couple of years, usually to offer cryptic advice when I'm grappling with a problem.

"Tyler! I feel like I'm being swept up by one of those punchy waves and I'm going to crash. I might drown. You have to help me."

I don't know why I ask Tyler for help. I guess it's because he's a spirit, so he should be able to see the big picture and know what matters. But his answers are always confusing, because he talks in surfer slang and I've never even been surfing. And when he shows up, he has his own agenda. Today was no exception.

"Ride your shortest board," he said. "The beach break is fast and steep. Turns quickly."

"No, Tyler. I need advice about my life, not about surfing. I'm stuck with helping this Moxie group find out what happened to Sabrina.

"Stay frosty, dude. Moxie has awesome energy, but they're about to fall into the pit. They can be sucked up by the barrel and get worked. Don't let them blow it."

"What are you saying? I have to save Moxie? Why? And from what?"

I was wasting my breath. Without another word, Tyler floated off toward the window and disappeared into the dark evening sky.

He brought up Moxie, I didn't. So he knows something about those women. Why did he say they have awesome energy?

I was so immersed in my thoughts that I almost didn't hear my phone. When I jumped up and grabbed it, I saw it was Elisa calling. I knew I didn't want to tell her that I was getting involved in another possible murder investigation. During the last one, she had given me as many dire warnings as Pablo had. But I picked up anyway.

"Hey, Cleo. What's up? You never called me yesterday with the lowdown on your lunch with Bruce."

"Sorry. I was depressed about a long discussion Pablo and I had about our future. I didn't have energy for anything else."

"Do you want to talk about that?"

"I do, but not right now. I'll tell you about Bruce, though. But you're not going to like it."

"Try me."

"You remember that woman who disappeared in the Indian Peaks Wilderness a few weeks ago? The one who was celebrating her fortieth birthday with a group of friends?"

"You mean Sabrina Larson?"

"Right. Do you know her?"

"Not exactly. It's complicated. You go on and then I'll tell you."

"Okay. Well as part of the celebration, the women all went off on individual personal journeys and Sabrina never came back. One of the women is Bruce's sister and Bruce wants me to help her try to contact Sabrina to see if she's dead. I think maybe she believes Sabrina was murdered."

I stopped and waited for Elisa to yell at me. She's not only my best friend, she's a psychologist like me, and she's my clinical supervisor when I need one. I can tell her anything, even about my clients. The upside—she keeps my confidences and supports me when I'm down. The downside—she's not shy about bawling me out when she thinks I'm heading off in the wrong direction. I expected dire warnings about how I need to stay away from anything even faintly resembling a murder investigation, how I have my professional reputation to think about, and how now that I'm pregnant I should be especially careful not to put myself in danger.

But instead she said in an uncharacteristically quiet voice, "Honey, we need to talk and we need to talk soon."

"If you're going to lecture me about staying out of trouble, I'd rather skip it," I said. "I already know the drill."

"Not this time, you don't," Elisa said. "That missing woman has a sixteen-year-old son and he's my daughter's boyfriend. Do you remember me telling you Maria has a new boyfriend? A snowboarder? Well, that's him. Ian Larson, Sabrina Larson's son. Like I said, it's complicated. If you're alone tonight, how about Maria and I pick up some takeout and come by your house for a talk?"

Chapter 5

Ian's an awesome snowboarder. He's in Breckenridge right now competing in the halfpipe Grand Prix. It's a serious competition." Maria paced around my kitchen, speaking with rapid enthusiasm, her long straight brown hair flipping from side to side across her face as she turned. She wore tight tattered jeans and a grey hoodie that said, "Music is an outburst of the soul."

Her words tumbled over each other as she continued to sing Ian's praises. "If he does well there, he moves on to major events in New Jersey and Idaho this winter where he could win money and maybe get a slot on the U.S. Snowboard Team. He's been snowboarding since he was five, and competing since he was ten. I mean if you saw him on the course, you'd be blown away."

Elisa and I listened quietly as she spread out containers of roasted vegetables, poached salmon and spinach salad and I sliced a baguette to put on a plate with a hunk of gorgonzola. When I sat down at the table, Elisa sat across from me, rolling her eyes.

"I saw that, mom," Maria said, as she finally ground to a halt, dropping down into the chair next to me. "If you have something to say, go ahead. We'll let Cleo decide who's right."

I've known Maria since she was a baby—I was her nanny for a few years when I was trying to make it as an artist—and her pacing was a behavior I recognized as a sign she was seriously upset. I never like to get in the middle of a disagreement between her and Elisa, but I love her like a daughter, and I wanted to connect. "Wait a minute, Maria," I said, putting my arm around her shoulders. "I haven't even gotten a hug from you."

"Sorry, Cleo," she said turning so we could hug. "It's good to see you."

"So Ian is your new boyfriend?" I asked. "What's he like?"

"He's tall with shaggy brown hair and huge blue eyes that are like deep pools of water," she said, looking dreamily off into the distance like she could see him standing there. Then she turned and smiled at me. "Cleo, I know you'd like him. He's sixteen like me, but he's so mature for his age. I think it's because he's been competing for years as a snowboarder like I have with violin. He has a clear focus, doesn't mess around with drugs or other stupid teenage stuff. He's the first guy I've met who gets why violin trumps everything for me. And I get why he has to be at this halfpipe competition," Maria finished, shooting a glare at Elisa.

"But his mother is missing," Elisa said quietly.

"Come on Mom, you know he cares about her a lot," Maria said. "And he misses her. But he says she's amazing at taking care of herself. He knows she'll be okay."

"But it's been almost three weeks. Where does he think she is? Isn't he starting to worry?"

"Mom, he can't take in negative energy right now. He needs to stay focused. His mom wouldn't want him to lose this competition because of her." Maria's voice was becoming shrill.

"So he's at the competition now and his mother is missing," I said, calmly. "He's still only sixteen. Did he go by himself?"

"He's with his coach. There are lots of times his mom can't go because she's working or whatever. He's fine. His aunt Brandi is fine with it, too."

"His Aunt Brandi?" I asked.

"Brandi is Ian's mom's sister. She was living at their house anyway, so she's handling stuff here at home. She's hilarious—sometimes she seems more like a teenager than Ian does—even though she's thirty."

I remembered what Gayle had said about how Sabrina had not wanted Brandi to be Ian's guardian. "Do Ian and Brandi get along?" I asked.

"Totally," Maria said with a grin. "Everything's fun when Brandi's around."

"But she must be worried about Sabrina too."

"Of course she is, but she gets that Ian needs his focus. And she knows Sabrina can take care of herself. Brandi is really good for Ian. She keeps him from getting down about his mom. Keeps him thinking positively."

Elisa sighed. She wasn't scowling or looking visibly upset, but I could sense a lecture on the way. Apparently Maria did too. "Okay, Mom," she said exasperatedly. Then, to me, "Cleo, Mom says I need to talk to you about how people act when they've lost someone. She thinks Ian isn't facing the situation, that he's in denial or pretending everything's fine when it isn't."

"What do you think?" I asked.

"I think Mom doesn't get Ian. I know what it's like to practice for days, months, years to get to a competition. Mom doesn't understand. He needs his focus."

Elisa finally lost it. "Maria, look at me," she said sharply. "We're talking about a serious situation here. Ian and Brandi are acting like his mom is away on vacation. I find that very strange. What is going on? Where does Ian think his mom is? Apparently he doesn't think she's still up at Indian Peaks injured or lost."

"Not really," Maria said. "After all the searches, they probably would have found her by now."

"So," Elisa went on, "do Ian and Brandi know something no one else does?"

Maria closed her eyes for a minute and took a deep breath. "You two are both psychologists so you understand confidentiality," she said looking us each in the eye in turn. "Everything Ian has told me is confidential, so I'm not going to tell you anything unless you agree to keep it that way. Do I have your word?"

"We can't make a promise like that, Maria," Elisa said sternly. "A woman is missing, your boyfriend's mother. Why wouldn't you want everyone to know everything that might help find her?"

"It's not my information to give out, Mom," Maria said, sounding close to tears. "I promised Ian to keep his secrets."

I thought about how committed Ian and Maria must be to each

other. Two intense focused kids like them could fall head-over-heels in love in a flash. It reminded me of when Pablo and I met in art class our sophomore year in college. We were instant soul mates deeply in love for the next three years until he broke my heart when he went off right after graduation to travel and find himself. I could imagine the fear Maria might be feeling at the thought of losing Ian if she betrayed his confidences.

I put my arm around Maria's shoulders again and gave her a squeeze. "It sounds like you're in a tough spot," I said. "I wouldn't ask you to betray Ian's trust. Maybe you could tell him your mom is worried? Maybe you and he could talk to your mom together?"

I pretended not to notice Elisa giving me the evil eye from across the table.

Chapter 6

Ilay in bed that night thinking about Maria's fierce, yet naive, love for Ian. Ah sixteen—such a romantic age. Again she reminded me of myself. I was only a few years older than she is when Pablo and I fell in love our sophomore year in college. We stayed together until we graduated. If this pregnancy had happened back then, Pablo and I might be married with a sixteen-year-old child today. Or—given all the ups and downs in our relationship—maybe we'd be divorced with a sixteen-year-old child. All of that is hard to imagine now.

I wouldn't have chosen to get pregnant at age twenty or twenty-one, but if I had, I would have had no hesitation about marrying Pablo. I loved him deeply, trusted him totally, and believed in our future together. I thought of him as my soul mate until that night a few days after our college graduation.

When Pablo said he'd saved up to take me to dinner at the pricey Flagstaff House to celebrate our graduation, I was sure he planned to propose. After all, the Flagstaff House is known as Boulder's most romantic restaurant, and widely acknowledged to be the best spot in town to pop the question. And we'd been together for three years. I intended to bring up my concerns that we were too young for marriage, that maybe we should wait a year or so. But I also planned to say "yes" to his proposal, because I knew we were destined to be together forever. I was floating on a joyous cloud as we walked into the elegant restaurant in the foothills.

Our table, next to a floor-to-ceiling window, gave us a breathtaking view of the city of Boulder 6,000 feet below. A stunning sunset matched my inner glow. I felt glamorous and grownup in my perfect little black cocktail dress, cut and gracefully draped to mold to my figure. I had spent more than I should have on it, but I wanted this night to be a magnificent memory. As I looked at Pablo, my handsome lover, looking especially delicious in a tie and jacket, I was in heaven.

We drank wine and ate amazing food in celebration of our newly minted fine arts degrees. We speculated about the acclaimed artists we would become. The future stretched endlessly in front of us. Everything was possible. When I look back now, it is with sadness for my naive former self who loved and trusted in a way I have never done since. And sadness for Pablo who had no idea of what I expected from him that night.

Just as I finished the last bit of my dessert—a chocolate torte I've never had a taste for since—Pablo took my hand in his, gazed soulfully into my eyes, and said, "Cleo, I love you so much. I hope you know how much I will always love you."

As I looked deeply into adorable brown eyes, I melted inside, waiting for the proposal I knew was coming. Except it didn't.

Instead, he said, "But I need some time away from Boulder, from everyone I know. I need to find myself as an artist and I can't do it here. I'm going to Mexico—to that artist's community, San Miguel de Allende." His face lit up and he dropped my hands. "So many artists live there. Galleries, art courses and workshops are everywhere. Diego Rivera painted there. Can you believe it?"

Shock nearly flattened me. All I could do was gasp out, "Why do you have to leave?"

He looked off out the window briefly, then turned back to me with a determined look. "For a while now, I've been focused on creating art that pleases others—like my teachers and judges of our student shows," he said. "But a lot of the fun has gone out of it for me. I don't know who I am as an artist anymore. My work doesn't have the energy I want it to, the energy of an artist freely exploring and creating." His voice gained intensity. "I need to reinvent myself as an artist, somewhere where art is in the air, where I can live cheaply, where I can devote all my time and energy to art."

Tears ran down my face. "Are you breaking up with me?"

"Cleo, I'd like to ask you to wait for me, but I won't ask that of you. I want you to be as free as I am to make whatever choices work for you."

No way. I couldn't accept that. I'd do whatever I had to do to keep him. "Maybe I could go with you. I'm an artist, too. I could study and learn there alongside you."

He shook his head no. "Much as I'd love to have you with me, Cleo, it wouldn't be fair to you, or to me to have you there. I need to live a solitary existence so I can create without distraction. I have to be able to follow whatever inspires me, to head off in a different direction any day I choose to, without any obligations."

"So you are breaking up with me." Now I felt anger growing inside me. He was so full of himself. How could he set me up this way? I didn't want to explode and make a scene in the restaurant, so I gathered my forces, stood up and said as calmly as I could manage, "Give me the keys. I'll wait in the car while you pay the check."

""Wait, Cleo. The evening doesn't have to end this way. You know I still love you."

Other diners were looking at us and a waiter was on his way over. It was tempting to sit down, but I stayed strong. "Give me the keys right now or I'm going to start shouting at you," I said.

He handed over the keys and I walked out with as much dignity as I could muster.

In the car on our way down the mountain, I asked the question at the top of my mind. "Why, the Flagstaff House, Pablo? Why did you take me there to break up with me?"

He sighed. "I didn't take you there to break up with you, Cleo. I took you there to celebrate our graduation and our exciting futures as artists." Then he launched into the "we can still be friends" spiel. I saw it as a sop to his guilt.

"Forget it, Pablo. Forget me, like I'm going to forget you," I said. "Have a good life."

We didn't speak or see each other again before he left. I didn't answer his calls, didn't go out where I might run into him. Of course I was nowhere near as blasé about his decision as I pretended. I felt blindsided, rejected and abandoned. Now that I'm a trained grief therapist I can look back and recognize the stages of grief I went through. First was shock, denial and isolation. I stayed home alone, cried, slept a lot, and was as miserable as I'd ever been. When I got tired of wallowing in self-pity, I moved on to anger. I burned all the pictures I had of him and threw out the things he'd left at my apartment. I started telling our friends what a shit he was.

The pain was intense for many months. I missed Pablo in so many ways and so many places. And I missed my vision of our future together. But I gradually let go of what was and moved on to what was to come. I committed myself to working intensely on my own art, painting with Gramma in her studio part of every day. I took a part-time job as a nanny to Elisa's one-year-old daughter, Maria. And I got involved in a relationship with Brian, a hunky graphic artist, who didn't want commitment any more than I did at that point, but who was always ready for a good time.

§ § §

Six years later, Pablo moved back here to help his parents after his brother got involved in a gang selling drugs and ended up in jail. He called me to meet him for coffee at The Trident one summer night. When I walked in, he was sitting at a quiet table reading a book, just like in our student days. But he looked different. Thinner, longer hair, face more finely drawn.

We hugged awkwardly, but we didn't kiss. I had thought about this day often over the years. More in the early years, less later. I had asked myself how I would feel seeing him again. Angry? Happy? Excited? What I hadn't anticipated was what I actually felt— nothing much.

We brought each other up to date on our lives at the moment, but carefully avoided talking about our shared past or about what we'd done in the six years he was away. Pablo told me about his brother's problems and the impact it had on his family. Then he said he had decided to go into police work to help keep kids like his brother out of gangs. He was already taking the Police Academy training. And he was living in Longmont with his family.

I said I had just started a doctoral program in clinical psychology at the University of Denver, because I wasn't making enough money from my art to support myself, and I didn't want to be a nanny for the rest of my life. I also told him how worried I was about my grandmother, who was becoming increasingly forgetful. At Grampa's encouragement, I had moved in with him and Gramma while I went to grad school. It would save me money and he needed the help now that Gramma was declining. He had offered to help me with school costs so I wouldn't have so many loans.

I think Pablo and I both had the same reaction. We were here, but the old magic wasn't. We were the past, not the present. With our respective family issues, and each of us immersed in demanding training programs, we rarely saw each other for the next five years. And when we did it was a "So, what have you been up to?" conversation that ended in, "Great seeing you."

§ § §

But deep down we never lost our love for each other. Finally, our stars exploded into alignment one night when I ran into him at a party at the house of some of our old college friends. It was one of those "across a crowded room" moments. I'm not sure why, but when we looked at each other, sparks flew. We weren't the strangers from the song, but we were different people than we had been. I saw the Pablo I had loved so truly ten years before. In the ten years since our breakup we had matured into capable professionals. He was a detective with the Longmont Police Department and I had my grief therapy practice set up.

We flew into each others' arms for a huge hug. "I've missed you, Cleo," he whispered in my ear.

"Me too," I whispered back.

"I was an idiot," he said, pulling me off to a corner of the room. "It's taken me a long time to realize what I gave up when I went off to Mexico by myself. I'd like to put the past behind us and try again. What do you say?"

"I say, I'd like to try that," I said. And I knew I was ready. I could look back at our nineteen-year-old selves and understand how a young man who felt a strong need to grow as an artist with no distractions, and a young woman who wanted commitment, were a terrible fit. Back then we had loved each other, but were both too self-absorbed and unsure of ourselves to see each other. Now we had mellowed into contented adults ready for a new relationship.

We ended the night at my place—my grandparents' house where I'd continued living after Gramma went into a nursing home and Grampa died. We came together, Pablo and I, with all the passion from our young romantic days, and all the compassion from life's lessons learned in the years since. Our hunger for each other was intense, and our joy at the satisfaction of that hunger was blissful.

Since then we've jumped in and out of this relationship like a couple of high school kids. Neither one of us has wanted a serious commitment, so we've been mostly drifting. We have fun together, and we have great sex, and we love each other. But I haven't had those old illusions about our relationship.

Now that I'm pregnant, he wants us to get married. But even though I love him, I have my doubts about whether marriage would work for us. I still have trust issues, and he still has independence issues, and in many ways we drive each other crazy. I think he's too bossy. He takes over and I feel swallowed up by him. He thinks I ask too many questions and push him too much. He also thinks I'm too flaky. And we have the issue of where we would live.

Some days I think we can get past all that, have a good marriage, and raise our baby in a happy home. Some days I don't. How do you know for sure? People say, "You just know." But that's too magical for me. I need to know we can fit together and stay together before I take that step.

Chapter 7

From: GayleWinfield@comcast.net
Subject: Moxie meeting
Date: November 28
To: CleoBoulder@yahoo.com

Hi Cleo. I talked to everyone about a group meeting with you and they agreed. Looked at the evenings you said you could meet & tomorrow (Wed 11/29) is best for us. My house, 7:00 p.m., 20XX Balsam. We'll bring food and wine.

I'm including a quick overview of the Moxie group to get you started:
- Diana Lesko - Physical therapist, massage therapist, rolfer, into boxing & bodybuilding. Age 42 - 2 kids: Amy(14) & Hugh(15).
- Hana Kim - Computer programmer, numerologist, climber, skier. Age 39 - one daughter, Carina(9)
- Lark Dove - Nurse, potter, climber, skier. Age 39 - one son, Darby(9)
- Paige Mosier - Yoga teacher, Wiccan high priestess (aka Rivka Ravenstar. Age 41 - two sons, James(12) & Mathew(13)
- Me, Gayle Winfield - Real estate agent, musician, runner. Age 41 - one daughter, Nicole(16)
- Sabrina Larson (former member?) - Nurse, runner, gardener. Age 40 - one son, Ian(16)

As I drove to Gayle's house, I realized I was looking forward to the Moxie meeting. Whatever happened with the Sabrina investigation, I was eager to meet this group of strong single mothers. I might be on my way to becoming a single mother myself—not a path I had consciously chosen. But at thirty-seven I knew my biological clock was ticking. And I knew I wanted this baby whether or not Pablo and I decided to get married, so single-motherhood was an option I was open to.

Gayle's house was exactly what I'd expect a smart Boulder real estate agent to own. A modern stone and wood two-story perched on a mesa in central Boulder with 360-degree views, and only blocks from downtown. When I got there at 7:00 p.m., I saw four cars parked in her long driveway, which told me that Moxie had probably planned a pre-meeting, most likely to prepare what they would say to me. Understandable.

Gayle answered the door dressed in skinny jeans and a black fitted t-shirt—the perfect outfit for her tiny body and black pixie-cut hair. "Thanks for coming," she said, hustling me through a sparsely furnished living room with floor-to-ceiling windows and white walls splashed with color from several large abstract paintings. I would have liked to take a closer look at the artwork, but Gayle darted off ahead of me, jabbering loudly to be heard over the din of female voices coming from a room ahead of her. "Everyone's here, in the kitchen eating, drinking and chattering away," she said. "We all have our theories about Sabrina, and quite frankly we're not agreeing on much. I'm hoping you can bring some clarity. First I'll quiet them down so I can introduce you."

In the gleaming eat-in kitchen, four women sat around a glass-topped table cluttered with plates, platters of food, and wine bottles. Gayle didn't need to silence them, because they all stopped talking as soon as we came in. I sensed a discordant vibe, as if unspoken harsh words hung in the air. But if Gayle noticed, she didn't let on. Just took advantage of the quiet spot to introduce me. "Okay, guys, this is Cleo Sims. And Cleo, this is Diana, Lark, Paige and Hana." She pointed at each as she named them. I concentrated on connecting their names to their faces, as I said hello to each in turn.

Diana was seated at the far end of the table. A stocky muscular woman with closely cropped brown hair and full lips. Next to her was Hana, a slim Asian woman with long straight black hair. Then Paige, whose long curly red hair had the effortless windblown look many women envy. Finally, at the end closest to me was Lark, a tall Nordic blonde with steely blue eyes.

Gayle moved toward the empty chair next to Diana and across from Hana, and motioned me to the seat next to hers, across from Paige and next to Lark. They passed the food and I quickly filled my plate with a variety of salads, bread, hummus, and cheese, but declined the wine.

"Maybe we could each tell Cleo a little bit about ourselves while she eats," Gayle said. She didn't mention why they'd gotten here early enough that they'd all mostly finished eating, but rather went right on setting out her agenda. "I've already spent some time getting to know Cleo, so how about one of you starts," she said.

No one spoke up. Hana looked at her plate, her long hair falling over her face. Paige and Lark sat quietly, their eyes turned slightly downward, eyeballs still, as if they had moved into a meditative state. Diana looked directly and intently at Gayle, issuing a silent challenge. Apparently the Moxie members hadn't signed on to the program.

I felt the tension but it didn't affect me. This was their show. I was there at their request—or at least at Gayle and Bruce's request. I was hungry and the food was delicious, so I let myself relax and enjoy the meal.

Gayle, on the other hand, became increasingly agitated. She fidgeted, drummed her fingers on the table, and looked around at the women in turn. Then she grabbed her wine glass and took a big swig. "Fine," she said. "We'll ask for what you want. But I don't think it's the way Cleo works, and I don't think you're making a fair request when you expect her to jump right in and help without getting to know us first."

Was Gayle the group leader now that Sabrina was gone? I remembered that she and Sabrina started Moxie. Clearly she intended to be in charge of tonight's meeting, and that might have worked if her phone hadn't rung just then.

"Oops, I have to take this," Gayle said, jumping up and heading down the hall to what I assumed was her office. "Have you decided?" she asked her caller. "You only have twenty-four hours…" her voice trailed off as she shut a door behind her.

The other four women lightened up a bit. Hana looked up from her plate and turned toward me. "Cleo, we mean no disrespect," she said. "If we had met under different circumstances, I'm sure we would have enjoyed sharing stories and getting to know you. But this isn't about us, it's about Sabrina. We need to find her before it's too late—if it isn't already."

Before I could reply, Diana jumped in. "Gayle told us about your Contact Project," she said, "and we all want to sit together with you tonight to try to contact Sabrina. We owe it to Sabrina," she said firmly. Her chin jutted forward, resting on her clenched fists. "Sabrina would do anything to help one of us, and we can't do any less for her."

Whew! A sticky situation. My head hurt just thinking about all the explaining and persuading it would take to get this group of women to fully understand and sign up as informed participants in the Contact Project. They were not only strong and determined, they were clearly used to getting their own way. I took a deep breath and offered them an option. "I understand that you feel desperate about Sabrina," I said quietly. "And I wish I could solve your problem right now. But I don't do group séances, or any kind of séances. I have a process and an apparition chamber that some people have used to contact dead loved ones. But only one person at a time can do it and it takes some preparation. So my suggestion is that if you all want to try to contact Sabrina, you each meet with me individually. I can give Gayle some appointment times so anyone who is interested can sign up."

They were all looking straight at me now. Even Lark and Paige had emerged from their inwardly focused trances. "How long will your process take?" Lark asked, pushing her long blonde hair back behind her ears. "I have a pretty heavy schedule at the hospital and my son Darby is only nine, plus I live up in Nederland, so I wouldn't have a lot of time for meetings."

"I know you're all busy," I said, looking around at all four of them. "How about if I just meet with whoever has the time and wants to do it?"

"Here's the thing, Cleo," Paige said. Her voice was surprisingly soft and musical but intense at the same time. "It's not just about our time. It's about acting quickly. Hana and Diana are right. We need to be in touch with Sabrina now." She leaned forward toward me from across the table, her mop of red hair skimming her wine glass. "And we all need to be part of it. Our combined group energy will be much more powerful than any one of us alone," she said, her green eyes looking intently into mine. "I understand that it's not the way you usually work, but this is a desperate situation. Surely you can make an exception." I wondered whether anyone ever said "no" to Paige. Her melodious voice and earnest demeanor touched me so deeply that I almost agreed to her appeal.

Fortunately, Gayle darted back in right then, which gave me a minute to regroup. What were they thinking? Their urgency told me that they still hoped to find Sabrina alive. But they wanted me to help them contact her spirit? As a grief therapist, I know that the intense pain of grief can lead to odd kinds of magical thinking. Like seeing someone in a crowd who resembles the dead loved one, and hoping that somehow a reported death is a mistake. Or telling yourself that the death was all a bad dream that didn't really happen. I've helped clients resolve these issues. But I couldn't do it in one evening with five women all at once. And I needed to stand firm and uphold what I believed to be ethical practice as a grief therapist.

"I can't make an exception," I said. "The process isn't designed to find missing persons. You need to ask yourselves why you feel this urgent need to try to contact Sabrina's spirit if you believe she may still be alive."

"That's what we want to find out," Gayle said. "Is she alive? And we want to find out as quickly as possible."

None of them were following my logic, but I wanted to honor Bruce's request to work with all of them. So I put my best offer out there. "I'm willing to meet with each of you like Gayle and I talked about," I said. "And then I'm willing to set up sessions in the apparition chamber for whoever is prepared and wants to do that."

Gayle grabbed the offer and took charge. I had already met with her and with her help I signed up the remaining four Moxie women to meet with me over the next few days. I would meet with Hana Thursday morning and then with Lark late that afternoon just before her hospital shift. Saturday afternoon I would meet with Diana, and Sunday with Paige.

Chapter 8

"Hey, Cleo. I need a favor. Would you be willing to come to my house for our meeting today? My daughter Carina is home sick with an ear infection." It was Hana Kim on the phone Thursday morning calling about our 11:00 meeting. "I've just taken her to the doctor and she's on antibiotics now, but she needs to stay home from school for a couple of days, and she's only nine. If you wouldn't mind meeting here, it would help me a lot. Carina will be downstairs watching movies, so we can talk freely."

I couldn't see any problem meeting Hana at her house, so I agreed to move our meeting there. It's not like she's a therapy client who I needed to meet in my office. And in my new status as mom-to-be, I was taking an expansive view of the needs of moms, especially single moms.

Hana's house was a split-level in the Table Mesa subdivision in south Boulder. I parked on the street in front and walked along a stone pathway through a partially-enclosed courtyard to the front door. I had a sense of how lovely the patio must be in summer. Even on this cold winter day, I could feel serenity emanating from the large rocks and stone Buddha statue at the end of the porch.

Hana opened the door before I could knock. The calm atmosphere continued as I walked through a small entryway to the living room. A bamboo fountain. Plants. Incense. She had tea and cookies set out on a black lacquered coffee table in front of a long low couch.

"I love this room," I said. "It has such a harmonious feeling."

"Thanks," she said. "I used feng shui to create the room. I like the calm gentle energy."

We sat on the couch. "I won't introduce you to Carina," Hana said. "Don't want to expose you to her germs. Like I said, she's downstairs watching movies. A rare treat for her. I limit her TV time pretty strictly, except when she's sick. Anyway, she's in her own world down there. Has a huge glass of OJ. So we don't need to worry about being interrupted." She poured tea from a red oval teapot into matching handleless cups, put one in front of each of us, then sat back and looked inquiringly at me. "Where would you like to start?"

"Tell me about Sabrina," I said. "What is she like?"

Hana bent her head forward, intently studying her hands. I admired her glossy coal-black hair, stick straight with bangs cut so evenly her head could be an avatar in some virtual universe.

She took a deep breath, sat up and turned toward me, her face composed. "I'm a numerologist—kind of fits with being a computer programmer, don't you think?" she asked, quirking an eyebrow. "Anyway, for me the best way to describe someone's personality is to tell you about their destiny number."

"Sounds interesting. I don't know much about numerology. What's a destiny number?"

"It's a number derived from all the letters in your full birth name that describes the potential, opportunities and challenges of your lifetime. Sabrina's destiny number is six. Sixes like to give help and comfort to those in need. They have a strong love of home and domestic affairs and make the finest, most concerned parents. Sixes are loving, friendly, and appreciative of others and they have a depth of understanding that produces sympathetic kindness and generosity."

My mind drifted briefly to the implications for my baby of the name I would choose for her or him. I had no idea that a name had this power. Surely Hana wasn't implying that I could influence my baby's personality by the name I gave her or him. "Are you saying that Sabrina has these traits because of the name her parents gave her?"

"That's complicated. What her number does is tell us about her character and motivation and describe the life tasks she faces using the name she was given."

"Is it all positive or do bad traits go with some destiny numbers?"

"All the numbers have their negative sides. For sixes that can be stubbornness, self-righteousness, or dominance. Also, sixes can demand too much of themselves or sacrifice themselves for the welfare of others. And sometimes they have trouble distinguishing helping from interfering."

"So all this fits Sabrina?"

"Yes, I think most of us who know her would agree that's a good description of her. She's a nurse, who works very hard at her job. She spends most of her free time with Ian going on weekend snowboarding trips to the mountains. She's tried over and over to help her sister Brandi, an ungrateful brat who uses Sabrina for whatever she can get. Sabrina's been a loyal friend to all of us, even when things got sticky."

I let the negatives about Brandi go by to keep the focus on Sabrina and the Moxie women. "By all of us, you mean the Moxie group?"

"Yes. Sabrina is the soul of Moxie. She and Gayle started the group, but Sabrina was the one who kept us on track."

"How did she do that?"

"She brought in a lot of self-help books that we all read and talked about. Reading books like Women Who Love Too Much helped us discover how we had ended up in toxic relationships with men and how to avoid repeating that pattern. She constantly reminded us to focus on being well and strong and to direct our energy toward making things happen rather than letting things happen. Unfortunately lately she hasn't been happy with the direction we've been going."

"Can you tell me more about that?"

Hana pressed her lips together and ran her hand through her hair. "Not really," she said. "I'd be violating the Moxie confidentiality code."

"Maybe this is a situation where the confidentiality code can't be the main priority," I said quietly.

Hana squeezed her eyebrows together and looked off into the distance. "I'll say this and this is all I'll say," she said. "We Moxie members believe in Karma—that it has a way of teaching people lessons. But after a while we realized Karma isn't enough. We might fix our own lives, but the problem with men who mistreat women is still out there. Other women are still being hurt the way we were."

She paused, her eyes darting nervously around the room. Then she took a deep breath, pulled her shoulders back, lifted her chin, and looked me directly in the eye. "At some point you have to go beyond surviving and turn around and face the problem," she said. "Sometimes action is necessary. We realized we couldn't count on Karma to right all the wrongs women suffer at the hands of men. We needed to help Karma along. We had to find the courage to act to make things better for all women. And we did that."

"Mom! Mom, I need help," Carina shouted from downstairs. "This DVD is stuck. It won't play."

Hana jumped up and turned toward the stairs. "I'll be right there, Carina," she yelled down. She turned to me. "Give me a minute. I'll be right back." then she disappeared down the stairs.

I sat quietly, reflecting on what I had learned from Hana. Sabrina—whom I noted Hana consistently described in the present tense—is or was a hard worker, responsible, caring, a loyal friend and parent who sacrificed her own needs to help others. But as Gayle had divulged a couple of days ago in my office and Hana had implied today, the joy had somehow gone out of Moxie, especially for Sabrina.

"I only have a few minutes left. Are we getting closer to trying to contact Sabrina?" I jumped at Hana's words. She had come silently back up the stairs and was standing on the other side of the coffee table.

"I'm not sure," I said. "Can you tell me what happened at the gathering in the mountains and what you think happened to Sabrina?"

Hana dropped down onto a large floor pillow across the table from me and tilted her head to one side. "What do I think happened to her? I think she worried too much and took too much responsibility for balancing an inharmonious situation, which brought out the self-righteous aspect of a six. This led her away from her destiny and she can't find her way back."

"Are you saying that metaphorically or practically?"

"Both, I suppose."

"Does that mean you think she's still alive and lost?"

"I think she's alive. I don't know about lost."

Chapter 9

M oxie was just what I needed for most of the last seven years, but I'm done with it now," Lark Dove said, shaking her head so emphatically that her long blonde hair almost dipped into her bowl of soup. Because Lark lives in Nederland forty-five minutes up the canyon from Boulder, we were meeting at Breadworks, a bakery cafe near the hospital where she works as a nurse. It was late Thursday afternoon just before Lark's twelve-hour shift and the cafe was pretty much deserted, except for staff cleaning up after the lunch crowd.

I leaned forward to hear her over the clatter of cutlery and plates. "I had decided to drop out even before Sabrina disappeared," she continued. "One thing you should know about me is that I think for myself. I don't let other people make decisions for me. But somehow every time I was ready to tell the others I was leaving Moxie, Sabrina talked me into staying one more week to see if things changed the way she hoped they would. Now that she's gone, I don't see Moxie in my future." She sat back, arms crossed, as if waiting for me to challenge her decision.

But I had no interest in questioning her plan to leave Moxie. I just wanted to keep her talking about Sabrina. I kept my face and voice impassive. "What was Sabrina hoping would change?"

Lark dipped a chunk of crusty bread in her white bean soup, took a bite, and chewed slowly before she responded. "Some members went off on a crusade that others of us don't totally agree with or support," she said, rolling her shiny blue eyes. "They have this strong feeling that Moxie is here for a reason they need to act on. We all believe in taking conscious action to be a creative force instead of a victim in your life, but their actions have gone too far." She shook her head dismissively.

Confusing. I had no idea what she meant. But her eye rolling and head shaking signaled defensiveness. I spooned some chicken noodle soup into my mouth and considered how to prod her into being more specific without making her clam up. Given what Hana and Gayle had said about Moxie's confidentiality code, I figured she'd back off if I pushed for details. I decided to explore her feelings about Moxie first, and then work my way up to more sensitive topics. "It sounds like you're clear that you wouldn't miss the group," I said.

She looked down at her soup as she crumbled some bread into her bowl. "No. I wouldn't miss it. I'm pretty much an individualist, not one to join groups. Like I said, I think for myself. My parents were hippies in the 1960s and basically still are. They raised me and my brothers in the mountains as self-sufficient free spirits, always outside, hiking, biking, climbing, and skiing. I like to do my own thing."

I spread some butter on a cranberry muffin as I decided what to ask next. Lark dug into a large salad of mixed field greens. "I'm not much of a group person myself," I said. "So I'm wondering how you happened to join the Moxie group."

Lark looked off to her left as she finished chewing, then turned back to me. "I joined Moxie mostly because of Sabrina," she said. "I met her at work—we were both nurses at the hospital— and we started eating together in the cafeteria when we were on the same shift. She was so cheerful and sincere and kept going on about this great group of strong single moms. And I was a single mom. My son Darby was two then. His father and I had a free and open relationship. Never married. Neither one of us wanted to be tied down."

This relationship sounded familiar. I could certainly relate to those feelings of not wanting to be tied down. Wonder how that worked out for her and Darby.

"Are Darby and his dad close?" I asked hopefully.

"No. Jacob said he would stay around and be a dad, but when Darby was a year old, Jacob got this great opportunity to travel with a band—he plays bass—and he never came back. That's why Moxie appealed to me. I was feeling kind of lonely and the idea of a group of independent women friends who were all single moms sounded good."

I felt a jolt of empathy for Lark as my own possible future flashed before my eyes. What if Pablo decided to go off again like he did years ago? Could I be a good enough mother to my baby if I was alone? Would I be like Lark— a lonely single mom looking for supportive friends? "That must have been awful having him leave you and Darby like that," I said softly.

Lark shrugged. "Not as bad as it sounds. I have a good job and a lot of support. That's one reason I still live in Nederland. My mom and dad are there and they help out a lot with Darby. By working three twelves, I have plenty of time to spend with Darby and time for climbing and skiing."

This woman did sound like someone who knew her own mind and acted accordingly. But yet, she let Sabrina influence her. Why? "If you were clear about leaving the group, how did Sabrina keep talking you into staying in Moxie?" I asked.

Before she could answer, the front door opened, letting in a gust of cold air and a group of five women, all about our age. They waved and smiled at Lark. "Nurses," Lark said softly as she waved back at them. "I can't talk anymore here. Are you up for a short walk?"

It was only about 4:45, but the sun had already set being that it was mid-December and close to the foothills. Walking along the storefronts of the small shopping center in the cold and the dark didn't sound very appealing, but I wanted the rest of the story, so I agreed. We got our jackets on, took our dishes to the bin, and headed outside. "Where were we?" she asked.

I was already shivering in the cold wind but Lark didn't seem to notice the temperature at all as she strode along. I hustled to keep up, hand in my pockets. "You were telling me what Sabrina said to keep you in Moxie," I said.

"Right. She'd remind me of the powerful friendship we'd all shared over the years, how we'd been there for each other when we went through bad relationships, sick kids, career crises, and other stuff like that." Lark sighed deeply. "Sabrina and I have always been close, working together and all. She has a way of reaching my soul, like she knows me in ways most people don't. Somehow I find myself going along with her even when that wasn't my original plan."

We'd reached the end of the sidewalk already, so we turned back in the direction we came from. By then I was too cold to focus. I hated to wimp out, but my car ahead promised warmth. "Let's go sit in my car and talk," I said. "I'll turn on the heat."

She gave me a puzzled look. "Oh, are you cold? Sorry, I didn't realize."

Once we were inside my Toyota and I relaxed into the warmth, we picked up the conversation. "Does Sabrina have this irresistible effect on all the group members?"

"Sometimes, but sometimes not. Who else have you met with from Moxie so far?"

"Gayle and Hana."

"Did they talk much about the problems the group was having?"

"They both told me the group had changed direction in some ways that Sabrina especially didn't like, and wanted to change. But they didn't give any details. They said Moxie has a confidentiality code that specifically prohibits talking to other people about what goes on in the group." I took a deep breath, then plunged in. "As a therapist, I certainly understand confidentiality, and I would keep your secrets if you'd be willing to tell me more."

Lark pressed her lips together, then lifted her chin and spoke in a slightly strained voice. "Okay. I'm not afraid to rock the boat. I'll tell you more about Moxie. The group is over now anyway, so its secrets don't really matter except for the ones that can incriminate specific members. But I won't betray people by telling you things that implicate them."

"I really only need to know about stuff that affected Sabrina. Whatever you feel comfortable sharing about that can help."

"Well, Sabrina had the vision for Moxie in the beginning. She and Gayle brought us together. All of us were fed up with being victims, so we didn't want to sit around sharing our miserable stories of how we'd let men walk all over us. Sabrina kept reminding us of Oprah's belief that your life is defined by your intention—that what you put out comes back to you."

I'm not an Oprah watcher, but that sounded positive to me. It's always better to move forward rather than obsessing over past injuries. "How did that work out for you?" I asked.

"Pretty well at first. Going on that path, we plowed through exercises from stacks of self-help books, and explored different spiritual paths and practices. One idea that kept emerging was 'concentrate your efforts on what you can control.' We got that this was about being good parents, taking care of our physical bodies, building or growing our careers, and looking forward with enthusiasm. Sabrina loved all of that and so did I."

"But that all changed at some point?"

"Yes, gradually Moxie turned sour. Some members wanted to get revenge against exes who had treated them like shit. These guys had lied and cheated, then denied everything when they got caught. Never apologized. Showed no remorse. Some of the Moxie members started thinking about the memories of these bad old relationships as clutter they needed to get rid of in their lives, the way feng shui gets rid of clutter in a room. They decided that getting revenge was a healthy way to clear their minds and build their personal power."

Hmmm…feng shui. That might be Hana. I still wanted more detail about these bad old relationships. "What kind of stuff had these guys done? Can you give me an example?"

Lark paused for a minute, leaning back, eyes closed. Then she straightened up and looked at me. "Okay. One ex was sleeping with someone else when his wife was pregnant, and blamed her for not being affectionate enough. This was when she was working sixty hours a week to support them both because he was unemployed. He spent money on whatever he wanted and told her it was none of her business what he did. He said she was nosey. Sometimes he hit her, but she stayed with him because she wanted them to be a family. When it got worse and she finally saved some money and decided to leave him, he found it and took it. Then she found out she was pregnant again. She decided to stay. She tried to get along with him but he found every excuse he could to have a tantrum and leave the house. Sometimes he stayed away for days. It took her another year to come up with the money to take the kids and leave. She's been really bitter about the whole thing."

"What did Moxie do to get revenge on guys like him?"

"They found out how to set up websites in a way that hides the owner's identity. Then they started creating sites about these guys telling what they had done in the past. They kept their own names out of it, but they told the truth. They used keywords so the search engines would pick up the sites and they'd come up if anyone googled the guy. Apparently it's not illegal as long as you're telling the truth, but it sure sends out a lot of negative energy."

"Is that what you and Sabrina were upset about?"

"We weren't happy about that stuff, but it was nothing compared to what came after it. Some Moxie members made it their mission to punish men who mistreat women. They made themselves the judges—kind of a warped worldview. It's risky and it's wrong and Sabrina was determined to change it. But that's all I can say about it, and I need to get to work."

She opened the car door and got out, leaving me sitting there wondering why Tyler had told me not to let Moxie blow it. It sounded like they already had.

Chapter 10

When I got home from my meeting with Lark, I had a sudden urge to start a painting of the Moxie women. I headed out my back door to my studio in the stone carriage house remodeled by my grandmother years ago. It's where I learned to paint in the peaceful summer mornings I spent there with Gramma during my childhood and teenage years.

I hadn't been doing much painting in the last couple of months, partly because since my pregnancy the smells of the pigments and thinners made me sick. But I was feeling good and I had a strong vision of how I wanted to portray the complex women as individuals and as a group. I knew painting them would help me get in touch with my subconscious insights about these multifaceted women.

The Moxie members began to take shape as a pack of sleek panthers, elegant and strong, each with the face of one of the women in the group. I painted the faces to sharply contrast the women's most distinct traits: Hana's analytical impassiveness, Gayle's vivid intensity, Lark's confident independence, Paige's earnest inclusiveness, and Diana's forceful confrontation. As the painting came together, I sensed their individual strengths contributing to the group energy but fragmenting it at the same time.

I was deeply absorbed when my cell phone rang. I didn't recognize the number, but decided to pick up in case it was one of the Moxie members wanting to change an appointment.

"Cleo Sims."

"Hi, Cleo. This is Brandi Peyton. I'm Sabrina Larson's sister and I really need to talk to you." Her warm friendly voice drew me in immediately.

But wait—this was Brandi. The sister Hana had called an ungrateful brat. The sister Gayle had said Sabrina didn't want taking care of Ian. But then again, also the sister Maria had said she and Ian think is hilarious and fun to be around. Another complicated woman added to the mix.

I kept my voice neutral and gave no indication that I'd heard anything about her. "Oh, hello, Brandi. I'm sorry for what you must be going through with Sabrina being missing."

"It's important to stay positive. I still believe we'll find her alive. That's what I want to talk to you about."

"Sure. Would you like to make an appointment to come into my office? I think I have an opening at 11:00 tomorrow. Would that work for you?"

"Maybe," she sad tentatively. "But I need to ask you a few things right now. This is a difficult time for me and for Sabrina's son Ian, and I'm afraid you're going to make it worse. Are you setting up some kind of séance for Gayle Winfield to contact Sabrina's spirit?"

"Brandi, I know this is a hard time for you and I certainly don't want to make it worse. And, no, I don't do séances."

"But you do help people get in touch with spirits of the dead, right?"

"Sometimes."

"How does it work?"

"That's way too complicated to explain over the phone, Brandi. But I'll be happy to explain it to you if you'd like to come in to my office."

"Is Gayle going to do it?" Her voice rose insistently.

"That's confidential. I can't talk to you about what I'm doing to help other people."

"So you are helping her. I knew it. Well, you should know Gayle is using you. She says Sabrina made a will appointing her as Ian's guardian and trustee. She's desperate to show that Sabrina is dead so she can get that will into court."

Whew! Brandi sure was working hard to suck me in to the conversation she wanted to have. But as a therapist I've had a lot of experience dealing with manipulation. She wasn't going to lure me into discussing her problems over the phone.

"Brandi, I have to go now. Would you like to come to my office tomorrow at 11:00 or would you rather check your calendar and call for another appointment?"

"You can tell Gayle that she's going to be in a lot of trouble if she keeps trying to take Ian away from me."

"I have to go. You can call back and leave a message about when you want to come in."

"No, wait. I'll come tomorrow at 11:00. And remember, I'm Sabrina's sister. Those Moxie women aren't family and they have no rights when it comes to Sabrina."

"I'll see you tomorrow at 11:00 —736 Pearl."

My enthusiasm for painting was gone, so I set about putting my stuff away, wondering whether Brandi actually knew something that made her believe Sabrina would be found alive.

§ § §

Brandi showed up promptly at 11:00. She had that fit and expensive Boulder look—skin-tight designer jeans, black high-heeled knee-high boots, and a white cashmere turtleneck topped with a fire-engine-red Montbell down jacket. Her long blonde hair hung loose under a black shearling sheepskin hat. Her makeup was skillfully applied to give the impression her looks were all natural. Sort of an eye-candy girl who looks the way she wants you to see her.

She had two fat leather photo albums in her arms, which she dropped on the table in front of the couch. Then she took off her jacket and hat and sat down. As she looked up at me, her whole face lit up in a warm smile. "I brought these to show you some pictures of Sabrina," she said. "I want you to know the special person that she is." Brandi's blue eyes showed a hint of tears, but her bouncy step and cheerful voice didn't fit the picture of a grieving person.

I sat next to her on the couch as she paged through pictures of her and Sabrina growing up, starting with cute shots of her as a toddler clinging tightly to her older sister's hand, then moving on to shots of them sharing happy family times as they grew up. "This was a trip we took to New York City when I was nine and Sabrina was fifteen," she said pointing to a page of snapshots of them in Central Park. "Sabrina and I had so much fun on that trip! Mom and Dad let us go off on our own on the subway to the Empire State Building, the Met, Rockefeller Center and all over. Sabrina acted like I was her best friend instead of a little sister six years younger than her. I felt so grown-up and special."

Brandi continued paging through pictures of holidays, birthday parties, and outdoor sports, many showing her gazing adoringly at Sabrina who was helping her with some difficult task or activity. But the pictures ended before Brandi became a teenager. "Our mom died when I was twelve and Sabrina was eighteen," she said. "No more pictures. Everything changed. Dad was overwhelmed and always working, so Sabrina watched out for me. She was everything to me in those years. Do you have a sister?" she asked, gently touching my arm.

"No, just a brother," I said, noticing that I was feeling a sympathetic connection to her.

"Too bad," she said. "A sister is very special."

Listening to her, I was beginning to wish I had a sister. I thought about Elisa who is like a sister to me.

"It sounds like you and Sabrina are very close," I said, carefully referring to Sabrina in the present tense.

She closed the album we'd been looking at, and turned sideways to face me. "Sabrina and I have a very strong bond," she said earnestly. "She and Ian are all the family I have since our father died two years ago. I've been living with her and Ian for the last eight months and we've had some great times together. Since we're both single, we help each other out and we share our worries and hopes for the future. Of course we have our differences, too, like all sisters do."

"Can you tell me about some of the differences?"

Her eyes narrowed. "One issue is those Moxie women. They think everything they do in that stupid group is a deep dark secret. Well it isn't. I know a lot." She tapped her fingers on the coffee table and continued sharply. "Like Sabrina's big mysterious birthday celebration.

I knew about it. She tried to make it out to be nothing. Said her big fortieth party with family and friends was the real deal. But I knew about the vision journey or whatever and I knew where they were going." She sat back, eyes closed, rubbing her forehead.

I gave her a minute, then asked gently, "You said last night that you're hoping Sabrina will be found alive. Do you know something about what happened up there that the police and the searchers don't know?"

She opened her eyes and her face brightened. "Missing persons do turn up alive, you know. Just because she's missing doesn't mean she's dead. The law considers a missing person alive unless there's proof the person is dead. Without proof, you have to wait at least five years before the courts declare the person dead, and that's what's driving Gayle crazy."

"Because she needs to prove that Sabrina is dead to get the court to appoint her as Ian's guardian?"

"Exactly. Which is where you come in. How does your process of talking to spirits work?"

I explained the apparition chamber and told her how it works for the person who is trying to contact a loved one who has died.

"So the person is in there alone. You don't stay with them?"

"Right."

"Then how do you know they really contacted the dead person they say they contacted?"

"That's really not my concern. The point of contacting the spirit is for the grieving person to resolve issues or accept the person's death. However that works for them is fine with me."

"But Gayle will lie and say she talked to Sabrina's spirit when that's impossible because Sabrina is still alive. Then she'll try to use that as evidence that Sabrina is dead."

"I seriously doubt that the court would declare Sabrina dead based on a report from Gayle that she contacted her spirit."

Brandi's mouth was smiling but her eyes oozed anger. "Well I don't want her going around saying she talked to Sabrina's spirit. We all need to think positively. We need to trust that whatever Sabrina's doing, wherever she is, she's where she's supposed to be and she'll come back to us when the time is right."

She jumped up, gathered her albums, hat and jacket, and gave me a look that sent chills down my spine. "I have to go now. You can tell those Moxie bitches they'd better not mess with me. If Sabrina doesn't come back soon, I'm going to petition the court to be named trustee of her property and to be Ian's guardian. Ian doesn't want to live with Gayle. He wants to stay with me. We're family and that trumps it all for both of us." She strode briskly to the door, head held high, and left the room with no backward glance.

Chapter 11

Saturday morning I pushed the whole Sabrina problem out of my head. I drove over to visit my 87-year-old grandmother at Glenwood Gardens, the cozy assisted living house she had moved into after her nursing home abruptly shut down two months ago. I cherish my visits with Gramma, even though Alzheimer's has taken away so much of who she was. Sometimes she can't quite remember who I am, but we still connect at a deep emotional level that grounds me in a way nothing else does.

I stepped lightly along the walkway to the door of the little house, rejoicing once again that she now lives in this homey place with plants, pets and people who love her. Mary Ellen, the RN who is one of the founders of Glenwood Gardens answered my knock and gave me a quick hug. "Martha's in her room listening to music," she said. "She was a little tired after breakfast."

I found Gramma sitting in her rose-colored easy chair; eyes closed, head tipped back, fingers clasped loosely together in her lap. The gentle strains of Schumann's Piano Concerto in A minor filled the room. As I moved slowly toward her, she opened her eyes and smiled. I sat on the arm of her chair, hugged and kissed her, then leaned back against the chair with my arm around her shoulders as we listened to the rest of the concerto together.

When the music stopped, I got up to turn off the CD player, and then sat on her bed across from her chair. "Hi, Gramma. Are you still tired?"

She looked bewildered. "Is it lunchtime?"

"No. We have some time to visit before lunch."

Her eyes wandered to one of her paintings of orange poppies on the wall above the bed. "I like this room," she said. "I like the flowers."

"That's one of your paintings, Gramma. I like it too. I think it's one of your best."

She turned her gaze back to me. "Cleo," she said. "How are you?" I saw a quick flash of recognition and awareness in her eyes that brought tears to mine.

Suddenly I wanted to tell her everything. I needed to confide in someone who loved me unconditionally, and would listen without pushing me, even if she couldn't understand what I was talking about. The words tumbled out like they used to when I was a kid with a big problem. "Oh, Gramma. I'm having a hard time right now. I'm pregnant and I really want this baby, but I don't know whether I want to marry Pablo. He wants us to get married, but I don't know if that's what I want." I stopped and took a deep breath.

"Babies cry."

Was that a random comment or was she actually cautioning me about the stress of being a single mom? "I know, Gramma. Babies are a lot of work. But I've been getting to know some single moms lately, who seem to have kept up with their professions and their kids pretty well, by supporting each other. Being a single mom would be hard but I could do it. And Pablo would help even if we weren't married."

"I'm married to James." Gramma doesn't remember that Grampa died five years ago, and I never contradict her about that. If her memories of their life together feel like today to her, why spoil her enjoyment?

"If I thought Pablo and I could be as happy as you and Grampa, I'd marry him tomorrow," I said sadly. Like an old home movie, a vision of them happy and in love living in the old house before Gramma got sick popped into my head. "But Pablo says he can't live in Boulder, so if we got married, I couldn't stay in your house. And we have other issues. Like trust. Years ago he deserted me to go off to Mexico to find himself. What's to say he won't do it again?" I didn't want to end up feeling like the Moxie members do about their ex-husbands.

Gramma looked intently at me. "Happy," she said. "Be happy."

"I want to," I said, my voice breaking. "But I don't know how you and Grampa did it so well. Sometimes I feel smothered by Pablo. Like this week. He's been in California for training since Monday. He's called me every night, full of questions and advice to make sure I'm taking care of myself. He acts like I can't manage on my own. And I haven't even told him what I'm working on for Bruce. I can't tell him, because I know he'd be mad. That says something."

Gramma patted my arm. She couldn't know what I was talking about, but she could tell I was upset. Much as I needed her support, it was time to pull myself together, before she got depressed or agitated. "You're such a sweetheart, Gramma," I said smiling at her. I moved back over to her chair and gave her another kiss and some hugs. "I think it's almost lunchtime. Let's go out to the kitchen and see what they're fixing."

§ § §

I had agreed to meet my fourth Moxie member, Diana, late that afternoon. She's a physical therapist and a massage therapist and she had invited me to come to her office to talk, after which she'd give me a massage. At first I thought I shouldn't accept, but then I figured why not. The Moxie women aren't my clients. Bruce is. And he just wants me to get information. And a massage sounded wonderful.

Diana works at Holistic Energy, a wellness and rehabilitation clinic that offers physical therapy, massage, Pilates, therapeutic yoga, and other helpful services. The clinic occupies a large section of a fairly new modern building in east Boulder. I sat in the waiting room for a few minutes along with a fit young guy wearing a knee brace and a young woman with a shoulder immobilizer. I figured Diana and the other therapists must be doing well. Boulder is full of athletes—both elite and aspiring—fertile ground for clinics like this one.

She came out wearing a sleeveless black tee shirt and loose gray drawstring pants, and took me back to a massage room equipped with comfortable chairs as well as a massage table. "I know you want to talk about Sabrina," she said as we sat down, "but I'm not sure what you want to know."

I took a minute to relax into the room's dim lighting and soft music, then pulled myself back to the reason I was there. "Just tell me about Sabrina," I said. "Anything you think might be important to finding out what happened to her."

Diana flexed the muscles in her right arm as she drummed her fingers on the arm of her chair. "Sabrina is a loving, caring person and a good friend, but she's so co-dependent—always taking care of people, rescuing people, always putting other people's needs ahead of her own." She rolled her eyes. "I hate to say this, but her helpfulness is her fatal flaw."

I'm not a fan of pop-psych jargon. Why pathologize the tendency to put others' needs ahead of your own by calling it co-dependency? As a nurse, taking care of people was Sabrina's job. I needed more information to see it as a flaw rather than expected behavior from a helping professional. "Besides being a nurse and taking care of her son Ian, who else does she take care of?"

Diana put her palms together in front of her chest, wrists flexed, and raised and lowered her arms several times. "I like to keep my muscles loose," she said. "Now what were you asking? Oh, right, who Sabrina takes care of. She'll take care of anyone she thinks needs something whether or not the person wants her help. When she started Moxie, she acted way overly maternal toward us. She'd take care of all of us, if we let her. But we didn't. Unfortunately there were other people in her life who were more than willing to play the needy role."

"Could you tell me about one or two of them?"

Diana laughed. "Where to start? Her ex? Worthless boyfriends?" She shook her head. "No. Let's start with her sister Brandi. Sabrina's been taking care of her since their mother died when she was eighteen and Brandi was twelve. Their dad was a total workaholic and he left it to Sabrina to keep Brandi out of trouble. Which she couldn't do. Brandi got pregnant at seventeen, manipulated the guy into marrying her, then lost the baby. She went back to her wild crowd and got a divorce. Sabrina convinced their dad to support Brandi even though he thought she should learn to take care of herself. It went on and on like that. Brandi would get into trouble, their dad would threaten to disown her, and Sabrina would come to her rescue and persuade their dad to keep supporting her." Diana stopped, got up and got us each a glass of water from a dispenser in the corner.

I thought about Brandi telling me about the strong bond she and Sabrina have, versus Gayle telling me Sabrina didn't want Ian left permanently with Brandi. What to believe? "How do Sabrina and Brandi get along now?" I asked.

Diana scowled. "Brandi's thirty-four now and Sabrina's forty and they're still doing the same dance. Brandi lurches from one disaster to another and manipulates Sabrina into rescuing her. Sabrina feels sorry for her, feels responsible for her."

A grin replaced her scowl. "But their dad got the last laugh. Two years ago, when he died, they found out that he had deducted all the money he'd given Brandi from her share of the estate. Sabrina got most of the money. Moxie had to work hard to convince her not to give half to Brandi. She was so resistant, we finally had to do an intervention. She only agreed because of Ian." She shrugged. "But now Brandi is living with her, sponging off her, taking everything she can get."

"So your intervention convinced Sabrina not to give Brandi half of her inheritance, but didn't persuade her to stop taking care of Brandi?"

"True, but a few weeks ago, we got her to give Brandi an ultimatum about finding a job and getting her own place. So the gravy train was finally coming to an end." Diana put her arms behind her, interlocked her fingers and pulled her arms up to stretch her shoulders. I could almost feel the tension roll off her.

Bells and whistles were going off in my head. Had Moxie's intervention led Brandi to get rid of Sabrina in hopes of getting control of her money before she was pushed out on her own? "Do you think Sabrina's relationship with Brandi has something to do with her disappearance?" I asked.

"Actually, no. Much as I dislike Brandi, I think she's too disorganized to pull off anything like that. I mostly told you about Brandi so you'd get how co-dependent Sabrina is. Where I think that's significant is with some of her worthless former boyfriends. Especially this guy, Erik, she was with last spring. He was such a liar and a con man, totally using her, but she couldn't see it."

"How was he using her?

"He had some holistic healing business and a deal where he sold people kits to grow herbs that they were supposed to be able to sell back at huge profits. She invested money and connected him with other people who invested money, but the whole thing turned out to be a scam. They all lost their investments."

I gasped. My heart raced as I struggled to speak. "You say his name was Erik?" I finally asked in a jittery voice. "What was his last name?"

Diana hesitated. "It started with a "V.' Maybe Vane? No, Vaughn. That's it. Erik Vaughn."

Omigod! Erik Vaughn. A wave of dizziness washed over me. Sabrina was involved with the sociopath I met last summer when I was helping Elisa's friend Sharon find out who murdered her husband? Erik didn't do it, but in the process of my investigation I uncovered a lot of his nasty past. And he threatened to some day make me pay for that.

"Are you all right?" Diana's voice sounded faint, as if I were in a tunnel.

I took a deep breath. "I know him," I said. "He's not a nice man. What happened with him and Sabrina?"

"He wanted to marry her. We were finally able to get her to break up with him, but I think she might have slipped and gone back to him if he hadn't suddenly disappeared. She was shocked. Even though they were no longer together, she couldn't believe he left her without saying anything. Plus he owed her and other people money that they'd invested n his business. The police called it a scam, but she didn't believe it. She was convinced something happened to him. She never heard from him again—or so she said—but she knew how we felt about him, so she might have lied about that. I think maybe he came back and she went off with him."

§ § §

Diana's massage was so what I needed after hearing about Erik. Her strong muscles and skillful hands wiped away the tension in my body and left me slack and smiling. I didn't ask her any more questions, just thanked her and went home. When Pablo called that evening, I told him I'd had a massage and was feeling great. Didn't tell him about Sabrina or Moxie, or anything else that might upset him. I figured Diana would call that co-dependent, but I called it a sweet and satisfying conversation.

Chapter 12

I woke up Sunday morning feeling relaxed and comfortable. No nausea. Got me wondering whether massage is the cure for morning sickness. I didn't enjoy Diana's dogmatic negative assessments of people, but her massage was so amazing, I was ready to go back tomorrow for more.

This morning I was going to Elisa's house in the foothills for brunch. As I drove up the winding mountain road, I wondered what the Moxie members would think about Elisa's and my relationship. Even though we're about the same age—I'm thirty-seven and she's forty—our relationship isn't exactly one of equals. She's been a psychologist way longer than I have, she has tenure at the university, and she has lots of money thanks to her husband Jack's skill at real estate development.

If they knew her, the Moxie women would probably remind me that she can be bossy and high-handed, but I'd remind them that she'd lay down her life for me if it came to that—which it almost did last summer. But more than that, we have some chemistry that creates trust at a very deep level. I can let go and be totally myself with her, which isn't easy for a therapist.

Elisa met me at the door with a big smile and a glass of ginger ale. "Hi sweetie," she said, handing me the glass. "This is in case you need to settle your stomach after the drive."

"You think of everything, as usual," I said, taking a sip. I was still feeling good. Smells of wood smoke and coffee drifting in from the living room didn't even bother me.

Elisa had a roaring fire going in the living room's moss rock fireplace and food set out on the coffee table in front of the couch.

The room had a cozy ambiance, despite the vaulted ceilings and the wall of soaring windows framing the mountain view that made their house worth the big bucks.

She took my jacket and motioned me toward the couch. "Sit, girl," she said. "I put the food out so we can munch. Didn't want to set a huge plate of food in front of you when you might be feeling nauseous, but I do want to be sure you eat for the baby." She had made an asparagus quiche and blueberry muffins, and put out a gorgeous fruit plate.

I sat and leaned back with a huge sigh. "Thanks," I said. "But I need to talk before I eat. This whole Sabrina situation is getting so complicated. I'm already beginning to feel like I'm in over my head."

She sat next to me on the couch and turned toward me smiling. "I'm all ears, girl. Catch me up on what's been going on."

I sighed. "I've been meeting with the five women who were up at Indian Peaks with Sabrina. They're actually a group called Moxie. A single moms' support group that they named Moxie to emphasize that they're gutsy adventurous women. I've met them all and had long conversations with four of the five. The whole thing is kind of spooky. They don't know whether she's dead or alive and they keep changing what they say. Which is especially confusing given that they want to try to reach Sabrina through my Contact project." I leaned forward to put some fruit on a small glass plate, then bit into a sweet strawberry.

"Tell me more about them."

"Okay, there's Gayle. She's a real estate agent and she Bruce's sister, and she says she is or was Sabrina's best friend. Then there's Hana—Asian, a computer whiz, and also a numerologist. She told me all about Sabrina's destiny number. There's Lark, a nurse who worked with Sabrina at the hospital—lives up in Nederland, very independent type, says she would have left Moxie a while ago but Sabrina kept talking her into staying. There's Diana—a physical therapist and a terrific massage therapist, also into boxing. Kind of confrontational and judgmental. Loves pop psych jargon. Told me all about how Sabrina is co-dependent and an enabler. Then there's Paige. I've only met her briefly. Yoga teacher and a Wiccan high priestess. One of those charismatic voices that can lead you anywhere. She's the one who set up the wilderness journey. They're all smart, strong, powerful women, but they're all over the place about Sabrina's disappearance. And they seem to think my apparition chamber will give them answers."

"Whew! That does sound like one strange group of women, Elisa said, pouring herself a cup of coffee. "I guess they think that if she's dead they can reach her and find out what happened, but if they don't reach her, that means she's alive."

"Something like that."

"I'm not telling you how to run your business, but you did tell them about how people don't always reach the dead person they're trying to contact?" Elisa said sharply.

"Not yet," I said wearily. "We can't really have that conversation right now. They're too distraught and confused to even think about whether to go right or left. They just want to plunge ahead, hoping for some resolution." I sipped my ginger ale.

"So now you're stuck right along with them? Is that a position you want to be in, girl?" Elisa asked, her voice rising.

"It's even worse than that," I said. "I found out from one of the women that Sabrina was involved with that sociopath, Erik Vaughn—the guy who was friends with your friend Sharon last summer. Remember him?"

Elisa shrugged. "The name's familiar, but I can't put it to a face." She bit into a muffin.

"Great face," I said, "but he was a big-time scam artist and worse. Selling people $500 herb kits they were supposed to grow and sell back to him, but then he disappeared without ever buying them back." I put a muffin and a slice of quiche on my plate and took a small bit of the quiche, which was delicious.

"Come on, honey! You can't be serious! Why would Sabrina get involved with someone like that?"

"For one thing, he has a hot body and a way of being charming that's hard to resist. I admit I liked him myself at first. But Pablo met him a couple of times and no way found him charming. I think his police radar picked Erik for a rat from the get-go."

Elisa polished off a piece of pineapple, raised her eyebrows and gave me that this-is-so-unbelievable look that I know so well. "So Sabrina fell for Erik's charms? Really?" she asked.

"I can only tell you what I was told," I said, trying not to sound defensive. I knew Elisa's questions were well intended, but I did feel kind of bombarded. I turned my face down to my plate and ate my muffin.

"Sure. Sorry if I'm being pushy. It's just hard to believe she'd be with him is all," Elisa said. "Anyway, what else do you know?"

"This is great food, Elisa," I said. "Anyway, here's what I know. Apparently Sabrina and Erik had a relationship last spring and summer. He had a nutrition and exercise practice, Vaughn's Holistic Healing, and he did some work at the hospital where she worked. After she got involved with Erik, she got friends and colleagues to invest in his herb-growing business. Of course they all lost their money when he left town."

Elisa frowned. "Did she break up with him or the other way around?"

"It sounds like she broke up with him. Somehow her Moxie friends were convinced he was a con artist and no good for her. She resisted but finally broke up with him. From my interactions with Erik, I know that wouldn't have been easy if he didn't want to end the relationship. He's very good at getting his way."

"So they think he came back after her?" Elisa cocked her head, which I knew meant she was skeptical.

"At least one of them thinks that. She could be right. Erik has a pattern of marrying women with money. The three women he married died or disappeared under mysterious circumstances, and he ended up with their money. Sabrina had an inheritance from her father. If she did marry him, it could be the worst choice she ever made."

"Do you think he convinced her to go off with him and get married without telling anyone, even Ian? Why would she do that?"

"The police were looking for Erik because of the herb-growing scam. Also, her friends are all totally against him. And they are some powerful women. She probably wouldn't have wanted to fight it out with them."

By then we were done eating. The sun was shining brightly, which in Colorado's altitude and dry climate warms winter days into feeling more like fall. We decided to take Maria's dog, Gustav, on an easy hike up a short trail just down the road from Elisa's house, and continue our conversation as we hiked.

The trail was icy in spots and muddy in others, so we climbed slowly, but it felt good to stretch my legs and work off some of the tension I'd been storing up.

"Okay, honey. You have a theory," Elisa said as Gustav strained his leash, trying to get her to move faster. "But it's not a very good one. I just can't see Sabrina leaving Ian that way. She would have known he'd be worried sick about her."

"But he's not worried sick, is he? From what Maria said, Ian and Brandi think Sabrina is okay and they aren't worried about her. Maybe she told them that she was planning to go off with Erik, but …Yikes!" My foot hit something hard that made me trip and fall to one knee. It was the skeleton of some small animal, picked clean and left on the side of the path. I shuddered as an image of Sabrina lying under a snow bank flashed through my mind. Suddenly I hoped she had gone off with Erik.

Elisa grabbed my arm and helped me up, while Gustav sniffed the bones. "Are you okay?" she asked.

"Fine," I said, ignoring a slight shiver. "I just got distracted and tripped on those creepy bones. Anyway, maybe Sabrina made Brandi and Ian promise not to tell because she didn't want her friends to know. Remember Maria said she knows something that's confidential."

"But what about the searchers? Would Sabrina go off like that knowing all those people would be searching for her? Would she let her friends go through the grief of thinking she's dead? That seems so cold and cruel."

I stopped dead in my tracks. I didn't want to see the truth in Elisa's points, but I had to face it. "You're right! I'm just spinning out possibilities without thinking through the details. When you put it that way, I see the conflict. Sabrina's friends all say she is a kind, caring, helpful person. How could she do something so thoughtless?"

"Maybe Erik came and kidnapped her," Elisa said. "He sounds like the kind of guy who could pull that off."

"Definitely he is. But that wouldn't explain Ian and Brandi not being worried. They have to know something."

The trail got a little steeper toward the top and we climbed silently for a few minutes, pacing our breathing. At the summit was a bench facing the stunning view below. We sat and took it in. A spectacular mountain view puts my world in perspective and clears my head of the fog of details swirling around inside.

I had a sudden flash of clarity, followed by intense foreboding. "Even if she is alive, I think she's in terrible trouble," I said. "I think someone needs to talk to the police about finding Erik."

"And I think we need to find out from Maria what Ian and Brandi know or think they know about where Sabrina is," Elisa said.

As we wound our way back down to Elisa's house, Gustav jumped and pulled on his leash, barking excitedly. "He sees Maria's car," Elisa said. "She's back from rehearsal. Let's go see if we can impress her with the urgency of Sabrina's situation so she'll tell us what she knows."

Maria was in the kitchen sitting on one of the high stools at the center island snacking on the remains of the food Elisa had put away before we went for our hike. We joined her. She sat on the floor and grabbed Gustav in a big hug.

I had mixed feelings about trying to get her to break her confidentiality agreement and tell us what she knew, but my concern for Sabrina won out. I told her why I was worried that Sabrina might be with Erik.

Maria burst into tears, jumped up and paced around the room, Gustav running frantically behind her. "I promised Ian I wouldn't tell anyone. If I could, I'd talk to him, tell him what you said about Erik, ask him if I could tell you." Her voice broke. "But he's up in Copper Mountain at a meet. I can't call him now. He's too busy to talk. Plus I don't want to upset him while he's competing. You'll just have to wait until he gets home." She continued pacing, her head in her hands.

"Waiting can be risky," Elisa said. "Don't you think he'd want you to tell us? Wouldn't his main priority be keeping his mother safe?"

"He thinks she is safe," Maria said, shaking her head in denial. "But of course he doesn't know all the stuff you told me. Actually Ian and Brandi like Erik. They said he's a good athlete and fun to hike with. They were sad when Sabrina broke up with him. Are you sure Erik is as bad as you say?"

"Absolutely positive," I said. "The last thing Erik said to me before he disappeared last summer was that someday when I least expect it he'll show up and make me pay for exposing him as a fraud. He said he'll never forget me and what I did to him and that he knows how to find me." I felt a surge of nausea—not pregnancy related.

"That's pretty scary." Maria stopped next to my chair, blew her nose into a tissue and wiped her eyes. Than she sat on the floor and gathered Gustav into her lap. "Okay, Cleo, I'll tell you what I know." She paused, took a deep breath and continued. "Brandi told Ian that Erik called right after his mom and her friends went up to the mountains for their celebration, and he said that he had a really special birthday surprise for Sabrina. So Brandi told him where Sabrina was. I guess he said he was going up there to find her, but he told Brandi not to tell anyone except Ian. She's sure Erik went up and got Sabrina and they went off—like maybe the surprise was a special trip or something."

"Has she heard from Sabrina?"

"I don't think so."

"Isn't that strange? Wouldn't she call if she was on a trip so everyone would know she's okay?"

"I guess it is a little strange, but Brandi wants to give Sabrina space to work out her relationship with Erik. She's sure Sabrina will be back soon. That's all I know. Don't ask me any more questions." She jumped up and headed off to her room with Gustav at her heels.

Chapter 13

I drove down the mountain from Elisa's house brooding about the Erik situation. My head throbbed with possibilities jumping over each other to be front and center. Should I confront Brandi to get the details of her phone conversation with Erik? Should I share Maria's information with the Moxie members? Or could I, given that it was told to me in confidence? Should I try to find Erik on my own? Maybe call his brother in Minneapolis? Or should I go directly to the police? But if Erik knew the police were on to him, there was no telling what he'd do.

I wanted to make a considered choice of action, rather than jumping in impulsively and making things worse. Part of me longed to discuss it with Pablo—especially since he knew Erik—but my sensible part warned me not to tell him I was involved in another possible murder investigation. I could hear his voice in my head reminding me, "Amateurs shouldn't get involved in police business. It's way too dangerous. Yada, yada, yada." He'd pitch a fit if he knew I was doing it again. I didn't want to hear it. I already had enough on my plate being pregnant and trying to work out my relationship with him.

"Yo, Cleo!"

"Tyler! Good grief!" I swerved sharply when I saw the surfer-dude spirit floating in midair outside my window. "Can't you see I'm driving? You need to get inside the car before I crash and end up as dead as you are."

"Chill, Cleo," he said as he drifted down through the roof of my car and perched cross-legged on the passenger seat beside me. "You're not even wet."

Easy for him to say. He's already dead. But I decided to forget about how he almost ran me off the road, and see if I could get some advice. "Tyler, I don't know what to do about Erik. Can you help me with that?"

"Heavies are coming in. Don't hotdog. You'll get pounded."

"So you're telling me to play it safe?" This was strange. Usually I'm the one worried about risks and Tyler is the one telling me to go for it.

"Sometimes it's cool to surf with a buddy."

"So I should get some help? Does that mean I should go to the police?"

"Sometimes the best place to catch a wave is your home swell."

I mulled that over as I maneuvered around a sharp curve. Amazingly Tyler didn't float away while I was thinking. Then I got it. "My home swell? You mean talk to Pablo instead of going to the Boulder police?"

"Keep your leash attached to your board, Cleo. Don't get axed." With that, he floated out the window, surfed up over the trees, and disappeared.

§ § §

I called Pablo as soon as I got home. I got his voice mail. Even though it was Sunday afternoon, he was in a training class. They don't take weekends off at these intensives. I left a message. "Hey, sweetie, hope you're having a good day. I need your advice about something, but it's a long story—too long for voicemail. I have a meeting this afternoon, but maybe we can talk later? Can you leave a message telling me when is a good time to call tonight? Love ya, bye."

§ § §

My afternoon meeting was with Paige Mosier, the last of the Moxie women. Looking back over my notes, I realized that Gayle's email introducing the women had said that Paige is also Rivka Ravenstar. That meant Paige had organized the personal journey gathering where Sabrina had disappeared. I wondered why none of the women had said anything about that when I talked with them. I decided her Rivka role would be the first topic I would bring up with her.

Paige had suggested we meet for tea at 3:00 at Boulder's Dushanbe Tea House. A pleasant sweet spicy scent of scented teas and Middle Eastern food surrounded me as I entered the restaurant. I always enjoy going there. The Teahouse—a gift to Boulder from our sister city, Dushanbe, the capital of Tajikistan—was hand carved by Tajik artisans, shipped to Boulder in pieces, then reassembled downtown next to Boulder Creek. The ambiance is both stunning and serene. Vivid colorful carved panels are everywhere you look—ceiling, columns, walls—and a central fountain with hammered copper sculptures splashes into a pool surrounded by plants.

I spotted Paige right away sitting at an isolated corner table with a squat black teapot in front of her. Hard to miss that striking mop of curly red hair. As I approached, she jumped up to give me a hug, even though I'd only met her the one time at Gayle's. It's the Boulder way. Despite her slender willowy body, her arms and shoulders were strong, which reminded me that she's a yoga teacher.

"I hope you don't mind that I already ordered tea," Paige said with a smile. "I got here a little early to relax and enjoy the atmosphere." Once again, I was struck by her lyrical voice, which drew me in right away.

I sat and ordered a pot of tangerine herbal tea while Paige got a refresher for the green jasmine she was drinking. She made idle chitchat about the beauty of the teahouse until our server was done. Then she sat quietly waiting for me to begin.

The teahouse was half empty and no one was close enough to overhear us, so I got right to the point. "If I have this right, you set up the personal journey gathering," I said. "You're Rivka Ravenstar, is that right?"

She showed no sign of surprise at my question. "That's right," she said. "Rivka Ravenstar is the name I use for my business—teaching yoga and conducting wilderness journeys for women. It's my Wiccan high priestess name. Do you know much about Wicca?"

I poured some tea from my teapot into my cup and took a sip.

Sweet, spicy and delicious. I knew very little about Wicca, but I tossed out what I could come up with. "Wicca is an earth-based religion that has rituals and ceremonies outside in nature, right?" I said tentatively.

She nodded. "Yes. We Wiccans feel very close to the earth. For us the soul of nature gives life to the universe." I leaned back and relaxed as the melodic quality of her voice turned her words into poetry. "Wicca is what got me into taking women on wilderness journeys," she said. "It's a way of giving modern women the opportunity to connect with the natural world the way land-based people of our past did. Dialoguing with nature in silence allows for inner reflection, discovery, and new perspectives."

Listening to her, I could hear that Paige was a natural at leading these women's journeys. I might become Wiccan myself if I listened much longer. "Are the other Moxie members Wiccans?" I asked.

Paige smiled, her green eyes sparkling. "No, I'm the only one. I've never tried to convert them. Wiccans don't proselytize. But the journeys aren't about being Wiccan. That's my framework, but the journey is personal for each woman. They bring their own beliefs and inner rhythm to the experience."

Much as I was enjoying listening to her talk about Wicca, I forced myself back to my plan to get some specifics about the gathering. "Can you tell me a little about how you set up the event?" I asked.

"Sure," she said. "I've told it to the sheriff and other rescuers so many times that it feels like a memorized speech. We went up to the Rainbow Lakes Campground in the Indian Peaks Wilderness on November sixth. It was a Monday evening. No one else was there. We all brought food to share in a community meal, and we had a big fire, and a ceremony where we declared our intentions to renew our lives and our relationships through our personal journeys. We shared positive feelings about each other, and each put forward our hopes for new visions for ourselves. It ended with a celebration circle with candles. Then we slept in our tents."

"Then you went on the individual journeys the next morning?"

Tears welled up in her eyes. "Yes," she said, her voice breaking. "Tuesday morning everyone gathered up their tents, sleeping bags and all their stuff and we locked it in my van. We each kept only our rain gear, a knife, water and some raw organic food bars. The starting place for each woman was mapped out. We each went off alone into the wilderness. I didn't see or hear any of them until we reassembled at sunrise Wednesday at the campground."

"Did you all get back there at about the same time?"

"Pretty much. Lark and Diana were there when I got there. Then Gayle showed up, and then Hana. We were supposed to have a circle gathering to share our experiences and personal insights, but we kept waiting for Sabrina to show up before we started. After a couple of hours, we got worried and started looking for her. We combed the area, calling and searching, getting more and more frantic. When it got to be noon and we still hadn't found her, I called the sheriff." Paige stopped and pulled out a tissue to wipe her eyes.

I waited until she looked calm, then asked softly, "What do you think happened to her?"

She shook her head. More tears ran down her face. "I have no idea. Nothing like this has ever happened at one of my wilderness journeys. I can't imagine how she just disappeared. I've gone over and over every minute of the time we were there. I'm obsessed. I blame myself."

"Do you think someone might have picked her up in a car? That maybe she went off with someone?"

"I guess someone could have picked her up, but she wouldn't just go off. Sabrina cared too much about being a good mom to leave Ian without telling him where she was going. She'd never do that. She knows what it's like to lose your mom as a teenager."

I didn't feel comfortable sharing what Maria had told me about Ian believing Sabrina had been picked up. Time to move on to another topic. I sipped my tea and thought about how to bring up the Moxie mess. Again I opted for the direct approach. "From my conversations with the other Moxie women, I've gotten the idea that Sabrina wanted the Moxie members to go on the personal journeys as a way of resolving some serious issues that had come up in the group. Would you agree?"

She closed her eyes briefly, then opened them and gazed directly into mine. "That was certainly a big part of it," she said, softly. "But Sabrina also had some personal issues that she wanted to work on. She was looking for a renewed vision—some kind of new direction in her life."

I kept the eye contact as I pushed on. "I know that's all very personal and confidential, but given what's happened, I'm wondering if you can tell me any more about what she was hoping for."

Paige checked her teapot and found it empty. She picked up a spoon, stirred the dregs in her cup, then placed the spoon carefully on the table. Finally she responded. "Has anyone said anything about the thirty-day plan Sabrina mentioned at the circle ceremony that night?"

Sabrina had a plan? Why was she the first to mention it? I stifled my surprise and answered calmly. "No. No one told me about that. What was her thirty-day plan?"

Paige turned her gaze inward. "I don't know anything specific," she said. "Sabrina said she was feeling overwhelmed and burdened by many people close to her, that she knew giving had been her pattern in life, and that she felt that she was giving too much." Paige stopped as if a wall had come up in front of her. But she pushed through it and went on slowly. "Apparently this all started when Diana told her she was an enabler, which Sabrina said she thought was ridiculous at first. But she said she had come to believe it and she wanted to change it. And she had a thirty-day plan to do that."

This sounded like some information that might help us figure out what happened to Sabrina. I wanted to know more. "Do you know what has happened to her plan? Sabrina's been missing almost thirty days."

Paige winced and her cheeks flushed. She cleared her throat. "Well…um…I know a little," she stuttered. "But I'll only speak for myself here." Her eyes darted around the room, then returned to meet my gaze. "I was part of the plan," she said. "Sabrina lent me some money a year ago so I could help my disabled brother. I haven't been able to pay her back, and she told me right before our gathering that I needed to repay the loan in thirty days." She rubbed her neck and looked away. "I don't really have the money, but I could get it if I had to. And I would get it and pay her back in a flash if she were here."

Tears filled her eyes as she continued. "I never meant to take advantage of her. She said she had the money to spare. Now I so wish I could give her back that money today. But I don't know what to do except pay it back to Ian or Sabrina's estate when we finally find out what happened to her."

I could feel Paige's pain. Grieving people who feel they have failed a lost loved one in some way have a strong desire to rectify that, to make amends. That can be very hard to resolve. When we said our goodbyes, I gave Paige an extra sympathetic hug.

Chapter 14

By the time I got home from my meeting with Paige, it was nearly five o'clock, and the sun had already set at my house by the foothills. The temperamental lock on my old front door is even trickier on a dark cold evening, but I finally got it open. I pushed my way in, dropped my jacket on the floor, and sagged onto my living room couch, wishing Pablo was sitting there ready to wrap me in his comfy, warm arms, and hold me tight.

But what I had was a voicemail message from him answering my voicemail. He said he'd be free at 6:00 p.m., so I could call him then. I used the extra time to take a hot shower and change into a robe, which cheered me up a little.

"Hi, hon," he said, answering on the first ring. "I hope you've been having as great a day as I have. This training is turning out to be amazing—and it doesn't hurt that we're doing it in warm, sunny southern California."

It warmed me just to hear his voice, but I couldn't match his perky mood. Also, I needed to get his take on the Erik thing and I needed to do it carefully. While I hated to keep Pablo at arm's length, I needed to give him just enough information to get his help—but not enough to give away my level of involvement in the case.

"My day can't match yours," I said. "I did have some great food for brunch at Elisa's this morning, and we went for a nice short hike after. But then I got a huge shock from Elisa's daughter, Maria. I found out that the mother of Maria's boyfriend may have gone off with that sociopath, Erik Vaughn. Remember him from last summer—the guy who scammed people with that herb-growing business?"

"Erik Vaughn is back in Boulder?" Pablo's voice dripped skepticism. "Hard to believe that when he knows the police are after him for that scam. But if he is back, please tell me you're not involved with him in any way, Cleo."

Uh oh. Just what I figured he'd say. Fortunately he couldn't see me rolling my eyes. "No, no, he's not here in town, at least not that I know of. It sounds like he may have snuck in and picked the lady up without anyone knowing. You remember that woman who went missing up at Indian Peaks last month? Sabrina Larson? Her son is Maria's boyfriend. And while searchers have been looking for Sabrina everywhere, her son Ian and his aunt have believed all along that Erik picked Sabrina up at the campground and they went off together."

"Why would she do that? And why wouldn't the son and the aunt tell the searchers what's going on?" I heard even more skepticism.

I sighed to myself, but not in a way he could hear. It's complicated. Apparently Sabrina was involved with Erik last spring and summer, probably right before we met him. They broke up and then he disappeared—you and I know why—and she never heard from him again. But apparently he called when Sabrina had gone to Indian Peaks and Brandi told him where Sabrina was."

"Wait, wait, wait. Who's Brandi?" Pablo's voice was rising. "And why wouldn't she have told the searchers by now if she thinks Sabrina went off with Erik?" he challenged.

This story was getting complicated. But I was into it now, so I had to go on explaining. "Brandi is Sabrina's sister and the aunt of Ian—Maria's boyfriend. Maria said Brandi and Ian have some reason to believe Sabrina wants them to keep it secret that she went off with Erik. But they don't know all that we know about Erik's past and what's happened to his former wives. I'm very worried about Sabrina. Like his other wives, she has some money, and I think that puts a huge target on her back where Erik is concerned."

"Cleo, just how involved are you in this situation? Why is it your responsibility?"

I leaned back, closed my eyes and worked on staying calm. "It's not my responsibility, but if she's with Erik, she's in danger."

"You could be right. But there's not a whole lot you can do about it. She has a right to go off with whoever she wants to go off with."

"But should I tell the police what I know?"

"What do you really know? You don't even know if she did go off with him. She may have fallen and hit her head in some isolated part of Indian Peaks. It's snowed up there since she disappeared. Her body could be covered up and they just haven't found her yet. Her family may be hanging on to the idea that she went off with Erik because they don't want to face the fact that in all probability she's dead. I've seen that reaction a lot. People will grasp at any straw to keep hope alive."

"But shouldn't I tell the police about Erik?"

"I doubt they'd do much. Missing adults don't get anyone very excited. There are way too many of them. The cops will figure she had her reasons to run away and there's no law against it."

I sensed Pablo's impatience with my continued questions, but I couldn't stop myself. I'm a Scorpio and when I have a question I keep probing until I get an answer. "But wouldn't the cops want to catch Erik?" I asked.

"They might, but we know how accomplished he is at disappearing. They couldn't find him last summer and I doubt they could now."

"I can't leave it that way, Pablo. If Sabrina marries Erik and then mysteriously dies. I'd feel responsible if I hadn't tried to stop it."

"I still don't see why this is your responsibility, Cleo. I want you to be careful. You're pregnant, honey. You know what I always say about amateurs and police work. But if you feel that strongly about it, I'll give the Boulder PD a call. They're more likely to listen to me than to you."

I heaved a huge sigh of relief and ended the conversation before he could make me promise to stay out of the situation from now on. "Thanks, sweetie. I owe you. Let me know what they say, okay?"

§ § §

I was suddenly starving, so I fixed myself a grilled cheese sandwich and a bowl of tomato soup. There's something so soothing about comfort food on a cold night at home. I turned on the TV, surfed around, and ended up watching Miracle on 34th Street, which seems to run nonstop in December. I love its uplifting message about believing in more than we can rationally explain.

Part way through the movie, Gayle called. I know the movie ending by heart, so I went ahead and picked up. "Cleo, I'm desperate." Gayle's voice shook. "You have to help me! I need to contact Sabrina right away before Brandi goes any further. Is there any way we can do it tomorrow?" she begged.

"Why are you desperate to do it tomorrow?" I asked calmly, trying to reel her in a little.

Her words rushed over themselves as her story tumbled out with hardly a pause for breath. "I couldn't stand worrying about Ian any more, so I went over to Sabrina's today to reason with Brandi about Ian. I hoped if she understood I wasn't after Sabrina's money, she might back off and let Ian stay with me until Sabrina is found. But Brandi screamed at me. Wouldn't even let me in the front door. Accused me of harassing her. Threatened to call the police and get a restraining order against me. Said she's filing court papers tomorrow to be appointed the executor of Sabrina's property and Ian's guardian." Gayle finally reached a stopping point, panting and gasping.

I thought she was overreacting. I doubted that Brandi had this much power. I moved on to the bottom line. "Isn't Ian old enough to tell the court where he wants to stay?" I asked.

"He's sixteen. I expect he'd have a say," Gayle said briskly. "But the problem is he likes Brandi. He's a teenager and she lets him do whatever he wants most of the time. Sabrina and Ian were having some issues about his grades before she disappeared. All he cares about is snowboarding and he's been letting his grades slide. Sabrina was making him spend more time studying. But Brandi doesn't care about schoolwork. Ian knows I'd push him like Sabrina was, so he'd probably choose to stay with Brandi. We can't let that happen!"

I wondered why Maria had never mentioned anything about Ian and his mom arguing about his grades and how much time he spends snowboarding vs. studying. But if that was an issue, I could see how he'd prefer Brandi's laissez faire approach to parenting over Gayle's stricter stance. In fact he might favor Brandi's style over Sabrina's.

Enough that he was in no hurry for Sabrina to come home?

"I guess that's one of the problems with giving a sixteen-year-old this sort of choice," I said. "You can't assume they'll choose what's in their best interests. But what about Sabrina's will? Can Brandi get the court to make her Ian's guardian when Sabrina has a will making you his guardian?"

"Apparently she can," Gayle said dolefully. "I called my lawyer and he said that right now Sabrina is a missing person not a dead person. The law presumes that a missing person is alive until the person is proven dead. Unless her body is found, the courts won't declare her dead for five to seven years. Meanwhile the court can appoint whoever they choose as executor and guardian. The fact that Brandi is living there with Ian and that's she's Sabrina's only relative is in her favor. So she'll probably get appointed."

I thought about whether I should tell Gayle what Maria had told me about Sabrina and Erik. But as Pablo said, I don't really know anything. Brandi could be lying or could be wrong. Sabrina might have died in the mountains. Maybe Gayle is right about trying to reach her. If she did, we'd at least have something to go on.

But is contacting a spirit proof that the person is dead? I had no idea. Could a living person project their spirit into the apparition chamber? I'd never thought of that, never tried to contact a living person there.

"I called all the Moxie members before I called you," Gayle said. "They agree that the situation is desperate and that I should go ahead and try to contact Sabrina as long as I report back to the whole group right away. If we can have the session tomorrow, Moxie can meet tomorrow night for my report."

I had some time free Monday afternoon, so I agreed. But I had a sinking feeling. Tyler had said I'm not even wet, but I was starting to feel the water closing over my head.

Chapter 15

Gayle showed up right on time Monday afternoon with the pictures I had requested of her and Sabrina over the years—some including other Moxie members, others of her and her daughter Nicole with Sabrina and Sabrina's son Ian. I asked her to reminisce about good times she and Sabrina had shared.

First she pulled out a photo of two grinning kids in grubby jeans and sweatshirts standing in front of a bright orange two-person tent. "Here's a picture from a camping trip when Ian and Nicole were about ten. They wanted their own tent, no moms in it, so we agreed. They were so proud that they put it up themselves. But in the middle of the night a raccoon pawed at their tent and woke them up. They were sure it was a bear, started screaming. Scared us to death. After we got them back to sleep, Sabrina and I sat up and talked about how precious our kids are, how we'd do anything to keep them safe. Sabrina never forgot that conversation, brought it up after her dad died when she asked me to be Ian's guardian if anything happened to her. I'm sick at the thought of letting her down, letting Brandi win."

Another griever feeling regrets at having failed Sabrina in some way.

The next picture she selected was of a younger-looking Moxie group at a restaurant table, arms around each others' shoulders, glasses lifted. Gayle smiled, looking inward at a fond memory. "That was five years ago," she said. "We went out to celebrate the second anniversary of starting Moxie. We were all so happy together then. We supported each other like a family—like the families we wished we'd had. We appreciated ourselves and each other in a way our shitty exes and some of our critical parents never did."

Her face fell. "Sabrina so wanted to get Moxie back to that level of support after the tension we've had in recent years. At the circle ceremony the night before she disappeared, she challenged us to remember our original dreams for the group, the support we've given each other in the past. She pleaded with us to return to that Moxie spirit. But now, without Sabrina, I don't know if that will ever happen."

I didn't follow up on that comment, because I wanted to keep Gayle relaxed and focused on positive memories of Sabrina. I've found that thinking happy thoughts about the loved one helps people make contact with the spirit.

We continued going through the pictures for a few more minutes until Gayle's phone rang. She grabbed it out of her purse and checked the ID. "Never mind, I'll let it go to voicemail," she said.

"You can't take your phone into the apparition chamber," I said. "So you may as well turn it off." She nodded, clicked it off and put it back in her purse.

"Are we ready now?" she asked.

I got Gayle set up in my apparition chamber. It's a small windowless room with an easy chair inclined backward facing a four-foot square mirror on the wall across from it. The mirror and the chair are surrounded by a black velvet curtain, which creates a small booth, so the sitter can gaze into the mirror and see only a pool of darkness. The only illumination comes from a fifteen-watt bulb in a small stained-glass lamp behind the chair.

If the process works, the person in the chair sees an apparition appear when gazing into the mirror's dark shiny surface. Sometimes the spirit comes out into the room, sometimes it stays in the mirror. Usually the spirit speaks, so they are able to have a conversation—although not always the conversation the person is hoping to have.

I gave Gayle the instructions I always give a person in the apparition chamber. "Take some deep breaths and relax," I said. "Try to clear your mind of everything except Sabrina as you look into the mirror. Don't try to rush it or make something happen. Just be here. You can stay as long as you want. I'll be across the hall in my office if you have any problems. When you're done, just come out and we'll talk."

An hour went by. The door chamber opened, but Gayle didn't come out. I heard loud sobbing coming from the room. When I went in, I found Gayle collapsed on the floor weeping. I held her until her sobs subsided, gave her tissues to wipe her face, helped her up and led her into the counseling room. I got her situated on the couch with a big glass of water, then sat in a chair across from her.

"Can you tell me what happened?"

"Oof. It was horrible."

My worst fears realized. Sabrina must have appeared to her in the apparition chamber, which hit Gayle with the undeniable fact of her death. I knew that however much Gayle wanted to contact Sabrina, she even more wanted Sabrina to somehow be still alive. Contacting Sabrina's spirit would kill her last hope.

"Can you tell me about it? Did Sabrina tell you what happened?"

Gayle jerked her head up, eyes wide. "No, no. It wasn't Sabrina. Sabrina didn't come. It was my mother. My crazy hateful mother back to demolish me one more time. Why did her spirit have to show up? It's bad enough that I have to fight not to hear her voice in my head. Now she's going to haunt me?" Gayle wailed. "Why didn't you tell me she could show up?"

Of course I had told Gayle that people sometimes contact spirits other than the ones they're trying to reach. But with her focus so much on Sabrina, she had probably brushed that aside.

Gayle pulled back and sat, face in hands, for a few minutes. Then she drew herself up, blew her nose, and faced me squarely.

"Do you want to talk about it?" I asked. "If you don't, I respect your privacy. It's your choice."

"I would like to talk about it," she said. "But it has to be completely confidential. I don't want my brother Bruce to know any of this."

"No worries. Anything you say here is confidential."

"My mother could be a real bitch. Hyper-critical. At least of me. She adored Bruce. Thought he was the golden child. He never understood why I had such a hard time getting along with her. I tried to tell him, but he couldn't see it. Said I took her too seriously. Ha!"

"Can you tell me about what happened in the apparition chamber today?"

"When I went in there, I was a little scared. I wanted to see Sabrina, but I also didn't want to—because if I saw her that would mean she was dead." Gayle stopped and sagged sideways, her breathing rapid and shallow. "I was sitting in the chair thinking about how much I miss her, when suddenly I heard, 'Gayle! It's your mother! Listen to me!' There she was in the mirror, glaring at me, just like she always did when she was upset about something I'd done."

Tears streamed down Gayle's face. "She said I'm a terrible mother. Reminded me she told me I should stay with Frank, that I shouldn't be a single mother. She said Nicole's problems are my fault. Maybe she's right. But it sure doesn't help for her to tell me that."

"Were you able to tell her how you feel about what she said?"

"No. She just dumped all that on me and then faded away."

"What would you like to say to her if she were here now?"

Gayle thought for a minute, a few more tears rolling down her cheeks. "I'd say, 'Mom, I thought my life would be different. I never planned to be a single mom. I know you see that as a failure. You never believed me about what Frank was like as a husband. I know you liked him. Most women did, unfortunately. He was charming. But he was a liar and a cheat.'"

Gayle was moving from misery to indignation. Her voice took on an angry tone as she continued. "Then I'd tell her that at least some of Nicole's problems are Frank's fault. In the ten years we've been divorced, he's never contributed to Nicole's support, hardly ever sees her. He sets her up. Calls and says he's going to take her on a trip, she gets all excited, then he cancels at the last minute. She's desperate for his love and approval, but he withholds it. No wonder she acts out."

"That's tough for her," I said. "When he does that she probably feels like it's her fault—even though it isn't. What sort of problems is Nicole having?"

"Nicole has been depressed this past year. Writes a lot of dark poetry Has piercings and tattoos and spiky hair dyed part blond part black. I let her do the piercings and stuff to express who she is as an individual. But maybe it's gone too far. I want her to talk to a therapist, but she refuses to go. I don't know what solution my mother thinks she has, but from my experience with Mom, I don't think it would be helpful."

"Do you have anyone you can talk to about this? Anyone who can help you think it through?" I asked.

"No. Sabrina was the only person I could talk to. Now I grab my phone to call her and then I remember what happened." Gayle stifled a sob. "I know I need to work though my issues with Nicole. I guess I need a therapist. Could that be you?"

"I really only do grief therapy," I said. "We can certainly work on your feelings about Sabrina. But your relationship with your daughter is outside my area of expertise. I can recommend someone, though."

She nodded. Sighed. "Okay, but first let's talk about Sabrina. I tried really hard to reach her in there. I thought about her, sent her love, asked her to come. But she didn't show up. Maybe that means she's alive. I don't want to go in there again. There's no way I want to risk seeing my mother one more time. And I don't want to try to reach Sabrina's spirit anymore. I think I need to think more positively, to have my intention be that she's still alive."

"It's certainly your choice," I said. "But just because Sabrina didn't appear in the apparition chamber doesn't mean she's still alive. Often I've seen people try to reach someone where it takes several tries before they do. And sometimes they reach someone else first."

Gayle stared off into space for a minute or two before she responded. "I hear you," she said slowly. "And deep down I don't believe Sabrina's alive. I can't imagine that we wouldn't have heard from her by now. She's not the sort of person who would run off and leave everyone she loves without a word. I know that, but I so desperately want her to be alive that hope creeps in and creates weird possibilities in my mind."

I thought about the weird possibility involving Erik, but unfortunately I couldn't tell her about that.

Chapter 16

Why didn't Sabrina come to me in Cleo's apparition chamber?" Gayle demanded. She paced rapidly around Paige's spacious living room, eyes darting from one to another of us as if we could unlock some secret code for her. "Was it my fault?" she asked. "Didn't I send her a clear enough message? Or did she just not want to talk to me?" The Moxie members and I were gathered around Paige's fireplace on that cold December evening to talk about the results of Gayle's contact session.

Diana jumped up from her spot on the couch, grabbed Gayle's shoulders and stopped her. Gayle struggled to keep moving, but Diana stood firm, her muscular arms holding Gayle in place. "Sit down, sweetie. Stop blaming yourself," Diana said calmly as she rubbed Gayle's back. "What you're saying is ridiculous on so many levels. We don't even know whether Sabrina is dead or alive, or what factors into whether a spirit shows up, or…Oh, come on, honey. Calm yourself and sit down." She gave Gayle a hug and dragged her toward the couch.

I thought about reinforcing Diana's message that it wasn't Gayle's fault that Sabrina didn't appear, but I decided to wait and see how the group dealt with the issue. I looked around at them. Diana had pulled Gayle down next to her on the bright red couch facing the fireplace. I was on Gayle's left in a comfy tan armchair and Paige was sitting in a rocking chair to sit on my left next to the fireplace. Lark and Hana were across from us in matching brown armchairs—Hana on Diana's right and Lark to Hana's right next to the fireplace. As I glanced at them, I tried to deduce their agendas for the meeting.

Lark's eyes were closed. I remembered her telling me she didn't see Moxie in her future, that she was done with the group. She certainly looked detached. Maybe she was wondering why she had come tonight, maybe wishing she hadn't. Or maybe she was just worn out from one of her twelve-hour hospital shifts.

Hana wore her usual inscrutable expression, but I knew her blank look didn't reflect indifference. A few days ago when she had told me that Sabrina was the soul of Moxie, she had spoken strongly about Sabrina's dissatisfaction with what Moxie had been doing to right what some members saw as the wrongs women suffer at the hands of men. Would Hana push the group to explore this as a possible explanation for Sabrina's disappearance?

Diana focused steadily on Gayle, who was taking slow deep breaths. I knew Diana believed Sabrina was still alive. And she seemed to believe Sabrina had gone somewhere willingly. A few days ago—before I knew that Brandi believed that Sabrina had gone off with Erik—Diana had suggested that explanation. Would she bring up that possibility tonight?

Next to me I could sense Paige shifting in her seat, getting ready to step in, to take on her Rivka Ravenstar facilitator role. And she did.

"Maybe we're all at fault here," she said, her voice silvery rich. She leaned forward to the group. "I wonder whether Sabrina would want to come back to us right now," she said softly. "Remember at the circle ceremony the night before she disappeared, Sabrina begged us to return to the Moxie spirit? Have we done that or even tried? I'm not feeling it."

Diana turned her gaze on Paige. "What do you want from us, Paige?" she asked sharply. "We're doing the best we can. None of this is our fault. Trying to guilt us into finding some fake unity isn't going to get you anywhere."

Whew! I remembered that Diana is a boxer. Clearly her skills extend to verbal as well as physical punches. I could feel Paige deflate and curl inward as she leaned back in her chair. But I figured she'd regroup quickly. These strong women continually circle each other for dominance, with no one member staying in charge for long.

Diana returned her focus to Gayle, leaning in to her and looking directly in her eyes. "What if Sabrina is still alive and that's the reason she didn't appear to you?" she asked. "You know how Sabrina takes care of people. She'll do anything to help someone who asks her. She keeps setting herself up for unhealthy relationships with narcissistic men."

Gayle drew back. "We've all had those relationships, so …"

Diana held up a hand and cut her off. "Okay, we've all had lousy exes. But we learned from those experiences. Sabrina didn't. She'll always fall for a sad story. Maybe some guy from her past—like that Erik from last summer—said he needed her, begged her to go off with him without telling anyone. She might have done that."

I noticed that Lark had opened her eyes and was watching the interaction between Gayle and Diana intently. Before Gayle could say anything else, Lark leaned forward and broke in. "Maybe she went off, but she didn't go with a man," she suggested. "You know Sabrina had some huge issues about Moxie. Things she wanted us to work out. Things I'm not sure we can work out. Sabrina didn't want to give up on us, but she was tired of trying to change Moxie. I think she told us what she wanted us to do—to return to the original Moxie spirit—and then she went off to see if we could do it on our own." Lark folded her arms, sat back and waited for a reaction.

Gayle jumped up and began pacing again. Her face was tight. "No. You're all wrong! Sabrina would never go off without telling anyone. She knows we'd all be worried sick about her. And she'd never leave Ian to worry this way. You know I want her to be alive as much or more than any of you. But it's false hope. You're looking for some possibility to cling to so you don't have to face the fact that Sabrina is dead. But we have to face it. And we have to contact her so we can find out what happened."

Paige stood up, walked over to Gayle and gave her a big hug. "I agree with you Gayle," she said. "I hate to believe that Sabrina fell and got hurt somewhere, that she's lying up there frozen in a snow bank, but I think it is probably what happened. We all know the mountains can be dangerous even when you're careful. I feel responsible because I organized the journeys, so I would especially like to believe Sabrina is still alive. But I think if she were alive, we would have heard from her by now."

After Gayle and Paige returned to their seats, Hana spoke up. "I agree with all of you in different ways," she said. All eyes turned toward her. "I agree with Diana that Sabrina has a tendency to attract people who need her. Her destiny number is six, so yes she's a caretaker type who is loyal, kind and helpful in relationships. If a man like Erik convinced her that he desperately needed her, she might go off with him. And I also agree with Lark that Sabrina cares so much about Moxie that she might do something extreme to force us to solve our problems. But I also think Gayle and Paige make a good point that Sabrina wouldn't go off without telling anyone. Sixes are loyal and responsible and trustworthy with their family and friends. If she went against that by disappearing, she'd be overwhelmed with guilt. We would have heard from her by now."

"So what can we make of that, Hana?" Gayle asked, impatiently. "Do you think Sabrina is dead or alive?"

"Actually, I lean toward thinking she's alive. I think if she had died up there, the searchers would have found her by now. So many searched so long and so thoroughly. So maybe Diana is right. Maybe she did go off with some guy. Maybe he won't let her call anyone. Bad things happen to women all the time. We all know that."

Lark had been nodding throughout Hana's comments. She looked around at everyone and said, "Maybe instead of trying to contact her spirit, we should focus on the Moxie spirit—see if we can come together the way she hoped we would. Maybe if we do that, she'll come back." I wondered why Lark put this challenge out there, given her expressed lack of interest in Moxie's future. Maybe out of loyalty to Sabrina?

We all sat in silence for a few minutes. I mulled over the idea of bringing up Sabrina's thirty-day plan. It might give us some clues. No one except Paige had mentioned it to me. Were any of the others in the plan? Then, as if we shared a wavelength, Paige tossed the issue into the ring.

"I told Cleo what Sabrina said at our circle ceremony about her thirty-day plan to stop giving too much to too many people in her life. Cleo said none of you had even mentioned it. I think it could be important. A step like that is a big change for Sabrina."

Silence. Dead silence. No one moved or reacted. It was as if Paige had sucked the oxygen out of the room.

Finally, Diana spoke up. First she turned to me with a fierce look. "No offense, Cleo. But what happened at our circle ceremony is confidential. As a therapist, I'm sure you understand that the assurance of confidentiality is a requirement for an environment of trust when people are sharing private information." She clenched and unclenched her fists as if flirting with the possibility of punching me.

But she was done with me and turned to confront Paige. "Paige, you of all of us should know that," she said sharply. "You set up the ceremony. Why would you share confidential information?" Diana kept her gaze focused on Paige as she waited for a response.

Paige held her gaze, eyes wide, face calm. "Diana, I understand your concerns about confidentiality," she said soothingly. "But there are exceptions. We have to think about priorities. If we have information that might help us find Sabrina, we need to share it and pursue any leads we find."

"I didn't mention the thirty-day plan because I didn't think it was important," Gayle broke in. "In fact I'd pretty much forgotten that Sabrina mentioned a thirty-day plan. It was probably just a thought that came to her mind for something to focus on during her personal journey."

"No, she had a plan," Paige said. "I know because I was in it. She wanted me to pay back some money she'd lent me last year. She was very firm about giving me thirty days to do it. She told me it was part of a plan to change her life. Were any of the rest of you in her plan? Or do you know who else was in it?"

A chorus of "no's" accompanied by headshaking all around. Then they all disengaged and sat quietly waiting. These were not people who jumped in to fill empty spaces with nervous conversation.

But Paige wasn't ready to let the subject go. "Gayle, are you going to try again to contact Sabrina?" she asked. "Because if you do reach her, maybe you could ask her about the thirty-day plan. Maybe she wrote it down somewhere."

Gayle winced. "I don't want to do it again," she said. "Maybe someone else should try. Paige, since you're the only one besides me who believes Sabrina is dead, maybe you should try."

Paige didn't answer, but Hana turned to me with a question. "Cleo, do we know for sure Sabrina has to be dead to contact us in your chamber? Could she come to us psychically if she's alive and trapped somewhere?"

I took a minute to consider. "I can't really answer that question," I said. "I don't know if that could happen. As far as I know it never has. At least not in my apparition chamber."

"But you teach a class in paranormal psychology at the university, right?" Hana said. "I googled you and read the description. Your class covers telepathy, telekinesis, clairvoyance, precognition, psychic healing, spiritualism, all that stuff. So you must know about telepathic ways to try to find Sabrina."

"I do teach that class," I said, "but what I know about most of it is academic, not personal. I'm not psychic. I can't see the future or find missing people. My only personal experience with the paranormal so far has been using my apparition chamber to contact spirits of some people who have died."

Okay, I wasn't telling them about Tyler. What would be the point? They wouldn't be able to see him and he doesn't answer questions in any way they could use.

"Maybe you should talk to a psychic," I said. "Boulder has plenty to choose from."

Hana stared at me blankly for a minute, then looked down at her watch. "It's after nine," she said. "I need to go."

A relieved chorus of "Me too's" replied, as the women stood up and prepared to leave.

"Let's do a group hug before we go," Paige said, "and focus our intent on working together to find out what happened to Sabrina. Come and join us Cleo."

The women glanced around uneasily, then slowly gathered in the center of the room, We stood in a circle, arms around each other. No smiles, not much eye contact. "Let's all take a minute to open our hearts, minds and spirits," Paige said softly. "Let's step back and acknowledge our mutual affection for Sabrina and resolve to help her the way she would help us."

We hugged like a unified group, but I felt the remnants of individual agendas hanging in the air.

Chapter 17

Tuesday I was too busy to think about Moxie or Sabrina. I had back-to-back clients scheduled until about 4:00 when I headed over to Glenwood Gardens to visit Gramma. I found her in the living room with a group of residents and high-school-student volunteers decorating a Christmas tree. Christmas carols played in the background, and a spicy, gingery smell filled the air. It was just what I needed after a stressful day.

Gramma and an animated blonde teenager were twisting white pipe cleaners through holes in cardboard rings to make retro snowflake ornaments. I joined them, giving Gramma a big hug. She smiled and hugged me back. "Christmas," she said. "I like it." Then a worried look came over her face. "I have to get a present for James." she said. "He's so hard to buy for. I never know what he wants."

Ouch. Grampa's been dead these ten years, so there's probably not much he wants. Or not much we can get anyway. But I didn't want to go there. I wanted to soothe her. "Don't worry, Gramma," I said. "We'll find something good for him. Now can I help with the decorating?"

I helped with the snowflakes, and then with making wreaths by stringing together squares of colorful wool recycled from thrift shop finds. Other residents and volunteers stuck mini candy canes into popcorn balls, which they then decorated with colored frosting. Some residents ate more frosting than they put on the ornaments, but no one cared. The tree filled up with pretty colors and the room filled with laughter.

Then it was dinner time. They always eat early at these places. I used to think it was disrespectful of the residents—done just for staff convenience. But I've learned that the residents like to eat early, just as they like to go to bed early. It's as if their interior clocks are set to a different time zone. Maybe because nothing holds their attention for long, they're always chafing to move on to the next activity on the schedule.

They were having meat loaf with mashed potatoes and gravy. It smelled homey and comforting. And baked apples—probably the source of the spicy, gingery smell I noticed when I first came in.

I helped Gramma settle in for dinner, then gave her a goodbye kiss and a hug. On my way out, Mary Ellen, the RN in charge, stopped me at the doorway. "Do you have a minute, Cleo?"

My heart dropped. "Is Gramma having a problem?" I asked fearfully, remembering the problems Gramma had a year ago when she was still at Shady Terrace. Like her habit of picking up other people's things and hiding them in her room.

"No, no. It's not about Martha," Mary Ellen said. "Martha's such a sweetie. But I need to ask you something. Can we talk in the living room for a few minutes?"

I followed her into a corner of the main room, where we sat together on the couch. "It's about Charlene who had the blue bedroom in the corner," she said, pointing off to her left. "You know she died last month after she went into the hospital with pneumonia."

"Yes," I said. "Gramma still looks for her."

"They all do," she said. "We don't try to make them accept that she died. We just say she's not here right now. But that's not what I wanted to ask you. It's about her family. Have you met her daughter, Allie?"

"Yes. I remember her from Shady Terrace. Very devoted to her mother. Like me, she was so excited that you started Glenwood Gardens and that her mom could move here."

"She was very devoted," Mary Ellen said. "And now Allie's having trouble accepting Charlene's death. I don't know whether she feels guilty or what. Not that there's any reason she should feel guilty. She did everything for Charlene. But, you know, family members so often feel they should have done more."

"True," I said. "It can take some time to work though those feelings, to be able to let go."

"Here's the thing," Mary Ellen said. "Allie is convinced that the staff at the hospital gave Charlene something that killed her. She says Charlene was doing fine one day and the next day she was dead, and that shouldn't have happened. I told her that pneumonia can go that way when someone is old and frail, but she won't accept that."

"Wow, that is a serious charge! Why would the hospital do that? Does she have a theory?

"She says the nurses kept asking her if she was sure her mom would want such aggressive treatment for pneumonia, given that she had Alzheimer's. She thinks the hospital staff thought Charlene's life wasn't valuable, and that she was suffering for no reason and would be better off dead. I've tried to get her to call you for grief therapy, but she's more interested in suing the hospital."

"Has she talked to the hospital patient advocates about this?"

"Several times. It sounds like they were very understanding and patient with her at first, but now they don't want to discuss it any more. They say they've investigated and found nothing out of order. Allie doesn't blame us here at Glenwood Gardens, so it's not really my problem, but I feel bad for her. She's so angry and upset. She calls me every few days to vent, and I listen. But I don't think that's helping her. She needs to find some resolution. Can you suggest something I could say to her to move her toward getting some grief therapy?"

"Maybe she'd go to a grief support group. Hospice runs some of those. Sometimes a group feels less threatening than individual therapy."

Mary Ellen fidgeted and shuffled her feet. "There is one other thing," she said, hesitantly. "I've heard you sometimes help people contact the spirits of their dead loved ones. Is that true?"

"Yes," I said, thinking to myself that I'd rather not have Allie in my Contact Project because of her anger. "But it's a complicated process and it's not for everyone."

Mary Ellen plunged on, going right where I feared she was going. "I was thinking that maybe if Allie could contact Charlene and she could see that Charlene is at peace, she'd be able to accept her death."

I tried to discourage her with a pessimistic answer. "You're right that seeing her mom at peace could help Allie accept her death," I said. "But the Contact Project is part of a grief therapy process. If Allie's intent on fixing blame, she probably won't want to invest the time and energy to work through her grief. So she's not a very good candidate for my Contact Project."

But Mary Ellen had made up her mind. "Would you be willing to at least talk to her about it?" she asked.

I hesitated. A few possible excuses for saying "no" flitted through my mind. But bottom line, I couldn't turn down a request from Mary Ellen. She's a dear and taking such good care of Gramma. "Okay. I'll talk to her," I said, "but I don't want to do it over the phone. Tell her if she wants to call and make an appointment to come in, I'd be happy to see if I can help."

§§§

Driving home, I thought about the difficulty of accepting that a loved one has died. Death is life's greatest mystery, and grief is one of the greatest psychological pains. Helping people find that acceptance is what my practice is all about. And that's also what the Contact Project is about. An encounter with the spirit of a dead loved one can bring peace by giving a grieving person a sense that the departed is comfortable, happy, and still with them spiritually.

I realized that in the past year I've gotten distracted helping people find murderers instead of helping them find acceptance. I've let myself get stuck in trying to place blame just as much as Allie is. Even though my investigations actually uncovered a couple of murderers, that's not what grief therapy is about. That's what police investigations are about. Suddenly I could see Pablo's point. He keeps reminding me I'm a therapist, not a detective. And he's right.

But now here I am up to my ears in another possible murder investigation. And it may involve Erik—the scariest guy I know. No wonder Pablo is worried about me. I have our baby to think about. In the other two murder investigations I've been involved with, I've found myself at the wrong end of a loaded gun. I've been lucky enough to escape unharmed, but if I keep putting myself in those situations, how long can my luck hold out? Is it fair to Pablo and the baby to take that chance?

As I pulled into my driveway, I decided I'd had enough. I had to change course. I would call Bruce right away and tell him I couldn't help Gayle and the Moxie women any more and that they should go to the police for help. After all, I could tell him that I had met with all the Moxie women and that Gayle had gone into the apparition chamber but had not contacted Sabrina.

Before I could change my mind, I grabbed my phone out of my purse, dashed inside, dropped my coat on the floor, found Bruce on my list, and punched call. He answered on the first ring. "Hi, Cleo. Go ahead. I'm listening."

I fumbled for a minute. No quick and easy way to say this. I wanted to be clear without sounding like I was blaming him for getting me into a messy situation. I paced around the room as I talked. "Um, Bruce. This whole thing with Gayle and Sabrina. It's really complicated," I stuttered.

"Right," Bruce said. "Don't worry about the cost. I know it will take a lot of your time."

"It's not the cost exactly," I said. "It's …"

"I have to go," he said. "We've got some serious problems in our programming on this software package. I have to solve it tonight."

"But I really need to …"

"Whatever you need, Cleo. No problem. Just fix this for Gayle. She's the only sister I have and I'll do anything for her. Talk to you later."

He hung up leaving me sputtering. Not acceptable, I told myself. I have to call him back and have the conversation my way. But before I could hit redial, a familiar voice interrupted.

"Yo, Cleo." Tyler surfed through my living room wall and perched on top of the TV.

I tossed my phone on the couch and plopped down next to it. "Tyler! I made a big mistake getting involved in helping Gayle and the other Moxie members try to find Sabrina. I need to stop."

Tyler pushed off on some invisible wave, surfing quick circles around my living room. "That's bogus," he said. "Don't bail your board. It's the wrong time to back down."

"No, Tyler. This is exactly the time to back down. Before it get dangerous."

"The dorkiest-looking wetsuit is a dry one, Cleo. This is no time to be a beach bunny. Surfs up. Time to paddle out and shoot the curl."

I whipped my head back and forth, trying to keep him in view. "But I thought you told me to listen to Pablo. What about our baby? Pablo thinks I'm putting it at risk."

Finally he came to a stop right in front of my face. "Babies float, Cleo. No problem there. You need to keep paddling, find Sabrina, and find the shark. Don't get blinded by the spray." With that, he vanished, back to whatever spirit surfer beach he calls home.

I picked up my phone again, but this time I called Pablo, not Bruce. I was set to pick him up at the Denver airport tomorrow, and I wanted to let him know I'd be there for him, for us, and for our baby.

Chapter 18

Wednesday morning I woke up excited about picking Pablo up at the airport. I was ready to have a long talk with him about our future, our baby, and this mess I'd gotten myself into with Gayle and the other Moxie members.

But when I looked out the window, my heart sank. Snow was falling thick and fast. What if I couldn't make it to the airport? For sure I'd need to leave early to meet Pablo's 2:00 p.m. flight.

Bundled up in boots, parka, hat and gloves, I trudged out to clean the white stuff off my car. The soft blanket of snow muffled the usual morning sounds and turned my yard into a winter wonderland of abstract white blobs. I took a minute to enjoy the peaceful silence surrounding me before I attacked my car with broom, brushes and scraper.

By the time I got done, went inside and looked at my phone, I had cancellation messages from all my morning clients. So no rush to get to the office. I went back out and shoveled my walk and driveway. While I shoveled, I thought about Pablo's concern that I might get snowed in all alone in my old house, and his suggestion that if I lived in Longmont, his whole family would be nearby to help me. I wanted him to see evidence this afternoon when we got back here that I can handle a snowstorm on my own.

When I finished the driveway, I was hot and sweaty inside my parka, but my face was icy and my nose was running from the cold. Time to go in for hot herbal tea and dry clothes. I turned on the radio. Schools were closed for the day. Nothing about the airport.

Outside my window the snow hadn't let up at all. We had at least eight inches accumulated already. Could be a hairy drive.

I started out for the airport at noon as planned, giving myself double the time I'd usually need. I figured I'd make it to the airport okay, since my Toyota has AWD and antilock brakes. Wrong. I had way underestimated this blizzard. We were slammed. No car was a match for Mother Nature that day.

The roads were much worse than I expected. Cars and SUVs were slipping and crawling through thick snow, sliding off into snow banks. My antilock brakes were doing yeoman duty. When an SUV in front of me suddenly skidded, I slid to a stop inches away from it. I managed to maneuver past the SUV, several sideways cars and a stuck bus, but when I finally got to the entry ramp for U.S. 36, a jackknifed truck had blocked it. No way to get on from that entrance.

I frantically considered other routes, cursing the truck driver who cut off my path. But traffic was barely moving. Visibility was terrible. I could only see a few feet in front of my windshield. I began to realize that I might not be able to get on the highway and, even if I did, the likelihood of getting to the airport through the storm was poor. More likely I'd get stuck on the highway for hours in this freezing weather. I hated to wimp out but I knew Pablo would agree that it would be foolish to risk our baby's life trying to meet him at the airport. I had to call him and tell him I couldn't pick him up, so he should take a bus or shuttle, whatever was running in the storm.

Too late. I got his voicemail. He was probably already on the plane. I left a message about the blizzard.

As it turned out the driver of that jackknifed truck did me a favor. No way I could have gotten to the Denver airport. I would have been stranded on U.S. 36 for hours along with thousands of other motorists. Some of them were routed off the road via on-ramps. Others abandoned their cars and walked to nearby hotels or Flatiron Crossing mall for shelter.

Worse yet, even if I had somehow gotten to the airport, I couldn't have picked up Pablo. His flight got cancelled when the Denver airport was closed to all incoming and outgoing flights. So my eagerly anticipated Wednesday evening reunion with Pablo was not to be.

I turned around and began making my way home. Snow drifts

obscured landmarks so completely that my familiar city looked like a foreign country. I drove slowly and carefully. Did not want to find myself digging my car out of a snow bank.

The radio was reporting more closings of businesses, government agencies, and schools. Everything was about the weather. "Get home before it gets worse. But stay off the highways. Boulder is on accident alert, so don't call police for fender benders. Just exchange information and report online or at a police station within seventy-two hours." Then came the news about the airport closing. I was so glad I wasn't stuck in traffic halfway there.

I was also frustrated, disappointed and lonely. I wanted to see Pablo. I wanted to have that conversation with him tonight, snuggled in each other's arms. I needed to do it now before I lost my resolve to tell him everything.

My phone interrupted my pity party just as I slid to a stop at the light at ninth and Canyon. Maybe it was Pablo. It would be so good to hear his voice, tell him how much I miss him, hear him tell me the same. But it was Elisa. "Hey girl, this is some snowstorm! No way Maria and I can get up to the foothills, even in the SUV. Can we crash at your place?"

Just the lift I needed. The company of good friends would be a welcome diversion. "Perfect. I'd love to have you and Maria stay over. And I have groceries because Pablo was supposed to get home today. I'm out in my car, but I'm almost home now."

My driveway was filling up again, but still passable. I pulled up to the front leaving room for Elisa's SUV. I figured we could all shovel later when the snow stopped. If it ever did. As soon as I got inside and got my boots and stuff off, they were at the door. "Whew, baby! Haven't seen a storm like this in years," Elisa boomed. "No day for driving. Thanks for taking us in."

We acknowledged the drama of the day by sharing our driving stories. Then we headed out to the kitchen for hot chocolate with whipped cream. While we were drinking it, Pablo called me to tell me his flight had been cancelled. He was at least as frustrated as I was. "We sat on the plane for hours, before they told us the Denver airport was closed," he said. "It's a madhouse here. They don't know when DIA will reopen, so they're not booking any flights to Denver." We commiserated sadly about our reunion, now postponed indefinitely.

While Pablo and I were talking, Maria's cell phone rang. She glanced at the caller ID and went off down the hall to the bedroom to take the call. In a few minutes she came back glowing. "That was Ian," she said with a dreamy smile. "They left Breckenridge after the snowboard competition ended last night to get back before the storm hit. Got back really late and then he crashed. They live close to here, so he's going to snowshoe over. I can't wait to see him." She was practically jumping up and down.

I was a little jealous that she was getting to share the snowstorm with her love. But I was also looking forward to finally meeting Ian.

He blew in to my front hall, covered in snow and exuding energy. Tall. Curly brown hair peeking out under a red wool cap. Adorable kid. No wonder Maria was entranced. Ian was excited about the blizzard and the great snowshoeing, wanted to share that with Maria. So after he and I were introduced, Maria borrowed my snowshoes and they struck out for nearby Eben Fine Park. Elisa and I opted to stay in and fix seafood lasagna for dinner.

I relaxed into the warmth of my kitchen, enjoying seeing the snow build up outside my windows. Very cozy. I love cooking with Elisa. We know each other so well we slip easily into a rhythm of shared tasks.

Once Elisa and I had our lasagna in the oven and salad in the refrigerator, we got a fire going in the living room fireplace, put on some CDs and relaxed companionably. I heard shoveling outside, looked out and saw Ian and Maria making short work of my walk and driveway. Sweet.

I wondered whether Maria had told Ian that she had shared his secret about his mom going off with Erik. If she had, he apparently wasn't mad. They were laughing and tossing snow at each other as they shoveled. Maybe Maria had postponed telling him in order to preserve the happy space between them for a while. I could relate to that strategy.

They came in, filling my front hall with wet boots, coats, and hats. Melting snow everywhere. I lent Maria some dry sweatpants but Ian had to dry as well as he could by the fire. When they were finally comfortable on the couch, legs touching, his arm around her shoulders, I invited Ian to stay for dinner. "That would be awesome," he said, grinning. "But would it be okay if I invite my aunt Brandi to come too. She's home alone and I've been away for a week and hardly seen her since I got back."

"Sure. But can she get here in this weather?"

He waved away my concerns. "No worries. She got Mom's car back from the cops. Subaru Outback. Skier's favorite car. You wouldn't believe the snow Mom and I have driven though in the mountains in that car."

§§§

Brandi arrived with a chocolate cake and a bottle of wine, which she handed to me so she could take off her coat and boots. "My big sister Sabrina bakes totally bitchin cakes," she said with a friendly smile. "This one was in the freezer, so I brought it to share. Thanks so much for the invite. I totally need to catch up with my outrageous nephew." She darted across to the couch, threw her arms around Ian, and planted a loud kiss on his forehead. "You next, Maria sweetie pie," she said, leaning over to kiss Maria. "It's been too long."

Maria giggled. Ian grabbed Brandi and pulled her down to sit on the couch on the other side of him from Maria. "I love you too, Brandi," he said. "But I need to introduce you to Maria's mom and her friend Cleo. So kick back for a sec, okay?"

My head was spinning at the thought of so casually eating a dead woman's cake. Or possibly a missing woman's cake. But really? My tongue was stuck somewhere in the back of my mouth waiting for my mind to clear.

But Elisa picked up the slack with her usual charm. She stood up, walked across the room to Brandi, and held out her hand. "Hi, I'm Elisa, Maria's mom. Thanks for bringing the wine. I was just wishing for a glass to enjoy by the fire."

"Hey, great to finally meet you," Brandi stood up and, ignoring Elisa's outstretched hand, threw her arms around Elisa's shoulders. Then she turned to Ian. "Cleo and I have already met," she said. "She's a friend of Gayle Winfield and she's been helping Gayle try to find your mom. They think she's dead up there in the mountains. I keep telling everyone that missing persons turn up alive all the time and Sabrina will come back when the time is right."

Oops. That was a conversation stopper. Elisa silently made her way back to her chair by the fire. Brandi sat back down on the couch. No one spoke. The only sound in the room was the music—"this'll be the day that I die, this'll be the day that I die." Madonna singing "American Pie."

The lyrics hung heavily among us in the room for several seconds until Elisa ventured gently onto the thin ice. "Ian, I'm thinking about your mom, how much you must be missing her. It's been what—a month she's been gone now?" she said softly. "And you too, Brandi, it must be horrible, not knowing."

Maria pulled away from Ian and glared at Elisa. "Okay, Mom, enough, okay," she said sternly.

Ian patted Maria's arm. "Chill," he said. "She's doing the nice parent thing."

"I wish," Maria said. "But what's real is my mom has an agenda here. She's backing me into a corner. Right, mom?"

Of course Maria was right. Elisa did have an agenda. But so did we all. Elisa wanted to talk with Brandi about Erik. I wanted to hear that conversation. Maria wanted to avoid it. But knowing Elisa as well as I do, I knew she wouldn't back down.

Sure enough, Elisa continued to push. "Maria, this isn't a game. It's a life and death situation. We all need to share what we know." Elisa said.

"Hey. News flash!" Brandi barked. "We know what Gayle thinks and that she wants me out of the picture. If that's what you have to share, you can skip it."

Just as I had seen in my office, Brandi's mood goes up and down like a yo-yo. One more way she's a challenge for Sabrina.

"No," Maria said, turning resolutely to face Ian. "This is not about Gayle. It's about Erik. I told Mom and Cleo about how Erik called Brandi, and how he said he had a surprise for your mom, and how Brandi told him where your mom would be, and how you think your mom went off with Erik." She wept softly. "I'm so sorry. I know I promised I wouldn't tell. But Mom and Cleo know stuff about Erik, really bad stuff. Your mom could be in trouble."

Then everyone was talking at once, sharing information and impressions of Erik—the good, the bad, the ugly, and the uglier. It took some doing, but Elisa and I finally convinced Ian and Brandi that my information about Erik was real, verified by personal experience.

As I described Erik's sociopathic behavior in detail, and talked about his three wives, who all died or disappeared under mysterious circumstances, Brandi went from vehement argument to strained silence, to tense, carefully worded questions. Finally she held her hands up to stop me. "Enough," she said, her jaw jutting forward. "I get that Sabrina could be in deep shit. But she's a smart girl, smarter than his ditzy wives. If he bullies her, she'll bust his balls for sure."

Ian had been silent for a while, eyes squeezed shut. His breath was shallow and rapid, his fists tightly clenched. Suddenly he jumped up and planted himself in front of Brandi. "This is weirding me out!" he cried. "Erik's a nutjob and Mom's with him. Seriously? We have to find her. We can't keep her secrets anymore. Seriously! We need to tell the police everything we know."

Chapter 19

Brandi jumped to her feet, shaking her head. "Don't worry, honey, we're going to find her," she said gently, embracing Ian and patting his back. "You have my word. I'll do whatever it takes."

Ian gradually relaxed into Brandi's arms. Slowly, she eased him back down onto the couch, next to Maria, who had been watching the interaction wide-eyed. Maria put her arms around Ian, squeezed him, and kissed him lightly on the cheek. Brandi collapsed onto a large pillow in front of the fireplace and gazed intently into the blazing logs.

My heart ached for this boy who I thought was trying so hard to stay strong. From what Maria had said, while he was away, totally focused on physical performance that required clear concentration, he had managed to keep worries about his mother out of his consciousness. Most likely his belief that Sabrina had gone off with Erik for a secret rejuvenating vacation had helped sustain him through his competition. But now that he was back in Boulder, I could see that Sabrina's absence was a huge hole in his life that he couldn't ignore.

Ian straightened up, regained his composure. "Sorry I freaked out," he said to Maria, grabbing her in a big hug. "Gracias for the support."

"No problem," she said, giving him another quick kiss. "Whatever I can do to help. Just let me know."

"Me too," Elisa chimed in. "I absolutely want to help if I can."

Maria jerked up away from Ian and glared at Elisa. "Don't you think you've done enough already, Mom? You just couldn't let me decide when to tell Ian and Brandi that I'd told you about Erik. You had to jump in and stir things up. We can't do anything about Erik right now. The police are busy with this blizzard. Why couldn't you let us have this evening before everything got all crazy?"

Elisa looked dazed, like Maria had thrown a huge wet snowball in her face. I could see her collecting her thoughts to respond, but I didn't want her to go from bad to worse. We needed a break to unwind. I stood up and turned to Maria and Ian. "You two must be starved after your snowshoeing. How about we have dinner before we talk more about all this?"

Relief all around. I could almost hear the tension release like air hissing out of a balloon. Everyone pitched in to set the table, slice bread, and put the food out, engaging in idle chitchat as we worked. Soon we were sitting around my kitchen table enjoying the delicious sensation of warm food in our bellies on a cold, snowy night.

Ian was plowing through his third helping of lasagna when Elisa turned to him with a sociable smile. "I'd love to hear about the Breckenridge competition, Ian," she said. "Your event is the halfpipe, right?"

He jumped and dropped his fork as if he'd forgotten the rest of us were there. "Sure," he said with a slow smile. "Breck has this totally perfect halfpipe. It was an awesome event. Highs and lows showed who's upping their podium percentages."

Brandi was bouncing in her chair, grinning. "C'mon Ian, tell them how you did. You should be so proud," she squealed.

Ian beamed. "Breakthrough!," he said. "I'm pushing myself harder this year. Last year I wanted to make the Olympic Team. I rode to a level I'd never gone to before, but I didn't get there. I learned what it takes, though, and I'm going to get there next time. So ..."

Brandi couldn't contain herself any longer. "But tell about the prize," she interrupted.

Ian stopped and glared at Brandi. "I wanted that to be a surprise for Maria."

Maria looked startled. "What surprise?" she asked.

"Like I told you earlier," Ian said, "I came in second place overall in the halfpipe, so I get points toward making the U.S. Snowboard Team." He stopped and gave her a loving smile. "But what I didn't say is I also got $3,000."

Brandi clapped gleefully. Maria flew out of her chair to kiss and hug Ian. "Really?" she screeched. "That's awesome. Why didn't you tell me?"

"I was planning to take you out somewhere nice and surprise you," Ian said. "But I should have warned Brandi not to spill the beans."

Brandi shrugged. "Sorry," she said, reaching over to give him a playful shove. "But, hey, speaking of surprises, I have a couple for you. Let's have some cake and I'll tell you what I've been up to."

We took our cake into the living room by the fire. Elisa and Brandi shared the last of the wine, while Maria, Ian and I had milk. I felt like I'd been demoted to the kids' table. This no-alcohol-no-coffee-while-you're-pregnant thing was already getting old. But I wanted to be a good mom to this baby, so I didn't take risks.

Ian focused his attention on Brandi. "Show-and-tell time," he said. "What's up?"

Their direct, good-natured communication style said a lot to me about their relationship—and it was all good. Neither took offense easily, or had to tread carefully, or beat around the bush. From what I could see, they "got" each other at some basic level. I began to worry that I was helping the wrong person. To hear Gayle and the other Moxie members tell it, Brandi was the bad guy here and Ian was her helpless victim. But that didn't fit with what I was seeing.

Brandi leaned forward, facing Ian. "Well," she began, "when Sabrina first went missing, you and I agreed that we should give her a few weeks to work out her shit before we panicked. That time is up," she said emphatically. "Last week, when the three-week mark came around, I decided to put her up on a website called FindaMissingPerson.com. I put up pictures of her, and information about her height and weight, when she was last seen, stuff like that. And guess what?" she squealed, gazing at each of us in turn. "Three people have already told me they've seen her—one in Dallas, one in Albuquerque, and one in Las Vegas. Looks like Sabrina and Erik may be moving around the southwest. We can pass that on to the police if you want, Ian." She sat back with a satisfied smile.

I doubted that the Boulder PD or the sheriff would follow up on tips like those, but I bit my tongue and kept quiet to hear what else Brandi would say.

Ian tapped a foot and nodded vigorously. "Definitely. We should tell them right away—at the same time we tell them about Erik's call to you. Seriously—like Maria's mom said, it's been a month. We can't just be waiting for her to show up." He hung his head and mumbled, "Because I think something must be wrong. She should have called by now."

"I agree," Brandi said. "We should tell the police what we know. And I have one more thing to tell them. A Boulder psychic named Dionysia called me. She said she had important information about Sabrina and she wanted to meet with me. I smelled a scam, but she said she wasn't going to charge me, so I got together with her." Brandi giggled. "Strange woman," she said, wrinkling her nose. "Totally fat. A hippo. All puffy and gross like she never goes outside. But she talked about Sabrina like she knew her, even though she said they'd never met. Said she can feel Sabrina's energy very strongly. She had an image of Sabrina in a white room, focusing her energy on a higher plane beyond daily life. Maybe Sabrina is at some sort of retreat where time has become irrelevant, and maybe that's why she hasn't called."

My skeptical side kicked in. A retreat like that didn't sound at all like Erik. "You have to be careful with psychics," I said. "I can't imagine Erik going on a retreat like that. Did the psychic get a sense of Erik being with Sabrina in the white room?"

"She didn't say. She did say she got positive loving energy from Sabrina directed especially toward you, Ian."

Ian sighed dejectedly. Maria whispered something in his ear. He squeezed her hand.

"And one last thing," Brandi said, firmly. "I filed the papers to be appointed Ian's guardian and conservator of Sabrina's property." She looked pointedly at me. "It's just temporary until Sabrina gets back."

Ian looked up sharply. "Did you have to get all legal about it?" he asked. "Couldn't we just go on the way we have been until she gets back?"

"No." Brandi said flatly, crossing her arms, eyes steely. "I had to do it. That pushy bitch Gayle Winfield keeps insisting that Sabrina is dead and that her will makes Gayle your guardian and puts her in charge of everything Sabrina owns."

Ian leaned forward, jutted his chin out and narrowed his eyes. "Oh, no. Not going to happen," he said shaking his head. "Not me staying with Gayle. No way I can live there with Nicole."

So Gayle was right that Ian would choose Brandi over her. Gayle had said he would choose Brandi because he would expect Gayle to be too strict about grades and studying. But he said it was about Nicole. I needed to hear more about that, but was too tired to think how to ask.

To my surprise, Maria kept the spotlight on Nicole. "Oh, Nicole Winfield," she said rolling her eyes. "She is kind of weird. Smart but strange."

"For sure," Ian said. "We kind of grew up together, since our moms are best friends. We got along great until last year. Then she totally changed, pretty much overnight. Started hanging out with the weird fringe. Got a bunch of piercings and dyed her hair half-blond, half-black. Became a vegan. She writes this dumb poetry that's all about how shitty life is. She's a dork—weirds me out."

"But it's more than that," Brandi said urgently. "Gayle and those Moxie gals are into some deep shit. They basically hate men. That's no kind of atmosphere for Ian to live in."

"What kind of deep shit?" I asked. "Does Sabrina know about it? She's a big part of Moxie. Is she involved?"

"It's not for me to say, but you should get your friend Gayle and the others to come clean with you. I think they're going down. You don't want to be dragged down with them."

I had no ready response. I was worn out, confused, and ready for the evening to be over.

Fortunately I wasn't the only one who was tired. Ian was slumped back, yawning, his eyes drooping. "Sorry," he said sleepily. "I'm still zoned from the trip."

Brandi stood up. "Right. We should go while I still have the energy to drive home in this storm. Thanks for the dinner and the company."

After they left, I accepted Elisa's offer for her and Maria to clean up the dishes, figuring they could use some alone time to work out their issues. I got out sheets and blankets for them to use on my futon couch, and left them to their work. As I headed off to my bedroom to call Pablo before I fell asleep, I could feel my resolve to tell him everything trickling away. I had to find out more about what the Moxie members were up to before I betrayed Bruce by sharing my concerns about them with a cop.

Chapter 20

Thursday morning the snow stopped, the sun came out, and the cleanup began. Elisa, Maria and I re-shoveled my walk and driveway before they took off for their house in the foothills on the newly plowed roads. I pulled on my fleece-lined Sorel boots and walked the six blocks to my office—partly for the exercise and partly just to be out and about.

We'd had two feet of snow, so school and just about everything else was closed. People celebrating their time away from the usual routine created a winter-resort atmosphere . Besides the usual digging out of cars and shoveling of walks, Boulderites were enjoying themselves with sleds, kids, and dogs. Cross-country skiers and snowshoers passed me in the street. Some kids were building a six-foot-high snow fort in the pocket park on Pearl Street. Restaurant owners greeted passersby as they swept the snow off awnings with brooms. Cheerful voices and laughter hung in the air.

But I wasn't so cheerful. So far all reports were that the Denver airport was still closed. Plows had managed to clear one runway this morning, but deicing areas and other stretches of the tarmac were still buried in snow. An estimated 4,700 travelers had camped out at the airport Wednesday night, according to a solemn news report.

Pablo called several times with increasing frustration about not being able to get the airline on the phone or to get on its website. For sure he wouldn't be getting home today. And the even worse news was that a new storm was heading our way, expected to drop another foot or more of snow on us tomorrow.

Since all my clients had cancelled, I had a good window to get some work done. I planned to use my time at my office to catch up on paperwork. As I walked along, I saw one of the kids building the snow fort taunting another one: "Liar, liar, pants on fire!" I stopped and stared at them, realizing that this morning could be a good time to meet with Gayle and get to the truth about Moxie. She wouldn't be showing real estate today and she could get downtown from her house on Balsam without too much trouble.

As soon as I got to my office, I called her and left her a message she couldn't ignore. "Gayle, I spent some time with Brandi last night, and I'm troubled by what she had to say about Moxie. I'm rethinking my level of involvement. I don't think I can help you any more until I know more about what Moxie is up to. We need to talk."

Sure enough, she called back in fifteen minutes. "Why were you hanging out with Brandi and what kind of trouble is she stirring up now?" she barked.

I filled her in briefly on my evening, leaving out the stuff Ian had said about not wanting to live with her and Nicole. "Look. I need you to come clean and tell me what's going on with Moxie. I'm at my office. Can you come down for a talk?"

She sighed. "I'll have to shovel out my driveway, but I'll get there as soon as I can."

While I waited, I reviewed what various Moxie members had told me about the group's problems. In the beginning Gayle said Moxie had turned into a nightmare. She also said she's afraid that what Moxie set in motion killed Sabrina. I'd been taking that to mean that Sabrina's distress about Moxie's issues had led her to arrange the retreat that she didn't come back from. But what if there was more? Maybe Gayle actually suspected one or more of the Moxie women of pushing Sabrina over a cliff. But why would they?

There was the secret Moxie mission some of them have alluded to. Could that somehow have led one or more of them to kill her? What did I know about that secret? Hana told me the Moxie members were taking action to right the wrongs women suffer at the hands of men. She wants to make things better for all women. Lark told me Moxie had turned sour and gone off on a crusade to get revenge against exes who had mistreated them. She said they started by setting up websites that revealed bad things those guys had done in the past, but went beyond that to some risky and wrong way of punishing other men who mistreat women.

If what they were doing was indeed wrong and possibly illegal, would Sabrina have threatened to expose them? At the group meeting, Paige brought up how Sabrina begged the group to return to the Moxie spirit. Lark agreed, saying that Sabrina might have gone off to see if the group could do that on its own. But what if Sabrina had been more forceful, given them an ultimatum? What if that was part of her thirty-day plan?

Chapter 21

Gayle breezed in, snowy and energetic, cheeks red from the cold. "I called Diana and Hana right after I talked to you." Gayle spoke rapidly as she pulled off her boots, hat, and jacket. "I told them I'm going to tell you everything, and if they want to be here for it, they should show up."

No sooner had the words left her mouth than Hana and Diana burst in, trailing snow all around my waiting room. "Gayle, you have no right," Diana said, grabbing her shoulders.

Gayle shook herself free, brushing off the snow Diana had dripped onto her arms. "I have every right," she snapped. "This is about Sabrina. We've wasted way too much time already." She pushed past Diana toward the counseling room.

Hana stepped in front of Gayle, impeding her path. "This is not about Sabrina and you know it," she said. "Think about what you're doing."

I elbowed past them all and stood in the doorway to the counseling room. "Enough," I said. "If we're going to have this conversation, you need to take off your snowy boots and jackets, come into this room, and sit down. If not, you can all leave, and it will be up to you to find Sabrina on your own."

They stopped squabbling long enough to get their stuff off and get seated in the counseling room—Hana and Diana on the couch and Gayle in the armchair catty-cornered from them. I turned on my electric teakettle, then sat in the wingchair across from the couch. They started right up again.

"You may be right that what's going on in Moxie has nothing to do with Sabrina's disappearance," Gayle said, glaring at Hana. "But we don't know that. One of those men may have made the connection and taken her."

"One of what men?" I asked.

They ignored me. "Gayle, that makes no sense," Hana said. "If someone took her to get back at us, they would have sent us a message. Otherwise what's the point?" She leaned forward, staring at Gayle.

"Let's start at the beginning," I said firmly. "Gayle, you said you're going to tell me everything. What is everything?"

Gayle took a deep breath and straightened in her chair. "Hana and Diana have a website that makes men suffer," she said.

Hana sat still, stonyfaced. Diana clenched and unclenched her fists. "Only some men, she said, scowling, "and those men have brought suffering on themselves."

Gayle lifted her palms to stop Diana. "Be quiet until I finish," she said. "Then you can make your case."

Diana pushed back. "You don't get it." Her expression hardened, as she dropped her voice down low. "We don't want you to finish. This is Moxie's confidential business. Why would you expect us to sit here quietly and let you talk about it?"

The teakettle whistled, jolting me out of the intense conversation. "The water's ready. I'm going to get myself some tea. Please help yourselves if you'd like some," I said, standing up and moving to the counter at the back of the room. I got mugs and boxes of tea bags out of the cabinet.

To my surprise, they all stopped talking, walked back to the counter, and quietly fixed themselves mugs of tea. Gayle's phone rang while she was pouring boiling water into her cup. She put down the kettle to pull her phone out of her pocket, but I stopped her before she could answer it. "If you can, let the call go, Gayle," I said. "We need to get on with this talk."

She glanced down at the phone, but let it go to voicemail. "Sorry," she said. "I keep it on pretty much all the time to be responsive to my customers." Her preoccupied look as she finished making her tea suggested the call had been one she hated to miss. Too bad. I'd been waiting long enough for some straight talk about Moxie.

After everyone was settled back in their seats, I put my cards on the table. "Look," I said. "Gayle is going to tell me what's going on. She invited you both here as a courtesy to hear what she says. If you don't want to hear it, you can leave. But if you stay, you need to let her talk."

Hana and Diana sat rigidly, but silently, on the couch. Hana stared down at her hands, while Diana looked off out the window across the room.

I turned to Gayle. "Can you give a brief summary, so we can go on from there?"

Gayle shifted in her chair leaning toward me, away from them. "Right," she said. "Hana and Diana's website is set up to punish abusive men. Here's how it works. Women report men on the site and provide details of the abuse. Diana checks out the story through a confidential network of investigators. If the story is true, Hana teaches the woman how to infect the abusive man's computer with a malicious software program called Zeus. Once Zeus is installed on the man's PC, it collects credit card information, online banking account passwords, and other financial documents and sends them to Hana's server." She stopped, leaned back, and looked over at them, as if waiting for a response.

Hana stared down at the low coffee table between us. Diana squirmed in her seat, looking like she'd rather be anywhere but here. But neither of them said anything. No denials.

I let the silence hang for a minute. Forced myself to breathe in and out before speaking. Their retribution website was way more complicated and sophisticated than I was expecting. I was shocked. Of course I knew Hana was a computer programmer, but it was hard for me to believe she could or would get people's information this way. I needed to hear more. "How does Zeus work?" I asked. "Just give me the simple overview."

Hana looked up, her face impassive. "Zeus is a data-stealing Trojan horse," she said, her tone and lack of affect fitting a lecturer addressing a Computer 101 class. "Once Zeus is on the man's computer, it installs modules that make his computer part of a botnet—a network of compromised computers under our control. Just think of it like an alien takeover. We turn the infected computers into zombies—called bots—that do whatever we want them to do. And what we want them to do is give us the man's financial information like account numbers and passwords." She stopped.

But clearly that wasn't the whole story. "What do you do with the financial information you get?" I asked.

Diana glared at Gayle, then at me. "We even the score," she said challengingly. "We use the stolen passwords to transfer money from the men's accounts into phony accounts, and we use the credit card information to make electronic withdrawals from their accounts. We send the abused women the money they deserve and need to live their lives and take care of their children. The rest of the money goes to charity."

I was stunned that these women were so far over the line. So Lark was right. They are making themselves the judges. And what they are doing is risky and illegal. No wonder Sabrina was upset. "This sounds like identity theft," I said quietly. "I can't believe no one has reported it. Why haven't the police shut your site down?"

Hana rolled her eyes. "You may have heard that identity theft is almost impossible to catch," she said. "And we know how to cover our tracks. The website is secret, passed along by women only to other women they know well. No one will stumble on it, and even if they did, all they'd see is an innocuous women's discussion forum. The real underlying site is protected by an elaborate system of passwords and logins."

"So this is what Sabrina wanted you to stop doing?" I asked. "Why didn't she report you to the police?"

Diana faced me, nostrils flaring. "Because it was Moxie, not just the two of us," she said in a carefully controlled tone. "We all signed on to this. It erupted out of mutual frustration and resentment. Individually we had once felt impotent, but together we became powerful. We couldn't just talk. It wasn't sufficient. We knew we were right to be angry. We wanted to stand up and help other women. We wanted to act, we had to act. We acted." She sat back, arms crossed.

Hana nodded and leaned forward eagerly. "After we give the abused women the money the men owe them, we give all the rest anonymously to shelters for abused women and to groups working for women's rights in societies where women are seriously repressed," she said. "So we truly are helping all women."

Apparently Diana and Hana don't have doubts. The end justifies the means for them. But how could the others go along? From the way they'd been talking, I had the feeling they had second thoughts about Moxie's activities. I looked at Gayle. "Maybe I'm missing something," I said carefully. "But to me it doesn't sound like all of Moxie did sign on to this. From what I've heard, Sabrina and Lark and Paige and you, Gayle, weren't in total agreement with what was going on."

Gayle grimaced. "No, Diana's right," she said, reluctantly. "We did sign on. It wasn't just Hana and Diana who wanted to help women who were suffering. We all had our reasons. Horrible exes, abused women we've known."

"Even Sabrina?" I asked.

"Definitely," Gayle said. "Sabrina's ex was an addict who couldn't hold a job. When Ian was a baby, Sabrina was working full-time as a hospital nurse, and he spent all the money he could get on drugs. She couldn't even leave Ian with him, so she had to pay for daycare. He kept telling her how much he needed her, how he would change if she stayed with him, but he never did. She finally left him. He disappeared into some druggie world, never paid any child support, never saw Ian again."

Gayle took a deep breath. "Then there's me," she said. "My ex had a child with another woman while he and I were still married. And he was convicted of tax evasion, which messed up our financial situation forever. I didn't hang on as long as Sabrina did. I had no trouble leaving Frank when I found out what he'd done. Never wanted to give him a second chance. Never looked back. Got a divorce and moved on with my life. But I had to take money from my brother to get a new start, and I hated Frank for putting me in that position. And I've hated him even more for how he's treated Nicole."

I could understand their anger and feelings of betrayal. Even their desire to get revenge. But to spread that outrage to men they'd never met? To set up their own kangaroo court that allowed the accused no defense or appeal? To punish them harshly and illegally? To put themselves and their friends in danger of prosecution and jail time? Is this where the strength of Moxie took them? To this dark side? What were they thinking?

"Diana, I hear your anger when you talk about the frustration the Moxie members felt as individuals. Can you tell me more about the power you felt?" I asked.

Diana nodded, her dark eyes cold and hard. "Feeling powerful is fairly new in my life," she said flatly. "My ex was physically abusive and I took it for years because deep down I thought I deserved it. My grandparents, who were very strict and religious, raised me. Hard work was expected. Laziness was a sin, and everything fun was laziness. They taught me I didn't deserve anything, that we're all sinners in God's eyes, that I could never be good enough. I rebelled by marrying a guy who was good-looking, charming, self-centered and spoiled. When he had affairs, took my money, hit me, and accused me of having sex with other men, I felt like it was my fault—that I deserved it. I was so powerless that all I could do was keep trying harder to please him."

Her face softened briefly. "I wanted us to be a family for our babies. I wanted Amy and Hugh to have the real family I never had," she said. Her eyes narrowed. "But the shitbag got worse and worse," she said bitterly. "He found every excuse he could to have a tantrum and leave the house. He'd yell that everything was a mess and he couldn't find his things. Then he'd empty drawers on the floor and storm out. Sometimes he'd stay away for two or three days. Finally a friend helped me see my codependency and my fears of leaving. I got in touch with my personal power and left him. I did it for my kids. I didn't want them growing up in that toxic environment thinking men can push women around any time they want."

Diana stopped and turned to Hana. "Your turn," she said.

Hana shook her head. "No. I'm not going to bore Cleo with the story of my ex," she said. She turned to me. "But you have to understand why we do this," she said. "We're not stealing, we're righting wrongs. Not just wrongs against us, wrongs against all women. Have you followed the sexual assault suits against the university football players and recruits? Those guys use women like sex toys, and get away with it. One woman was gang-raped at a recruiting party, but football boosters used their power to whitewash the whole thing. The police, the district attorney and the grand jury investigated her claims, but the prosecutors decided not to file sexual-assault charges."

Diana was nodding vigorously. "Exactly," she said. "My ex is long gone but he messed me up in a lot of ways. After all I went through with him, I'm not interested in a relationship with any man. My physical therapy and massage practice is doing well. And my feelings about abuse have become stronger over the years. Intimate partner abuse is the number one cause of injury to women—more common than muggings, stranger rapes and car accidents combined. I see victims in my practice. Even though they don't admit they're being abused, I recognize those bruises. So yes, I'm on a crusade to stop this."

Miserable stories. I felt myself joining their anger. But I couldn't go there. I looked off at one of Gramma's paintings on the opposite wall for a minute to restore my sanity. It was time to take a principled stand. "I sympathize with your anger and frustration," I said. "I also hate domestic violence. But I can't endorse your tactics. You can't simply take the law into your own hands like this."

Then I turned to Gayle. "How did you all agree to this extreme solution?" I asked.

Gayle's face reddened. "The thing is," she said, "we've all seen enough abuse of women. And society isn't doing much to stop it. In Moxie, we spent years trying to let go and rise above our angry feelings, but finally we began to ask ourselves whether overlooking and letting go was the best way. We kept coming back to the idea that rising above and almost ignoring the behavior of an abusive man is like accepting their behavior, which in turn sounds like giving them permission to carry on. We decided we weren't willing to tolerate it any more. So we had to act."

"But some of you have had regrets since?" I asked. "Some of you want it to stop?"

A battle took place on her face. Then she squared her shoulders and looked straight at Diana and Hana. "Yes," she said. "Sabrina and I realized that being involved in this illegal activity was risky for us and for our children, even if it was for a good cause. She planned to do what she could to stop it. Did she tell you that?" she asked them.

Diana and Hana looked at each other for a long moment. Then Diana shrugged. "Okay, I'll admit it. Sabrina did have a thirty-day plan. And Hana and I were part of it. She said we had thirty days to dismantle the website, the accounts—all of it—or she was going to report us to the police. But if you think we pushed her off a cliff or something to stop her, you're wrong. In fact we don't even think she's dead. Go ahead and try to contact her again. If she is dead and you talk to her spirit, you'll find out we didn't have anything to do with it."

Chapter 22

Waves of nausea overwhelmed me. I knew that if I stood up or even moved I would vomit on the floor. Partly morning sickness, but more Moxie. I felt sick about Moxie's illegal activities and petrified about what my involvement with them could mean for me and my baby.

But I stayed in therapist mode. I closed my eyes and took a deep breath to settle my stomach. "I appreciate your telling me the truth about the website," I said as evenly as I could manage. But at this point I don't know what to do with this information, or whether I can be involved with any of you any more. You all need to leave now so I can think. I'll let you know tomorrow what I decide."

Diana leapt to her feet in front of me, muscles tensed, nostrils flared, eyes cold and hard. "Don't underestimate us," she said forcefully. Waves of anger poured off her, headed straight at me. "We've done some investigating. We know your boyfriend is a cop. If you even think about telling him any of this, you'll regret it for the rest of your life. You know what we're capable of."

As I struggled with how to respond to Diana's threat, Hana stood up next to Diana and put her arm across Diana's shoulders. "I think what Diana means to say is that one step in the wrong direction will cause you a thousand years of regret," she said quietly. "That's a proverb worth remembering. Now we will leave as you requested." She pulled Diana off into the front room, where they put on their coats and boots and went out the front door.

"Be smart and keep your mouth shut," Diana yelled back at me on her way out.

I sagged back into my chair, feeling sicker than ever. Gayle sat quietly in her chair next to me. When I collected myself enough to look over at her, she was looking down at the floor, her shoulders slumped. We sat together in stunned silence for a minute, as if part of some botched meditation exercise. Then Gayle spoke haltingly. "I'm so sorry. I never should have told you." She straightened in her chair. "But you insisted on knowing," she said firmly, "and now that you know, you're in as much trouble as the rest of us."

But I'm nothing like them, I thought. I'm not on some vendetta to punish men. "Do the Moxie members hate all men?" I asked.

"No, of course not," she said. "Except for Diana, we've all been in good relationships with men. Some of us still are." She took a deep breath and looked off across the room. "If luck had been with me, I'd be happily married to a guy I met a few years after I got divorced from Frank. His name was Stuart. He was sweet and funny and a terrific dancer. My soulmate. But he got cancer—lymphoma. He fought so hard to live, never complained, went through chemo and radiation, all the nasty side effects." Her voice broke. "When Stuart died, it felt like the end of my world. I haven't found anyone like him since, but I know there are lots of good, kind, gentle men out there."

Pablo is a good man, I thought. Okay I was hurt when he left me years ago, but I got over it. And now we're together and I love him and he loves me. Poor Gayle. She'd had more than her share of bad breaks when it came to men.

"I'm sorry that happened to you, Gayle," I said. "But I'm glad to know you see more than one side of this story."

"Moxie may have gone off the track," she said leaning forward toward me, "but it's for a good purpose. We're not crazy or stupid or irrational. If we're guilty of something, it's caring too much—which puts us in a Karma-free zone. We so desperately want to help abused women."

My head was spinning. I held up my hand to stop her. "Look Gayle, I can't talk about this anymore right now," I said wearily. "You have to go. I'll talk to you later."

She stood up and turned toward me to offer parting words. "Cleo, I know you've gotten way more than you bargained for when you agreed to my brother's request to help find out what happened to Sabrina. But please don't give up on us. I have to know whether Sabrina is dead or alive."

I didn't answer. She waited a minute, then walked off toward the front room.

When I heard the door close behind her, I got up slowly, went to the front door and locked it. Then I bolted into the bathroom and puked my guts out. After which I didn't feel up to walking home, so I took a nap on my couch.

§§§

I woke up energized, hungry, annoyed and confused. Was it really as easy as they said it was to get away with identity theft? Now that I knew what they were doing, what should I do about it? Was I putting myself—and my baby—in danger if I turned them in? I had no idea what they might do, but I took Diana's warning seriously. I wouldn't underestimate them. On the other hand, I didn't want to think about Pablo's reaction if he found out that I knew what Moxie was doing and didn't report it. I needed more information to help me think this through.

I fixed myself a peanut butter sandwich and headed for my computer to do Google searches on identity theft. The information was not encouraging. I discovered that identity theft affects millions of households in the U.S. every year, mostly through credit card and/ or bank account misuse. But in most cases, the criminals are never identified, partly because by the time theft victims realize their information has been compromised and report the theft, the case is cold, partly because the cases often cross state lines and jurisdictions, and partly because the thieves are too smart to leave a paper trail. Without any details on Diana and Hana's scam, how could I possibly prove what they are doing if they deny it? And would it be worth risking their retribution to try?

Then I thought maybe I could find Hana and Diana's website. But Google found millions of domestic abuse victims' discussion groups, and I had no criteria to narrow the search. I went on some of the sites and read women's stories, many of whom wrote about how hard it is for them to leave the abuser, either because they believe the abuse is their fault, because they are afraid to lose the relationship, because they feel guilty at the thought of leaving, and on and on. They just keep taking the abuse, while somehow hoping the guy will change. As a therapist I'm familiar with these dynamics, although I don't generally treat abuse victims. Nevertheless, reading victims' stories reminded me of the horrific emotional and physical pain so many women live with.

A little whisper inside me said if Moxie has the courage and the ability to act against some of these abusers, good for them. I'm not saying I agreed with what Hana and Diana were doing, but I wasn't ready to turn them in to the police. As my clients, the Moxie women were entitled to confidentiality unless they were threatening physical violence to themselves or others. And in truth, I could see how they had come to judge the morality of their actions based on the outcomes. Sometimes the end does justify the means.

But sometimes it doesn't. If they had pushed Sabrina off a cliff to keep their secret, they had to be held accountable. Diana's words rang in my ears: Go ahead and try to contact her again. If she is dead and you talk to her spirit, you'll find out we didn't have anything to do with it.

And that's what led me to call Gayle for the second time that day, and once again invite her to come to my office.

§§§

Gayle showed up right away, surprisingly willing to go into the apparition chamber, even though she had said she never would again after her last experience. "Your Contact Project was the reason Bruce brought me to you in the first place," she said. "And I agree that I need to try again to reach Sabrina. I'm not afraid of getting my mother. If she shows up this time, I won't listen to her. I'll simply stand up and tell her to go away."

I got Gayle set up in the apparition chamber, reminding her to relax and think positive thoughts about Sabrina. I had no energy for paperwork, so I went into the counseling room to think and listen to music while I waited. As before, I worried that if Sabrina appeared to her in the apparition chamber, Gayle would be hit hard with the undeniable fact of her death. Even though Gayle had been saying that she no longer believed Sabrina was alive, being face-to-face with her spirit would be a shock.

I had almost dozed off, when I heard, "Yo, Cleo."

Tyler swooped across the room, spinning his board to a graceful stop on the coffee table. "No waves today," he said, frowning. "Bummer. More paddling than surfing."

I straightened up, moving slowly so as not to push Tyler away. "Huh? What do you mean, 'no waves'?" I asked.

"Gayle's sitting there like a duck, bobbing around."

"What are you saying, Tyler? Does Gayle need help?"

"No. She's not surfing. A wannabe. Like a waxboy on the beach."

Before I could figure out what to ask next, he and his board rose up and away. "Later!" he said as he surfed off through the wall, leaving me to try to decode his cryptic message as usual.

I still hadn't figured it out when I heard the chamber door open about an hour later. Gayle walked slowly into the counseling room, looking sad and resigned, but showing no signs of shock or deep grief. She sagged into a chair, her head in her hands.

I got up and brought her a glass of water, but said nothing—just waited for her to begin. She raised her head, mumbled "thanks for the water," and took a sip. She lapsed into silence again, eyes glazed.

I waited.

Finally she exhaled deeply and looked at me. "I saw her," Gayle said in a monotone, "but she was very far away. I said 'Sabrina, what happened to you?' but she didn't answer. She turned away and said, 'Not Brandi. Not for Ian.' I told her I'm doing everything I can to keep our agreement and take care of Ian, but Brandi is making it very hard. Sabrina got this very sad look and said, 'You have to stop her. Brandi is wrong for Ian.' Then I couldn't see her or hear her anymore."

Gayle sat back, eyes closed.

I didn't react right away, because I didn't know what to say. Gayle's reaction was not only unexpected, it was peculiar. Seeing Sabrina did not bring up the intense grief I was prepared for. Furthermore, Gayle showed none of the amazement, awe, or intensity I've seen in other clients who have reached a loved one in the chamber.

"How did you feel when you saw Sabrina?" I asked, finally.

"Sad," Gayle said. "And guilty because I haven't been able to get Ian away from Brandi. And confused because I still don't know what happened to Sabrina."

I was confused also. Gayle's reactions weren't ringing true to me. For the first time since I'd started the Contact Project I found myself doubting a client's report. While it was possible that Gayle's reaction could be this subdued, I was skeptical. Maybe Brandi was right when she predicted that Gayle would lie about reaching Sabrina as a way of proving she is dead and to get Ian away from Brandi. Maybe this was what Tyler was trying to warn me of when he said Gayle wasn't surfing, that she was a wannabe on the beach.

But I couldn't express those doubts, certainly couldn't accuse her of lying. And there was no way to verify what she had experienced in the chamber.

These Moxie women were full of surprises and they always seemed to be one step ahead of me. But at this point I was determined to hold my own with them to find out who was responsible for Sabrina's disappearance.

Chapter 23

Friday morning I got a desperate call. "Cleo, this is Allie Hecht." Her voice broke. "My mom, Charlene, was at Glenwood Gardens with your grandmother." She paused and took a couple of deep breaths. "You probably know Mom died last month." Another pause. "I'm having a hard time. Mary Ellen at Glenwood Gardens suggested I call you for grief therapy. And I really need some."

I remembered Mary Ellen telling me Allie was angry because she thought the hospital had deliberately hastened her mother's death. She'd said Allie wanted to sue the hospital. Knowing that, I wasn't eager to add Allie to my client list. Helping someone move through anger and blame in their grieving can take a long time. And I had a lot going on. But I had told Mary Ellen I'd talk to Allie if she made an appointment.

"Of course, Allie," I said. "Charlene was so sweet. I know Gramma and all the residents miss her. I'm so sorry for your loss. Would you like to set up an appointment to come in?"

"I would," she said softly. "I thought I'd get over it on my own, but with the holidays coming up, I really miss Mom. And today is her birthday, which makes it even worse. Is there any way I could come in today?"

I heard her pain and swallowed my reluctance. "Sure. I've had some cancellations because of all the snow, so I could see you at 1:00 this afternoon."

§§§

I'd always thought of Allie as attractive. She's petite, with thick wavy blonde hair and laugh lines that crinkle when she smiles. But today she was a wreck. Her face was splotchy, her eyes were red, and her limp hair badly needed a shampoo.

She collapsed into a slump on my couch. "My brother keeps telling me I should be over it by now," she said, "but I don't know how to do that." Her face contorted in an attempt to control her emotions, but she lost the struggle, breaking down into heavy sobs.

"It takes time," I said passing her a box of Kleenex. "And the amount of time is different from one person to another."

Allie wiped her eyes, blew her nose, took a deep breath and continued. "Mom was in her eighties, and sick, so I guess I should have been prepared to lose her. But I wasn't. I miss her every day. I cry. I can't sleep. I don't want to get out of bed in the morning. My friends don't understand why I'm having such a hard time. They tell me it was Mom's time to go. They say it's good she's not suffering anymore. They try to cheer me up by inviting me out. But I don't want to go. I'm not interested in doing things just to help me forget Mom."

"Of course you don't want to forget her," I said. "Can you tell me about some of the good times you and your mom had together?"

Allie brightened as she talked about her mother who was a teacher, a loving grandmother to Allie's three children, and a valued volunteer at the local historical library before Alzheimer's stole away her mind. "It was painful to watch her fading away, but even in these last few years when she mostly didn't recognize me, I felt her spirit connecting with me at some deep level. You must know what I mean from when you visit your grandmother."

"I do," I said, thinking of how I cherish my time with Gramma even now that so much of her is gone.

Allie's face darkened. "But I don't think the doctors and nurses at the hospital understand that," she said. "They think a person whose mind is gone is a useless person who doesn't deserve to live." Her voice was angry, her eyes hard. "I don't think it was Mom's time to go. She was getting better with the antibiotics. Then all of a sudden she was dead. I think someone gave her something that killed her."

I kept my face and voice impassive. "What makes you think that?" I asked.

She gave me a withering look. "It was pretty obvious that some of the nurses there thought I should let Mom die. They kept asking me if I was sure I wanted such aggressive treatment for pneumonia, given that Mom has Alzheimer's. They said she might be suffering. They'd ask if Mom had ever said what she'd want in this situation."

"But she was continuing to get the antibiotics?" I asked.

"I think she was," Allie said. "At least they said she was. But I think someone put something else into her IV." Her face quivered. "I wasn't even with her when she died. The hospital called me in the middle of the night and said she had passed. I couldn't believe it."

"Have you talked to her doctor about your suspicions?" I asked, thinking that the physician might help her accept the rapid deadly course pneumonia can take in a frail elderly woman.

"Yes, but it doesn't go anywhere. He pretends to listen, but I'm pretty sure he thinks I'm just a hysterical woman who can't face reality."

I thought to myself that he might think that. Anger and blame so often accompany grief. And he might well believe that a woman in her eighties who doesn't recognize family members isn't a good candidate for life-prolonging measures. It's possible that he discussed that with Allie before Charlene died, but once she was gone, he'd be unlikely to have that conversation.

But the hospital couldn't ignore her so easily. "How about the patient advocate at the hospital?" I asked.

"I did talk to the advocate several times. And I filed a written complaint. But she won't tell me anything except that they're investigating. What I think is that one of Mom's nurses did it. I suspect that woman who disappeared in the mountains last month—Sabrina Larson. She was Mom's nurse some of the time in ICU and she was one of the ones who questioned me about the antibiotics. After Mom died, I asked Ms. Larson a lot of questions. She acted anxious and defensive. Denied trying to influence me about the antibiotics. I think the hospital administration did investigate and made an accusation against her. I bet she disappeared or committed suicide rather than face it. She couldn't stand the shame."

I struggled mightily not to show any reaction to Allie's accusations of Sabrina. My involvement with Sabrina's disappearance had no place in this therapy session. But I was shaken and shocked. Could Sabrina have been a suspect in a hospital investigation? Would she have run away because of it? I wanted to know more. "So no one at the hospital has told you anything about their investigation?" I asked.

"Of course the hospital won't tell me anything. They're covering their butts. Last week I talked to a lawyer about suing them. I'm not going to stand back and do nothing while elderly patients are being quietly euthanized. I can't bring Mom back, but maybe I can save someone else—it might be your grandmother."

At this point I felt we had gone as far with her suspicions as was likely to be helpful—especially if she was planning legal action. I had been careful to give Allie the opportunity to express her anger without any judgment from me. Now what she and I needed was time to explore her special relationship with her mother, so I could help her accept her mother's death. That would be her first step toward moving on to remembering her mother while living in a world without her.

"I can't help you with what might have gone on at the hospital," I said. "I'll leave that part to you and your lawyer. But we can work on your grieving process and ways of getting through the holidays if you'd like to do that."

She agreed, so we spent the rest of our time talking about the ups and downs of her relationship with her mother over the years. Then we set up a series of future appointments and I left her with a piece of homework. "Finding a way to acknowledge and remember your mother on her birthday and special holidays like Christmas can help you keep a positive connection with her on those days. This week try visiting a special place that you shared with her, going to her gravesite, or making a gift to an organization or charity that was important to her."

§§§

After Allie left, I got myself a cup of tea, sat down, and thought about her accusations against Sabrina. From what the Moxie women had told me about Sabrina—that she was a loving caregiver who liked helping and comforting those in need, that she believed that what you put out comes back to you—she didn't sound like the Dr. Kevorkian type. But people are complex. And I'd never even met Sabrina.

I decided I should pursue these accusations to find out more about Sabrina. But how? The hospital patient advocate wasn't going to violate confidentiality by discussing Allie's complaint or any subsequent investigation with me. Mary Ellen at Glenwood Gardens wouldn't be a good source either. She had pretty much dismissed Allie's suspicions of the hospital as a symptom of unresolved grief.

Then I thought of Lark, a Moxie member, Sabrina's good friend, and a fellow nurse who worked with her at the hospital. I called her on her cell to see if we could meet. Conveniently, she said she'd be off at 3:00. I live right at the base of the canyon, so she'd basically be passing my house on her way home to Nederland. It only took a little arm twisting to get her to agree to stop by for a short talk. I hustled home, made coffee and tea and got out some cookies. One of Gramma's lasting legacies will be, "when you want a favor, feed them."

Despite the weather, Lark showed up wearing green scrubs and New Balance walking shoes, with only a light down parka for warmth. No hat over her long blonde hair pulled back in a no-nonsense ponytail. Mountain people are hardy.

We sat at my kitchen table with our mugs—coffee for her and tea for me—and a plate of ginger cookies perfect for dunking. "This is awkward," I said. "But I've promised to do what I can to find out what happened to Sabrina, and now I have a question you're the only one I can think of who might be able to answer."

"Sure," she said, her gaze direct and open. "Anything for Sabrina. Ask whatever you want. I'll do my best to answer."

Before I could reply, my phone rang. Caller ID said "Brandi." I let it go to voicemail and turned off the phone.

"Sorry for the interruption," I said. "Anyway, the question I need to ask you is, do you know how Sabrina feels about euthanasia?"

Lark stared at me as though I had slapped her. "Why do you ask that?" she gasped.

I couched my information carefully so as not to violate Allie's confidentiality. But I put my question out there. Time was short and I needed answers. "Someone whose relative recently died at our hospital believes that a nurse might have been involved in the death—and that nurse might have been Sabrina. If it's true, it could be a reason Sabrina disappeared."

Lark shook her head. "Oh, I know that woman. She's the one whose mother in end-stage dementia came in with pneumonia. The mother had no idea what was going on, but the daughter wanted everything done. Mom got IV antibiotics, but she died anyway. The daughter's been all over the hospital blaming the nurses."

I didn't acknowledge the accuracy of her description. "Was Sabrina that patient's nurse?"

"That patient was in ICU for a couple of weeks before she died. All of us in ICU took care of her."

"Did Sabrina think the patient shouldn't be getting the antibiotics?"

Lark threw up her hands. "Look," she said. "There are worse things than death. End-stage dementia is one of them. Most nurses don't believe a person in end-stage dementia who has no quality of life should be treated with antibiotics. Most of those patients can't recognize family members and friends, can't tell anyone what they need, and can't swallow solid food. They're incontinent, and often wheelchair or bed bound and prone to bedsores and infections."

I had asked Allie's question for her and for myself. Now I paused, thinking about Gramma and what I would do if she ended up in that situation. "Is that because the nurses think those patients' lives aren't worth saving?"

Lark sighed. "Mostly it's because demented patients don't understand why they are being poked and prodded or hooked up to beeping machines. Sometimes they fight the IVs and have to be tied down to keep them in. Sometimes they wind up on a ventilator with an endotracheal tube down their throat. Sometimes the pain caused by the treatment is worse than the pain of the illness. We don't want to be doing that to them."

"But it's your job, so you have to do it, no matter how you feel?"

Lark nodded. "Exactly. We don't have a choice. If the physician orders the treatment, we have to provide it. But the antibiotics are really prolonging the death rather than prolonging the life. Even if we cure the pneumonia, most of these patients will have another episode soon and be back in the hospital where we have to torture them again."

"I can see where that would be uncomfortable for nurses," I said. 'Why do physicians order antibiotics for these patients?"

She grimaced. "Most people don't have advance directives. Most families don't understand that a long life isn't necessarily a good life. Some of these family members believe in aggressive care always, and will fight ferociously to get the patient every possible intervention, even when there's no quality of life. The physician can advise comfort measures only, but it's not the physician's choice." She looked at her watch. "I really need to get going."

"Sure," I said. "I appreciate your answering my questions. Just one more thing. Do you think there's any chance Sabrina might have gotten fed up and taken action to put the patient out of her misery?"

Lark gave me a stony look. "Of course not," said. "Sabrina's a licensed nurse. She could have her license revoked for even neglecting a patient. As far as willfully endangering a patient's health in a way that resulted in death, she could go to jail. That's not Sabrina."

Chapter 24

I was in the kitchen still trying to decide how I felt about Lark's critique of the medical treatment of Alzheimer's patients when I heard loud knocking on my front door. Figuring Lark had forgotten something, I ran in to the living room and pulled the door open without looking out to see who was there.

My heart jumped into my throat when I saw Brandi and Erik Vaughn. I would have guessed he had a gun in her back, except he was in front of her. And they were both smiling.

I tried to slam the door in their faces and lock it so they couldn't get in. But Erik was too fast for me. He stuck his foot in the doorway so I couldn't shut it. Then he pushed the door open and walked in. Brandi followed. Why would she be with him after I'd told her how dangerous he is? "I called you six times," she said. "But you never picked up."

"Oops, my phone's turned off," I said. I realized it was still sitting on my kitchen table and headed out to get it. But Erik went around me and blocked my way.

"Hey, Cleo. Good to see you," he said, coming toward me grinning, his arms stretched out for a hug.

I backed off like I'd seen a snake. Which I had. A snake in the grass. The usual Erik, all glib and charming on the outside, but evil and manipulative on the inside.

Why would he be so friendly when the last thing he said to me last summer was that he'd come back and make me pay for exposing his scams? He must want something. But what?

I gave him my fiercest glare. "I know it's too much to expect that you came back to Boulder to make restitution to victims of your herb-growing scam. So, what do you want?"

He grinned. "Whoa! Ease up there lady. Why do you always see the worst in people? Investments go south all the time. That doesn't make them scams. Investors take risks. That's life. I don't owe anyone anything. I came here out of the goodness of my heart to help Brandi find her sister."

Brandi sat on the couch, uncharacteristically silent, smirking at us like we were a reality show devised for her entertainment.

I took a step toward Erik, shoulders back, spine straight, trying to make myself look bigger. "Do you know where Sabrina is? Did you take her somewhere and do something to her?"

He shook his head slowly like I was a two-year-old throwing a tantrum. "There you are with the negative again. No, I didn't take her somewhere. I haven't seen her since last summer. I haven't even been in Boulder since last summer."

"Why would I believe that?" I folded my arms across my chest. "As I recall, you have very little regard for the truth."

"Believe what you want. I am telling you the truth." His cold eyes belied the innocent expression on his face.

"Brandi said you called her when Sabrina was going up to the mountains with her friends and you said you had a surprise for Sabrina, so she told you where to find her."

Brandi squirmed in her seat and looked down at the floor.

Erik laughed. "I didn't call Brandi. I haven't talked to Brandi since Sabrina broke up with me last summer," he said.

Omigod! Who do I believe? Is anyone telling the truth here? They both strike me as antisocial personalities—impulsive, manipulative, and lacking concern or remorse for people they mistreat. Erik is an accomplished scammer who has been lying to anyone and everyone since he learned to talk. Brandi is impulsive and irresponsible, but I don't have direct experience of her lying. If I have to choose one of them to believe, I'll choose Brandi.

I turned to face her. "Brandi, why is Erik saying he didn't call you about Sabrina?" I asked.

She looked up at me, rolling her eyes. "Because he didn't call me."

She raised her eyebrows as if to say "duh."

"I made up the phone call. Okay? Everyone was so sure Sabrina was dead. But I knew she was still alive. I knew she'd be back. But no one would listen to me." She shrugged with a cocky little tilt of her head. "I didn't want Ian to think she was dead. I made up the phone call to help him believe Sabrina could still be alive."

"You say you knew she was still alive." I speak slowly and deliberately, as though that will eke the truth out of Brandi. "How did you know?"

Brandi crossed her arms and looked away. "I just knew," she told the wall. "I felt it. Even now, I can feel her presence out there in the world. I just don't know exactly where."

I could see that line of inquiry was going nowhere, so I turned back to Erik. "If you didn't call Brandi and you haven't seen Sabrina, what do you know about the situation? In fact, how did you even know she's missing?"

"I have a Google alert set up for my name," he said. "It notifies me when my name appears somewhere on the web. Last week it took me to Brandi's YouTube video."

"What YouTube video?" I asked.

"After I put Sabrina up on the missing persons' website, I made a YouTube video," Brandi jumped up and went to my computer in the far corner of the living room. "Boot up your computer. I'll show you."

I sat at my desk and they stood behind me as we watched the two-minute video. Brandi, wearing a clingy white sweater, faced the camera holding a picture of Sabrina. "I need your help," she said in a teary voice. "My sweet sister Sabrina has been missing for a month. The police have no leads. I'm pretty sure they think she's dead. But I believe she's still alive. I believe she went off with a man named Erik Vaughn. He may be dangerous. My sister is a beautiful, caring person. I need your help to find her. Look carefully at this picture of Sabrina. If you've seen her, send me information at the website www.FindSabrinaLarson.com. I'm offering a $5,000 reward for information that leads to finding her. And Sabrina, if you see this, I want you to know that I miss you very much. Please call and let me know you're okay."

I swiveled around in my desk chair so I faced the room. Brandi went back to the couch. Erik backed away from my desk but remained standing.

I stared at Brandi. She showed no embarrassment at all at being caught in her lie, which she even put in her video. Apparently the end always justifies the means in her world. I could hear Gayle's voice ringing in my head. Brandi, with only a high-school diploma and no responsible work experience, is ill equipped to take care of herself. Brandi desperately needs people to believe Sabrina is only missing, not dead, so she can stay on in Sabrina's house, controlling Sabrina's property.

I pushed harder. "If you made up the phone call from Erik, why did you say in the video that Sabrina may have gone off with him?" I asked.

"Because I really thought Sabrina might have gone off with him. She'd keep it a secret because her Moxie friends don't like him," Brandi said. "But then, after what you told me about him, I was worried about what might have happened to her if she was with him."

Erik pointed at me, his hand mimicking a gun. "We need to talk, Cleo. Why are you telling malicious lies about me to Brandi and Ian and anyone else who will listen?"

I ignored him. "So you came to collect the $5,000 reward?" I asked him.

"Maybe. Even if I haven't seen her, I might know something about where she is," Erik admitted.

"See, I told you she's still alive," Brandi said. "And Erik can help us find her."

"How can Erik help?" I stood up, pushing my chair out from behind me. "And why are you both here at my house?" I wanted them gone. "If you know where she is, why aren't you out finding her or giving your information to the police?"

"You know I don't want to have anything to do with the police," Erik lowered his head and dropped his voice an octave. "The reason I'm here is to get some help calling off Sabrina's feminazi friends. Those bitches never liked me. They're the reason she broke up with me last summer. Then this fall, someone hacked into my online accounts. I know it was them. I know about their website. I got it out of Sabrina when we were together."

Brandi nodded like a jackhammer. "Erik says those Moxie women are stealing money from his bank accounts and credit cards," she said. Her eyes darted to Erik, then back to me. "He's willing to help us find Sabrina once you get them to give back his money. That's why we came." Her voice softened to a pleading tone. "Cleo, you know I don't have any influence with those women. But they like you. You can convince them that they need to give back Erik's money to help Sabrina. Please say you'll try." She sounded like a puppy begging for a treat. "If they care about Sabrina as much as they say they do, they'll cooperate."

My head was spinning. I decided to play dumb. "I have no idea what you're talking about," I said. "And I have no reason to believe Erik knows where Sabrina is. Why do you believe him?"

"Because he …" Brandi began, but she stopped as the front door swung open, letting in a blast of frigid air, and Pablo loaded down with a backpack and a suitcase.

A shot of energy exploded in my chest. I squealed, sprinted across the room and leaped into his arms. "Hey babe," he said, dropping the luggage and enveloping me in a bear hug. "I got a last-minute standby seat. Tried to call you from DIA when we got in, but you never picked up."

I was still locked in Pablo's embrace when Erik and Brandi grabbed their coats and scurried past us out the front door like the rats they were.

Chapter 25

"Why didn't you arrest Erik last night?" I asked Pablo the next morning. We were snuggled under my cozy down quilt as winter winds howled outside. We were finally ready to talk. The night before pent-up passion had pushed us to the bedroom, bypassing the all the catching up and explaining I had planned.

We had a lot to talk about.

"I will call Boulder PD to let them know Erik's in town," Pablo said, "but I couldn't arrest him. As far as I know, there aren't any outstanding warrants for his arrest."

"What about how he never bought back those starter herb kits he sold people? The whole thing was a scam. He promised the investors big profits and then skipped town."

"The Boulder PD did want to question him about that, but they never had enough evidence to show probable cause that he had committed a crime. Investment scams require a lot of investigation. Maybe some of his investors have filed civil suits against him, but I don't know anything about that."

I pulled back and raised up on one elbow so I could look him directly in the face. "How about the fact that three women he married died or disappeared under mysterious circumstances, and he ended up with their money?"

"Come on, Cleo. We don't even have evidence that those women's deaths were homicides." Pablo pulled me back down into his arms. "Now it's your turn to answer questions. What was Erik doing here at your house? And who was that woman with him?"

I told him about Brandi and how she'd lied by telling us that Erik had called her right before Sabrina disappeared. I told him about

Brandi's YouTube video and how it got Erik's attention and brought him to town. I told him about Erik's claim that he can help find Sabrina, and how excited Brandi is about that.

The only thing I left out was how the Moxie women had hacked into Erik's accounts and how he wanted me to get his money back from them. I didn't want to turn Hana and Diana in to the police. I was very clear that what they were doing was illegal. But I wasn't so clear it was wrong. If Moxie could punish an evil guy like Erik who had very likely gotten away with murdering several wives for their money, how could that be wrong? He's a callous, cold-blooded, conscienceless criminal who is clever enough to avoid getting caught. If vigilantism is the only way to effect justice and get some small measure of revenge for the women he's hurt, I'm good with that.

"So how did you get involved with Brandi?' Pablo asked.

"Remember I told you that Sabrina Larson's son Ian is the boyfriend of Elisa's daughter Maria? Brandi is Ian's closest relative now and she's living in Sabrina's house and taking care of him. Elisa and Maria were stuck in town during the blizzard and came over here to stay. Ian came over to see Maria, and Brandi came along for dinner."

"So you've ended up in the middle of trying to find this missing woman—Sabrina Larson? Does this have something to do with your Contact project? Are you planning to go into your apparition chamber, contact her, and find out what happened?"

"Of course not. The apparition chamber is for contacting the spirits of people who are dead. We don't know that Sabrina is dead. Plus, I don't know Sabrina personally, so why would she show up to contact me?"

"Is Brandi going to try and contact her?"

"Definitely not. Brandi believes Sabrina is still alive."

Pablo squeezed me tighter. "Enough, Cleo." He laughed. "I know you too well. There's more to this than you helping Elisa's daughter's boyfriend. You're hiding something and I'm not going to let you go until you tell."

I struggled, pretending to try to get loose from his muscular arms. Then I joined his laughter. "Okay, Mr. Policeman. I surrender. Here's the truth. I do have another connection to Sabrina. It turns out that her best friend, Gayle, is the sister of Bruce—the guy who funds my Contact Project. He asked me to help."

"Help how? Does this involve your apparition chamber?"

"Yes, Gayle has gone in twice trying to contact Sabrina. The first time she didn't reach her. The second time, she says she did talk to Sabrina, but I'm not totally sure that really happened. She may not be telling the truth."

Pablo groaned, let me loose, and rolled away. "Good grief, Cleo. Now you have clients lying about seeing spirits? This whole missing person thing looks like a mess you'd be better off out of."

"I'll admit I've thought that myself lately," I said. "But what about Bruce? He wants me to do this. I owe him, and he's never asked me for anything. And to be perfectly honest, I need his funding. His money not only keeps me going in this town full of therapists, it makes it possible for me to help people through the Contact project."

"If he believes in your work, he won't take away your funding just because you can't find his sister's friend," Pablo said. "Most likely he'll respect your choice."

"Bruce is a results guy," I said. "His way of dealing with issues is to get the facts and find a fast solution. He wants me to solve this for Gayle. He's willing to pay whatever it costs. He's made that clear. But I don't think he's going to accept me dropping out."

"Okay, let's consider the worst outcome. Say he does withdraw his funding. You can still help people without his money. And you won't be able to work as much anyway after the baby comes. I know that. And I'm expecting to contribute more than you do to our expenses and the baby's expenses."

Oops. Our expenses? I didn't want to get into the living together or marriage conversation right then, so I steered him back on topic. "What about Maria? She's like my own daughter. She loves Ian. I can't just back away from helping them find his mother. It would hurt Elisa as well and she's done so much for me. I have to stay involved."

He threw off the quilt. "It's getting late. I'm going to jump in the shower. We can talk about this more over breakfast."

But we didn't. In fact we didn't even have breakfast. When I got out of the shower, Pablo had the TV on to the local news and he was talking on his cell. Newscasters were showing shocking pictures of a twenty-five-car pileup last night caused by what they called a "wall of blowing snow" on U.S. 36 east of Boulder. Three people were killed and thirteen others were injured. Police closed the highway in both directions for four hours. The Colorado State Patrol blamed "ground blizzards," which occur when fresh snow and high winds create blizzard conditions under clear skies.

I sat mesmerized watching video of smashed cars, vans, and trucks being towed from the pileup. "And this was only the start of accidents and congestion last night in Boulder County," the TV anchor announced. "Wind gusts that reached 115 miles-an-hour washed blinding waves of snow over other Boulder County roadways, icing streets and creating whiteout conditions. Ground blizzards caused multiple accidents; gusts swept trucks off the road and knocked trees into power lines."

"Wow, that was some accident on highway 36," I said. "I'm sure glad you got back from the airport before it got so bad."

"Me too." Pablo clicked off his phone. "But here's a shocker. I just called Boulder PD to tell them that Erik Vaughn is back in Boulder. But—get this—turns out Erik was one of the people who died in that pileup."

I was stunned. "No way! What was Erik doing out on the highway in that weather?"

"Probably on his way to the airport," Pablo said. "I'm guessing that after he ran into me, he decided to get his ass out of town ASAP. We'll probably find out more about that later. But I've got to go." He laced up his boots and grabbed his jacket. "Sorry, no time for breakfast. I have to get out to Longmont, turn in that car I rented last night to drive in from the airport, and get to work. They're calling everyone in because of all the accidents." He gave me a sweet goodbye kiss and was off.

As soon as he shut the door behind him, I grabbed my phone and called Brandi. "Have you heard about Erik?" I asked.

"Heard what?" she asked.

I gave her the news. "Are you sure it was him?" she asked.

"Pablo got the news from the Boulder PD," I said, "which I'd say is a reliable source. So unless someone else was carrying his ID, it was him."

Silence on Brandi's end.

"Did Erik tell you where he thinks Sabrina is or what he knows about her disappearance?" I asked.

"He told me one thing, but he said the rest would have to wait until the Moxie women give him back his money."

Another long silence. I could almost hear the wheels turning in Brandi's head. Finally words came gushing out. "Wait a minute! He doesn't need the money now." The words gushed out of her mouth. "So why wouldn't he tell me what he knows? I think he would. I'll go in your apparition chamber and contact his spirit and he'll tell me everything. How soon can I try it? I can be right over."

Omigod. Of course she'd ask for this. And of course I'd refuse. "Stop, Brandi," I said firmly. "No one is going to try to contact Erik in my apparition chamber. Not you, not anyone. It was bad enough having Erik around when he was alive. There's no way I want to try to bring back his spirit."

Chapter 26

It was Saturday, a day I usually visit Gramma, so I headed over to Glenwood Gardens. She was in the living room with several other residents and a perky teenage volunteer, all singing along with a CD of "You Are My Sunshine." It never ceases to amaze me how music reaches residents with dementia who ordinarily sit slumped in a chair, not speaking or moving. When they hear a favorite song, they suddenly come alive, rocking rhythmically and singing along. It's truly inspiring to watch.

I was ready for a break, so I sat and sang along with them through several more old favorite songs. After the music was over, I sat next to Gramma so we could talk. She's always more alert and communicative right after music. "Cleo," she said, "Are you okay?"

"I'm just tired," I said. "How are you feeling?"

"I miss James," she said. "He hasn't come for a long time." I saw tears in her eyes. What to say next? In fact, Grampa had died before Gramma moved to Glenwood Gardens from Shady Terrace, but I don't like to remind her that he's gone. "He's been busy," I said. "I'll tell him you miss him."

She smiled. "He works hard," she said. "He's a good man. He loves me."

My mind drifted off to Pablo, a good man who loves me. We're not a perfect couple like Gramma and Grampa, but we love each other. I need to think hard about whether I want to risk losing what we have, especially with the baby coming.

When I looked back at Gramma, she'd fallen asleep in her chair. I gave her a soft goodbye kiss and gathered up my stuff to leave. Sadness hit me as it always does when I leave her, but it's mostly the familiar sadness about how Alzheimer's has taken her away.

Just as I got to the front door, Allie Hecht came in. "Cleo, I'm so glad you're here. I came to talk to Mary Ellen. But it would be great if you could join us. Do you have a minute?"

"I have a bunch of stuff to do," I said, "so just a quick minute."

When we were all three squeezed into Mary Ellen's tiny office, Allie leaned forward and spoke softly. "I told you both I've been planning to sue the hospital because I'm not getting anywhere with the complaint I filed about Mom's death. So this is all totally confidential, just between us, but yesterday my lawyer told me the hospital is offering to settle with me to avoid bad publicity." She paused to let that sink in, then continued. "They're not admitting any fault or wrongdoing, just saying they want to put this behind them and they're willing to offer me a settlement if I sign an agreement not to sue them and to keep all the information relevant to the case confidential."

"So should you be telling us about this?" Mary Ellen asked.

"I know neither of you will tell anyone," she said. "You both knew Mom, and I need your advice. What should I do? I figure the hospital must have found some evidence that I'm right about patients being euthanized in the ICU. Otherwise why would they offer to settle?"

"It could really be just like they say, to avoid bad publicity," Mary Ellen said. "A scandal like that can cost them a lot more than settling the case with you."

Allie looked at me. "What do you think, Cleo?"

"I can't really advise you. It has to be about what you think will make you feel better," I said. "What would you like to do?"

"Basically I'm not inclined to accept the settlement. Money's not what I'm after. It won't bring Mom back—nothing will. I want satisfaction for her death—the satisfaction of them admitting they're wrong. I want that nurse Sabrina Larson to get the blame she deserves. And I want to prevent what happened to Mom from happening to other patients."

"It could be very expensive to sue a hospital," I said. "Are you ready to spend that kind of money to get satisfaction?"

Allie sighed deeply and closed her eyes for a minute before she answered. "That's exactly what my lawyer asked me," she said. "He's recommending I take the settlement. But have I really gotten justice for Mom if I do that?"

"Maybe you could use the settlement money for a memorial in honor of your mom," Mary Ellen said. "How about a donation to the historical library where she volunteered? That way she'd be remembered for the good work she did."

"Maybe," she said. "But if it's all covered up, if there's no real investigation, would other older people be safe at that hospital?"

"It sounds like you need to sit down with your lawyer and discuss what's likely to happen if you settle," I said. "Then decide whether you can live with that."

We all sat silently for a minute, tuned into our individual thoughts. Then Allie gathered her things and stood up. "I've taken enough of your time," she said. "Thanks you guys. I'll let you know how it turns out."

§ § §

When I got out to my car and turned on my phone, I had three voicemail messages. One was Brandi, begging me to let her try to contact Erik in my apparition chamber. I hit "delete." The next one was Pablo, saying he was swamped with work, would have to work late tonight and go in early in the morning, so he planned to stay in Longmont for the night. Damn.

The last one was Paige. She sounded shocked. "Cleo, you're not going to believe what I found," she said. "It's Sabrina's thirty-day plan! You have to see it. I haven't told anyone else, so please keep it confidential. I want to show it to you. You're probably not at your office on Saturday but can we meet somewhere this afternoon?"

For sure I wanted to see that plan. This could be the breakthrough we'd been waiting for. I called her back and arranged for her to bring the plan to my office at 2:00, which gave me time to go home, grab some lunch, and get down there.

Paige showed up promptly at 2:00, waving a small red spiral notebook. "Here it is," she said. "Like I said, I found it in her locker."

"What made you decide to look in Sabrina's locker?" I asked. "And why hadn't the police already checked it?"

"I'm sure no one thought about checking her yoga locker," Paige said. "I know I didn't. But today I had some extra time at my studio because of classes cancelled due to the snow, so I was cleaning out old abandoned lockers for the new year. The lockers are rented by the month, but some people stop paying, go off and leave locks on lockers, and never come back to claim their stuff. So I have them sign a contract in advance that includes a statement saying if they haven't paid for three months without making arrangements with me, I will cut off the locks and remove the contents."

"So you decided to cut off Sabrina's lock too?"

"Exactly. When I came to her locker, I thought—hey maybe there's something in there that could help us find her. I didn't really think there would be, but I figured that if she comes back, she'll understand why I'd cut her lock off to check. So I did. And there was this notebook. Take a look."

Paige handed me the notebook. I opened it to the first page. There it was. Sabrina's handwritten thirty-day plan.

My 30-Day Plan
Sabrina Larson
November 1

Next week I turn forty—a major milestone that will be the beginning of my new life. It's time to make some major changes. I've come a long way, but I still have a long way to go. I'm not the person I was in my twenties. Back then I spent a lot of time depressed, broke, floundering, trying to make screwed up relationships work, trying to be the person I desperately wanted to be. My thirties were better, but I still made a lot of mistakes, especially by naively trusting people who were using me to further their own causes.

I take care of people. It's what I do. It's in my DNA. I'm a nurse. I've taken care of my sister Brandi practically all my life. And my friends rely on me to be the strong one, the careful one, the responsible one. And

I am. I'm always there to give and give, expecting very little in return.

And men. Men have used me. I break up with them, but they beg me to come back. I feel so guilty, I can't say no. I go back, and guess what? Nothing changes. By the time I finally break up for good with one of those jerks, I'm wrung as dry as an old washcloth. I always vow to never again get myself into that situation again, but somehow I do.

For years Diana has been telling me I'm co-dependent. Deep down, I know she's right. I like to be needed. I give everyone the benefit of the doubt. And I am extremely loyal, remaining in harmful situations too long. But I'm tired of following other people's lead. I'm tired of feeling used. I'm going to change my life.

Now, on the doorstep of age forty, I feel calmer, more experienced, more competent. I'm ready to toughen up, stand up for myself, and be a friend to myself first.

I plan to celebrate my fortieth birthday with a Moxie getaway retreat, which will be the beginning of my new life. I've already taken some steps by telling people in my life what has to change in my relationships with them.

I've made this 30-day plan to give them the opportunity to make changes on their own. Some of them are involved in illegal and unethical activities. Others are using me to make their own lives easier. They think that because I care about them, I won't act against them. But I will. I have to. If they continue as they are, there will be consequences.

Here is what I've told each of them so far. I'm writing it here as a record for myself of what I've said to them. I'll put this notebook in a safe place where none of them is likely to accidentally run across it.

Hana and Diana: *You crossed the line in exacting retribution. Your vigilantism is not only unethical, it's illegal. By standing by and letting this go on, I feel tainted and dishonest. It's over. You have thirty days to take down your website and compensate your victims, or I will post details of your cyber-crime along with your names and contact information all over the internet.*

Paige: *I admire your devotion to your brother, but if you choose to support him, you need to do it on your own. A year ago, I loaned you money for what you said was an emergency. You said you'd pay me back* quickly, but you haven't, even though you seem to have money for vacations and a new car. I've let that go by, but now I'm asking you to repay that loan within the next 30 days.

Lark: You took an oath. You are violating it. You have 30 days to make a change or I will report you to the state board of nursing.

Brandi: I've coddled you too long. It's time for you to become a self-sufficient adult. You have 30 days to move out of my house and find a way to support yourself. If you choose to ignore this warning, I will take steps to force you out.

Ian: You've been neglecting your schoolwork and expecting me to give you a pass on that so you can put all your energy into snowboarding competitions. But I need to step up as a mother and make you consider your future beyond riding. You have 30 days to improve your grades or I will seriously curtail the amount of time you spend riding.

Erik: You're harassing me. There's a reason I broke up with you. I don't trust you and at this point I don't even like you. I'm not even going to give you 30 days. Stop calling me, stop contacting me in any way at all, or I will give the police and anyone else who is interested any information I have that will help them track you down.

Getting my relationships straightened out is the beginning. From there I'll take care of myself and Ian, but others in my life won't be leaning on me. Caring will always be part of my life, but only a part. I plan to leave nursing. It's not as rewarding as it used to be. I can afford to take some career risks. And I have the confidence to try new paths. Turning 40 will be about freedom, being true to myself, letting myself be who I am.

Chapter 27

I closed the red notebook and wiped the tears from my eyes. My heart ached for Sabrina. "After all that self-examination, goal-setting, and planning, she didn't get a chance to implement any of it," I said shaking my head as I looked over at Paige.

"I know," she said, her voice quivering. "I cried when I read it, too. She was so open about her past vulnerability and so determined to start fresh in her forties, and then …" She stopped, closed her eyes and took several deep breaths before she opened them again. "But maybe she's still alive. We don't know for sure. Maybe she can still have that new life that she planned."

I wanted that chance for Sabrina. Or at least I wanted justice for her. I cared about her now in a deeply personal way. A surge of determination energized me. "We have to find out what happened to her," I said. "She deserves that. Let's call Gayle and get her over here to help us decide what to do next."

"Why Gayle?"

"Because she's not mentioned in the plan, so whatever happened to Sabrina, she probably wasn't responsible. Plus she's the one who got me involved in trying to find Sabrina. And she's Sabrina's best friend, the one she wants to raise Ian if something happens to her."

§§§

Twenty minute later, Gayle dashed in, face flushed, eyes wide. "You have it? Omigod I can't believe it. Let me read it. I have to read it right now."

Paige handed her the notebook. We watched in silence as Gayle sat on the couch turning pages with a dazed look on her face. As she read, she alternately gasped, nodded, slapped her hand against her cheek, or shook her head "no" and then "yes." When she finished, she looked up with an incredulous stare. "Sabrina never told me this stuff," she said softly. "She did talk about forty being a milestone and wanting to make some changes, but not this, not these ultimatums. She says she felt used. Was she angry? You're in the plan, Paige. Was Sabrina angry when she told you she wanted you to pay her back in thirty days?"

"No," Paige said. "She was clear and determined, but I didn't get any sense of anger from her. But it's not like she'd been pushing me for the money. This was the first time she'd asked and I promised her she'd have her money in thirty days like she wanted. But she might have felt differently about some of the others. It sounds like she'd been asking them to change, but getting nowhere, and she was losing patience. She might have been angry with them."

"Maybe we should think about which of them was likely to have been angry with her," I said. "Several people in the plan have good reason to want Sabrina to disappear. Who looks most likely?"

"Ha!" Gayle barked. "Brandi's the one." Her face hardened. "That irresponsible flake would have been penniless and homeless at the end of Sabrina's thirty days and now she's got everything Sabrina owned, or at least she does until there's actual proof that Sabrina's dead. She set it all up to keep it looking like Sabrina's missing. We know she lied about Erik calling her. Who knows what else she's lying about? I say we go after her and push her until she cracks. She's not as strong as she pretends to be."

"I agree," Paige said, her usually melodic voice taking on a firm tone. "Let's go see if she's home."

§§§

I was not optimistic about confronting Brandi—figuring she'd just stonewall us—but Gayle and Paige were so insistent that I went along. They also convinced me to go up ahead of them and ring the bell, saying that if she saw them at the door, she might not open it.

After a few minutes, Brandi answered wearing a purple down robe and fuzzy green slippers. No makeup. Messy hair. Very un-Brandi-like. "I've been thinking about Erik ever since you called," she said. "I can't believe he's really gone, when he was here just last night. It's such a shock."

Gayle and Paige got out of the car and started up the walk behind me. Brandi recoiled when she saw Gayle. "What's she doing here? You have no right to bring her here."

Paige stepped up beside me. "I found a notebook Sabrina left at my yoga studio," she said, smiling warmly. "I think you'll find it interesting. It has some very important information that might help us find out what happened to her. If you'll let us come in, we'll tell you about it."

Brandi glowered and stood her ground. She pointed at Gayle. "She's not welcome in my house."

"Oh put a lid on it, Brandi," Gayle snapped. "What can I really do to you with Cleo and Paige right here?"

"We just want to talk a little," I said. "We're trying to find Sabina and we need your help."

Brandi backed grudgingly away and let us in. The living room was trashed. Dirty dishes, soft-drink cans and empty chip bags covered the tables. Stacks of what looked like dirty laundry balanced in one corner. "I'll give you five minutes," she said, as she gathered up a bunch of papers from the couch so we could sit. "If what you have to say doesn't interest me by then, you're out of here." She sat down in a chair across from us and folded her arms across her chest.

Paige smiled at her again. "Did you know Sabrina had a thirty-day plan to change her life?" she asked.

Brandi glared at us. "She never said anything about that."

"It was in the notebook I found in Sabrina's locker," Paige said.

"Why would I believe you bunch of liars know more about my sister than I do?" Brandi said with a sneer.

Gayle lost what little cool she had, jumped up and stood in front of Brandi, legs planted wide. I shuddered as angry words erupted from her mouth like lava from a volcano, but it was too late to stop her.

"It's a real plan that Sabrina made and you're a big part of it," Gayle said pointing at Brandi. "Sabrina said she gave you thirty days to move out and find a way to support yourself. Now isn't it just too convenient that Sabrina is missing and you've got control of her money."

Any hope of a rational conversation with Brandi was over at that point and I knew it. But I watched transfixed for another couple of minutes as the vitriol continued.

Brandi jumped up facing Gayle. "I've had enough from you," she screamed. "Get out and stay away from me, or I promise you I'll file a harassment suit against you so fast it will make your head swim. And if you think you can get Ian away from me, think again. I'll find Ian's dad and have him file for guardianship and that will leave you up shit creek."

Then she turned her attention to us, waving her arms wildly. "And you," she said, pointing accusingly at Paige. "What were you doing going in Sabrina's locker? You have no right. Any property of hers that you found belongs to Ian and me. So hand it over or I'll sue your ass too."

Before she could turn her wrath on me, I stood up and looked her directly in the eyes. "Enough, Brandi," I said firmly. "We hear you. We hoped to get your cooperation, but clearly that's not an option. So we'll go."

I could only hope that Gayle and Paige would follow me to the door, and fortunately they did. We all ignored Brandi's shouts. "Give me that notebook right now. It's not yours to keep. You'll be hearing from my lawyer." She threw a couple of soft-drink cans at us as we went out. They clattered down the walk behind us.

§§§

Back in my office, we congratulated ourselves on our decision to leave the notebook locked safely in my office when we went to Brandi's. "If one of us had it in our hands, that bitch would have gotten it away and destroyed it for sure," Gayle said.

"Well that didn't happen," I said. "But nothing useful happened either."

"Sorry," Gaye said. "I screwed up. I thought we could crack her, but I went at her too hard and too fast."

"Never mind," I said. "Getting information from her was always a long shot. Let's move on." We sat silently for several minutes. Then I knew what we had to do. "Paige, I think you should go into my apparition chamber and try to reach Sabrina," I said.

Paige blanched. "So you think Sabrina is dead?"

I looked at Gayle who was looking down at her feet. "I think she must be," I said, "because Gayle reached her spirit in the chamber two days ago."

Paige gasped. "Gayle! You contacted Sabrina? Why didn't you tell us? What did she say?"

Gayle squirmed and rubbed the back of her neck, continuing to look down. She looked like she had swallowed something slimy.

"Gayle," Paige said softly. "Was it so upsetting that you can't even talk about it? Maybe Cleo can tell me." She turned to me. "What did Sabrina say to Gayle?"

I sat back and let a minute go by. "It's not for me to tell," I said. "It's up to Gayle whether she wants to share what happened."

Gayle sat up straight, arms crossed over her chest. She stared at me and took a deep breath. "Okay, Cleo," she almost whispered. "I think you know what I'm going to say next. I didn't actually contact Sabrina. You knew that all the time, didn't you?"

"What?" Paige asked, tilting her head to the side. "Why would you lie about that, Gayle?"

"It was the only way I could think of to undercut Brandi's story that Sabrina is missing, but alive," Gayle said.

I wasn't surprised at Gayle's lie—only a little surprised that she admitted it with so little prodding.

"That's what I figured," I said. "You thought if you pretended to contact Sabrina's spirit everyone would believe she's dead and by the terms of her will, you'd have control of Ian and Sabrina's estate."

"That's right," Gayle said, her voice flat. "But afterwards I couldn't go ahead with it. That's why I didn't tell anyone else. I don't want Sabrina to be dead. I want to be thinking positively, to have my intention be that she's still alive." She bent forward again, covering her face with her hands.

Paige wrapped her arms around Gayle. "It's alright, Gayle," she said soothingly. "This is a terrible time for all of us and we're all cracking a little under the stress. But if you and Cleo think I should go in the chamber and try to reach Sabrina, I'm ready."

Chapter 28

An hour later, Paige stumbled out of the apparition chamber, pale and trembling. "We have to go back," she said, her voice choked with tears. "All of us. Back to Indian Peaks." She stood shakily in the middle of the room, staring past us, blinking as if a spotlight shone in her face.

Her stunned look told me she had contacted someone in the apparition chamber, and the experience had deeply shocked her. I walked slowly toward her and put my arm around her shoulders. "Rest for a minute," I said, guiding her toward a chair. "Then tell us what happened."

Paige twitched and shook free of me. "No," she said, her eyes darting around the room. "We can't waste time resting. We need to get all the Moxie members together and go up there now." She darted out to the waiting room.

I followed. She was already pulling on her boots when I got out there. She kept getting the left boot twisted on her foot, shaking her foot to get it off, and trying again with jerky hands. Her agitation worried me. I could see she was in an altered state after her contact session. I couldn't let her drive into the mountains in this blizzard. I stood in front of her, took hold of her shoulders and pulled her to face me. "Paige, stop," I said firmly. "Think for a minute. It's 4:30 in the afternoon in December. It's already dark in the mountains and we've just had a blizzard. You wouldn't be able to get to the campground, and even if you did, it would be too cold and snowy to do anything."

She stared blankly at me. Then her face crumpled and she began to sob. "Sabrina is dead," she wailed. "And she told me to bring Moxie back together up there. I have to do it."

I put my arms around her and hugged her as she sobbed on my shoulder. I wasn't surprised that Paige had reacted strongly and viscerally to the contact session. A creative, spiritually-attuned person like her can easily let go of inhibitions and relax into an experience.

"I have to do this one last thing for Sabrina," she wailed. "I have to."

Gayle had followed us and was watching quietly from the doorway. Tears ran down her face. "You're sure, Paige?" she asked. "You're sure she's dead? You're sure you talked to Sabrina's spirit?"

Paige pulled herself back from my shoulder. She looked like she had come out of her fog. She spoke softly. "Yes, Gayle. I know it was her."

My heart ached for them. Although they had both said earlier that they thought Sabrina was dead, they had still kept a glimmer of hope alive for her survival. Now that glimmer was gone. They needed time to grieve, but it was also important for Paige to tell us about her experience while it was still fresh in her mind. "Let's go back in the other room and talk about what happened," I said. "Then Gayle and I can help you find the best way to honor Sabrina's request."

Paige let me lead her back to the counseling room and we all sat down. Paige looked down at her lap, running her hands through her hair, alternately pulling it back and letting it fall forward again into her face. Gayle and I sat across from her watching quietly.

"Spirits can be confusing," I said. "When they suggest something, they may not mean it as literally as you think. Can you tell us exactly what happened and what Sabrina said?"

Paige squared her shoulders and sat up. She looked intently at us. "Okay. Here's how it went," she said slowly. "I was nervous when I first got in there. I wanted to see Sabrina and yet I didn't want to see her. But I knew I had to try to reach her, so I focused on my breathing and got centered. I let my eyes go into a soft focus, looking at the mirror and waited."

She sighed deeply and wiped her eyes before she continued. "After a bit I saw colors all over the mirror and then I began to see scenes of past Moxie gatherings. They felt real to me, as if I had gone back in time. I could feel the powerful love and support that we had in Moxie for so long. I was happy." She leaned back and smiled to herself as if the scenes were replaying inside her head.

"Was it like a dream seeing those scenes?" Gayle asked.

"A little like a dream, but more real," Paige said. "It's hard to describe." She thought for a minute. "No, it was more like a movie. I knew I was awake and I was aware of myself sitting in the chair watching the scenes. Then the scenes faded into the background and I saw Sabrina in the mirror. That wasn't like a dream at all. It was real. She was right there in front of me. I was looking right into her face. I was sad because I knew she must be dead. But she didn't look sad. She was smiling, kind of glowing. She told me not to worry about her, that she's fine. I could feel love from her." Paige's face softened and she paused, gazing off into space.

I waited silently. I wanted to let Paige tell us about her contact experience in her own way, as I always do when someone comes out of the apparition chamber. To facilitate that, I listen attentively, nod encouragingly, but interrupt rarely.

Gayle, on the other hand, followed a different script. She fidgeted, tapped her foot, clasped and unclasped her hands. Then she broke the silence. "Did you ask Sabrina what happened to her? Did she tell you how she died?" she asked.

Paige hesitated as if deep in thought. Then she turned her attention back to us. "Yes," she said, "I asked Sabrina questions. And she talked to me, but it was inside my head. It was like I thought of a question and she answered it before I could ask her. I didn't exactly hear her speak, but I knew what she was saying. I asked her how she died. She said it was an accident, a mistake. I asked her to tell me about it, but all she said was, 'Moxie has the answers.'"

"Gayle shook her head vigorously. "Oof! What kind of answer is that?" she asked. "What kind of accident? Why didn't the searchers find her body?" Her tone sharpened. "How can Moxie have the answers?"

Paige leaned forward toward Gayle. "I know it's frustrating, Gayle," she said. Her eyes tightened and her voice rose a bit. "But I can only tell you what she said."

Paige took a couple of deep breaths and then went on with her description. "I asked her how we could find the answers, but all she said was 'Moxie.' So I told her I found her thirty-day plan and asked her if the answers are in it. She said, 'It's about Moxie. You all have to finish it. Go have another circle ceremony. Return to the Moxie spirit. Fix it.' Then she faded away and I couldn't talk to her anymore." Paige closed her eyes and leaned back.

"It's crazy to try to have a circle ceremony at Indian Peaks in this weather," Gayle said. "Anyway, did she say we should go up there? You said she said we should go have another circle ceremony. Why would it have to be there?"

Paige opened her eyes with a start. "Sabrina wants us to go there. I know she does."

"But did she actually say that?"

"It's what she meant," Paige said, turning to me. "Cleo, do spirits say everything they mean or do they just pass on the feeling and trust you to understand?" she asked.

"That I can't answer," I said. "I have no way of knowing what spirits want us to understand. I do know that people have different experiences with spirits. Some have clear specific conversations. Others say the spirits talk very little or not at all, but they have a strong sense of why the spirit is there. Some people say the spirits ask them to do something. Others just get a feeling of peace and support."

"Exactly," Paige said. She may not have said the words 'Indian Peaks,' but I know she wants us to go there."

Gayle got up, went over and sat next to Paige on the couch, putting her arm around Paige's shoulders. She spoke softly. "Paige, isn't it possible that what she wants is just for you to bring Moxie together in another circle ceremony? You're Rivka Ravenstar, so you're the one to set it up. But couldn't we have it inside, since it's the dead of winter and freezing up at Indian Peaks?"

Paige tilted her head to the side and pulled on her ear, as she took time to reflect. "You're right, Gayle," she said, finally. "I am Rivka and I can decide. Nature isn't welcoming for an outdoor ceremony right now. And it's not the space where the ceremony takes place that's important. It's the intent behind the ceremony and the open hearts of participants that make it sacred. We can have it at my studio tomorrow. It's Sunday, so no classes are scheduled. You find out when they can all come, and make sure they get there. I'll set up the ceremony."

Gayle hugged Paige enthusiastically. "Perfect," she said. "And I think Cleo should come too, because I know they'll have lots of questions about your contact with Sabrina."

Paige nodded. "Will you join us tomorrow, Cleo? We'll get back to you with the time."

"I will," I said. "Do you think we should share the thirty-day plan with all of them? I Xeroxed some copies while you were in the chamber."

"Yes," Paige said. "I think we should. Sabrina said the plan is about Moxie and that we all have to fix it."

"But wait a minute," Gayle said. "The plan isn't just about Moxie. Ian and Brandi and Erik are in it too. What should we do about that?"

"We already tried to talk to Brandi about it," Paige said. "And that got us nowhere. And Erik is dead. But Ian is a different matter. I don't know about talking to him about the plan, but shouldn't we tell him that I contacted his mother's spirit—that we know Sabrina is gone?"

Gayle jumped up. "You're right," she said, pacing the room. "We have to tell Ian. But omigod, this will devastate him. Brandi has him totally convinced that Sabrina is still alive. We'll be wiping out his hope." She turned to me. "How should we tell him, Cleo?"

Tricky. Oh so tricky. No way I wanted either of them going to Ian to tell him Paige's contact session was proof that his mother was dead. "We have to be very careful," I said. "Contacting a spirit in my apparition chamber doesn't prove the person is dead."

"But I saw her!" Paige said. "She was a spirit floating in that mirror. What else could it mean?"

"Some people would say you hallucinated her image," I said. "Or even worse, that the three of us conspired to show Sabrina is dead so we could get Ian and Sabrina's estate away from Brandi. I'm sure she'd say that."

Gayle scowled. "So you think we shouldn't tell Ian? Wouldn't it be just as wrong to keep it a secret from him?"

"Yes," I said. "I want to let him know what Paige saw. But I'd like to tell him myself so I can tell him about the apparition chamber and answer his questions. You two go ahead and set up the Moxie meeting and I'll talk with Ian."

Chapter 29

Saturday evening

Awave of exhaustion swept over me on my way home from meeting with Paige and Gayle. As I picked my way along the icy sidewalk to my car, shivering in the cold, dark evening, I realized that I wasn't yet used to the toll pregnancy was taking on my energy. Probably just as well that Pablo was working and staying in Longmont tonight. I barely had the energy to scramble myself some eggs and collapse in front of the TV.

Which was exactly what I did. And then promptly fell asleep on the couch.

"Yo, Cleo."

I jolted awake and saw Tyler crouched on his surfboard, knees bent, legs wide, arms outstretched, as an unseen wave tossed him around my living room. I felt seasick.

"Tyler! Slow down. You're making me dizzy and sick to my stomach."

He cruised back over to the couch and hovered just above my feet.

"Don't blow it, Cleo. Grab Ian's wave before he takes a nosedive."

"I barely even know Ian. What kind of nosedive is he about to take? What do you want me to do for him?"

"Ian hits the surf like the Duke. He's outrageous. But he's in the fog. Doesn't know which line to take. Don't let him get swallowed."

"Doesn't know which line to take? What do you mean? Are you talking about what happened to Sabrina? He's not the only one. No one knows."

"You're in the channel, Cleo. Don't bail on him."

"If you're saying I should tell him about Paige contacting Sabrina in the apparition chamber, I'm already planning on doing that. As soon as I get a chance."

"Tick, tock," Tyler said as he floated away through the wall.

I looked at my watch. 7:30 p.m.

My phone rang. "Hey girl, what's up with you?" Elisa boomed. "I haven't heard from you since Maria and I left Thursday morning."

I filled her in on Brandi and Erik's Friday night visit and how Pablo walked in just at the right minute. Then I blew her mind with the info about Erik's fatal collision in the icy pileup. She waited until I got through it all before she exploded. "Whew, girl! You've been busy. I can't believe you didn't call right away about Brandi and Erik showing up on your doorstep, and her YouTube video, and Erik's claim that he might have some information about where Sabrina is. You know how I like to be kept in the loop."

"Sorry," I muttered, "I was ..."

"Never mind your excuses. You didn't even call about Erik's crash! Now that's some news. You must feel relieved."

"I hate to say I'm glad someone's dead," I said. "But in his case, I admit..."

Elisa interrupted again. "Don't apologize. I want to sing the wicked witch is dead myself. You know I worry about you and with Erik gone for good, I can breathe a little easier. How did Brandi take the news? Have you talked to her?"

"Oh, yeah. Get this. She wants to go into my apparition chamber to try to contact Erik. Says she still believes he knows something about where Sabrina is. Of course I said no, and of course she's furious."

"Do you think she's right that Erik did know where Sabrina is?"

"I doubt it. They're both big-time liars who will say whatever they think will get them what they want. Brandi admitted she lied about Erik calling her when Sabrina and her friends went up to Indian Peaks. And she admits she did it so people would believe Sabrina is still alive."

"Do you think she actually believes Sabrina is still alive?"

"I don't know. She says she can 'feel' Sabrina's presence."

"What do you think?"

"Paige went into my apparition chamber today and contacted

Sabrina. She was very clear that she saw Sabrina's spirit and talked to her and that she really is dead."

"Whoa! Does Brandi believe Sabrina is dead now that Paige had that contact session?"

"Brandi doesn't know about it. Besides Paige and me, you and Gayle are the only ones who know right now.

"Are you planning to tell Brandi?"

I updated Elisa on the visit Paige, Gayle and I had made to Brandi after Paige found Sabrina's thirty-day plan. "She threw us out and threatened legal action," I said, "so, no, I don't plan to call her. Anyway, it's not like someone found Sabrina's body. A contact session isn't proof of death."

"True," Elisa said. "So you won't be telling the police either?"

"I can't imagine the police would take me seriously," I said. "Even Pablo is skeptical about my spirit contacts. But I am thinking I should talk to Ian. It seems wrong not to at least let him know what Paige saw. What do you think? You know him better than I do."

Elisa was silent for a minute, then said, "Actually Ian is one of the reasons I called. Apparently Brandi has decided that she and Ian are moving to Park City, Utah. The top-rated snowboarding halfpipe coach lives there, and he's agreed to coach Ian. Maria is having a complete meltdown. But Ian is excited about the move, says Maria can fly out for weekends. No way I'll be letting her do that, given the type of supervision Brandi is likely to provide. So Maria's even more pissed at me than she was the other night." Loud sigh.

Uh-oh. This must be what Tyler was talking about when he said Ian's in the fog and I have to help him. But what could I do? Of course Ian would be excited to work with the best coach. And, given what Sabrina had written about him in her thirty-day plan, he'd probably be glad to be in a new school that might be less demanding, as well as continuing to live with Brandi who won't make him put school-work first.

"Wow! Brandi's taking Ian and leaving the state," I said. "I'm thinking she wants to get Ian as far away from Gayle and the other Moxie women as she can. You wouldn't think she could take him out of the state, but she's been working with a lawyer so I assume they have it all figured out."

"And they're not wasting any time about it," Elisa said. "She's planning to go right away so Ian can start school there after the holidays."

Uh, oh. I realized that my chances of talking to Ian were going down the drain quickly. This must be what Tyler meant by "tick, tock." I had promised Gayle and Paige that I would tell Ian about Paige's contact with Sabrina, and the push from Tyler had added to my resolve. But I was still a little nervous about doing it.

"How do you think Ian would react if I tell him about Paige contacting his mom in the apparition chamber?" I asked.

"That's a hard call." Elisa said. "I don't know him that well. He mostly talks about sports—at least when I'm around. Aside from that night at your house, we haven't talked about his mother. You're the grief therapist. How do you think he might react?"

"Probably not well," I said. "He might be devastated that there's a sign that his mother isn't alive, or he might think the whole thing is a fake, or he might be upset that someone other than him talked to his mother's spirit. But I think I have to tell him."

"I agree," Elisa said. "Other people know, so he should too. Ian and Maria are hanging out with some friends in Boulder tonight. Do you want me to call her and see if they can stop by your house?"

I didn't really want to see them right then, but I knew it wouldn't get easier by putting it off. And, Tyler's "tick, tock" rang in my ears.

"Okay," I said, "if they can come before 9:00. But don't give them any specifics, okay? Just say something like 'a few things have come up about his mom that I'd like to talk to him about.'"

§§§

Maria and Ian were on my doorstep at 8:30. Maria was scrunched into her coat, her face barely visible. "My mom said you had some important news about Ian's mom," she said, her words rushing out. "Do you know where his mom is?"

Ian hung back silently, his face serious, brow furrowed. My heart rate went up. Maybe this meeting was a big mistake.

I ushered them into the living room where I had a fire going and hot chocolate and cookies ready. We sat—them on the couch, me in a chair. "Thanks for coming by," I said. "What I have to tell you may seem a little strange to you, Ian. Feel free to accept it or reject it. I just feel like I have to give you this information."

"Sure," he said, stiffening a little.

His wariness before I even told him anything concerned me. I could see I wasn't getting off to a good start with him. I decided to back off and talk to Maria in hopes he'd relax a bit. "Maria, you know a lot about my Contact Project," I said. "Have you told Ian anything about it?"

She shook her head, and looked down at her hands. "Not really," she said. "It's kind of hard to explain."

Not what I was hoping to hear. Looked like I'd have to start from the beginning. And, like Maria said, it's hard to explain. I started with Grampa, how much I loved him, how much I missed him after he died, how I finally tried setting up the apparition chamber to see if I could contact him, and how good I felt when I talked to his spirit. Ian avoided my eyes, mostly looking down as I talked. Maria held his hand but remained silent.

I plunged on, going through my use of the apparition chamber with grief therapy clients and how contacting spirits of loved ones had helped them accept their losses. Ian jiggled his foot while I talked, then held up his free hand, palm facing me. "Stop," he said. "Are you trying to tell me I should go into your chamber and try to contact my mom? Because I don't want to do that."

"No," I said. "Even if you wanted to do it, I couldn't let you because you're a minor. And at this point it's not even clear who has the authority to sign a consent form to let you do it."

Ian pulled his hand free from Maria's and turned to her. "Why did you bring me here?"

She pulled back. Tears ran down her cheeks. "I'm sorry," she said, opening and closing her mouth a few times as if struggling to find the right words. "My mom said Cleo had something important to tell us." She looked at me, her head tilted to one side. "Do you have something to tell us, Cleo? What did you tell my mom?"

None of this was going the way I had hoped, but I was too far in to turn back. "Here's what happened," I said, and then I told them about Paige's contact session. "She was sure she saw your mom and talked to her," I said, "and she and Gayle and I decided it would be wrong not to share that with you."

Ian shrugged and gave me a polite smile. "Look," he said. "I know you're Maria's good friend and her mom's good friend, and I'm sure you mean well. But I don't believe in ghosts or spirits or whatever you call them. And I believe my mom's still alive. So unless you know where she is or you have a clue about where she might be, you can't help me."

He turned to Maria. "We need to get over to Kirby's before it gets any later," he said. "They'll be wondering where we are." He pulled her up.

She put her hands on his shoulders and looked into his face. "No, wait, Ian," she said. "Think about it for a minute. Your mom has been missing for a month now. If she's alive, wouldn't she have called you or sent you an email or something? Wouldn't she want you to know she's safe?"

He sagged. "Maria, we've been through this." He pulled away from her, frowning. "Just because I haven't heard from her doesn't mean she's not alive. Maybe she's being held prisoner somewhere, or maybe she hit her head and wandered off and doesn't know who she is, or maybe she's just off somewhere with a really good reason not to let anyone know. That's as real as some room with phony ghosts."

He walked over to the front hall and grabbed their jackets, then came back to the couch and handed Maria hers. "Are you coming?" he asked.

"Sure," she said, putting her jacket on. She walked over and gave me a quick hug. "Thanks, Cleo," she said. "I'll talk to you later."

After they left, I sat by the fire, rerunning the conversation in my head. What had I been thinking? I was so focused on giving Ian the news that I totally overlooked exploring his interest in hearing it. My agenda, not his. Very un-therapist-like behavior.

Chapter 30

Sunday afternoon

Focus on Sabrina," Paige said, her melodious voice soft and soothing as usual. "Hold her in your heart." She paused to give us time to do that. Then she continued. "I asked Gayle to let you all know I saw Sabrina in Cleo's apparition chamber yesterday." Tears ran down Paige's face. "It was amazing and I want to tell you exactly what it was like."

I was at Paige's yoga studio, Inner Poise, sitting on a yoga mat in a circle with the five Moxie members. I had been nervous about how this meeting would go. But as soon as I arrived at the studio I had picked up a calming vibe, perhaps from all the yoga sessions that had been held there over the years. I had let myself relax into the place as I looked around.

The studio was on the second floor of a south Boulder building, affording a stunning view of the mountains. The sparsely simple classroom was mostly space, with white walls, hardwood floor and large windows. A table at the front of the room held an Ikebana flower arrangement of three deep purple irises and green leaves in a flat black bowl.

Paige had gotten us started with breathing exercises to help us get centered and find focus. She looked fit in deep turquoise spandex yoga pants and a tank top of a lighter shade of turquoise. She had pulled her long red hair back into a ponytail, but curly tendrils escaped to frame her face. Because of the tank top, I was able to see that she had a saying tattooed around her upper left arm. It said, "Live the life you love, love the life you live."

The rest of us were also dressed comfortably, following Gayle's suggestion when she had called us to set the time for the meeting. And—except for Lark who had come from a hospital shift wearing blue scrubs—we wore comfortable workout clothes. Gayle was in black as usual—spandex pants and a long-sleeved scoop-necked top. I didn't see any pocket for her phone in her form-fitting outfit. Maybe she had it under her legs.

Diana wore the loose gray drawstring pants she wears at her physical therapy practice, topped with a fitted "Proud to be a feminist" black tee that showed off her amazing muscles. Hana wore black leggings and a drapey coral tank that hung to her hips and was the perfect backdrop for her long shiny black hair. I wore my favorite navy yoga pants and a soft loose-fitting ivory shirt.

As Paige began to tell about her experience in the apparition chamber, I noticed that Lark's head was bent toward the floor. I couldn't tell whether her eyes were open or closed and wondered whether she was dozing after a long hospital shift. Diana fidgeted and looked around the room. Gayle, Hana and I sat quietly cross-legged, eyes on Paige as she began to speak.

"I started out sitting in the dark in Cleo's chamber, looking into a lighted mirror," she said. "I saw colors all over the mirror and then I began to see scenes of past Moxie gatherings. I could feel the powerful love and support that we had in Moxie for so long." Paige stopped and let her glance flit across our faces, embracing us with her smile. Then she turned her look inward as she continued. "I saw Sabrina in the mirror," Paige said, shaking her head slowly. "She was right there in front of me and I was looking into her face. I felt sad because I knew she must be dead. But she didn't look sad. She was smiling, kind of glowing. She told me not to worry about her, that she's fine. I could feel love from her."

Diana had shifted position again, squatting back on her heels with her head jutted forward. "Excuse me, Paige," she said. "I'm sure this was a profound experience, but how do you know it was real? It sounds like a dream or a hallucination to me. I don't see how we can decide that Sabrina is dead based on what you think you saw."

Lark sat up straight, her arms folded over her stomach. "Diana has a point," she said. "You are very suggestible, Paige."

I wasn't surprised to hear the skepticism. I've heard plenty of doubts and disbelief about my Contact Project. Which is why—even though I firmly believe the spirit contacts are real— I don't go around promoting the process or touting its results.

But Gayle wouldn't let me sit back. "No," she said. " Tell them, Cleo. You know it was real. I saw Paige when she came out and I heard her talk about it. She saw Sabrina."

I was between a rock and a hard place. I couldn't testify positively either way. "I wasn't in there with Paige," I said. "So I only know what she told us. But in my experience, people feel very strongly that they do make contact with spirits in the chamber. And the way they describe their experiences is very similar to what Paige told us."

Hana shifted her legs in front of her, pulled up her knees and wrapped both arms around them. A slight frown flitted across her face as she turned toward me. "Look, Cleo," she said. "You seem to be an honorable person, but I have to bring this up. So many psychics have been found to be frauds. How can we know you and Gayle didn't set up a computer to project a digital image of Sabrina into that mirror? I know Gayle wants to have Sabrina declared dead—not that you want her to be dead, Gayle, but that you believe she's dead and you want to prove it so you can get Ian away from Brandi."

Gayle jumped to her feet and began pacing the room. "Good grief, Hana! You think I'd do that? I thought we were friends."

"It's not that I think you'd do that or that Cleo would either," Hana said. "But I'm a scientist. When something unusual happens, I look at as many explanations as I can think of and try to find the most likely ones. It's how I've been trained."

Paige narrowed her eyes as she looked at Hana. "Well that explanation may seem likely to you," she said. "But it's totally wrong. What I saw couldn't be a fake. It wasn't just an image. I asked Sabrina questions. And she talked to me inside my head."

"So you didn't actually hear Sabrina talk?" Hana asked.

Paige frowned. "No, I didn't exactly hear her speak, but I knew what she was saying."

Hana didn't back down. "What did you think Sabrina was saying?" she asked.

"I asked her how she died. She said it was a mistake. I asked her to tell me about it, but all she said was, 'Moxie has the answers.' She said 'Go have another circle ceremony. Return to the Moxie spirit. Fix it.' Then she faded away."

Gayle, who was still pacing, came to a stop in front of Hana. "I can't believe you'd accuse us of lying about Sabrina's spirit, Hana. Just because you and Diana mislead and defraud people doesn't mean the rest of us are like that."

"And if you want to talk about lies, what about Sabrina's thirty-day plan?" Paige said. "When I brought it up at our meeting at my house on Monday, you three—Diana, Hana and Lark—said you weren't in it and that Sabrina hadn't talked to you about it. But that turns out not to be true. All three of you are in it. Sabrina had specific things in there that she said we all had to do."

"Stop," Diana said, jumping up and holding her hands out as if directing traffic. "Is this something else Sabrina's spirit told you? Because I've heard enough of these ghostly accusations. I'm leaving. You can call me when you have some actual evidence."

Gayle stopped pacing and stood directly in front of Diana. "As it turns out, we do have some actual evidence," she said. "Paige found Sabrina's thirty-day plan in her yoga locker. You're all in it and we brought copies for each of you." She turned to me. "Can you pass out the copies, Cleo?"

I got the copies from my bag in the corner and gave one to each of them. We all sat down on our mats again and read, mostly silently with a few gasps and exclamations. Then Diana spoke up. "It's about time she admitted she's co-dependent. I've been telling her that for years. She totally lets men walk all over her. It's disgusting."

"That's all fine, Diana," Gayle said. "But what about what she says about your website?"

"What about it?" Diana challenged.

"She was going to expose your illegal activity if you didn't take it down and compensate your victims," Gayle said.

"We told you and Cleo that on Thursday," Hana said. "So how is this news? Yes, Sabrina did threaten to expose our website."

"Okay. You knew about her plan, and now the thirty days are up," Gayle said. "Have you taken the website down, quit infecting men's computers with software that collects their financial information, and stopped stealing money out of their accounts?"

Diana thrust out her chest and leaned forward, fire in her eyes. "Of course not," she snapped. "We have a mission to stop abuse of women. Our work has just begun. We've found a way to even the score for some women and we're not going to stop just because some of you got cold feet." She glared at Gayle.

I squirmed and bit my lip. Diana's anger had swept away the calm in the room. We were all sucked up in the argument swirling around us. My instinct as a therapist was to try to defuse it, but Moxie had a long history as a group and it wasn't my history. I was sure they had their ways of coping.

Sure enough, Paige, in her Rivka facilitator persona, tried to pour some calm on the flames. "Diana, I know you and Hana care deeply about helping women," she said. "But remember how often in Moxie we've talked about how revenge isn't in anyone's best interests and it doesn't heal your heart. And in this case you could go to jail. The best revenge is getting your life together and moving on. I think Sabrina was trying to help you let go of your desire for revenge and step into a better future."

Hana had been shaking her head no, all during Paige's talk. "It would be wonderful if the world were really like that," she said. "But we're not there yet. So many women around the world are living desperate lives—abused, prisoners in their own homes, even trafficked as sex slaves. We can't stop now. We have so much more ..."

"We don't want to stop, and we don't intend to stop" Diana broke in, her face red. "We intend to settle the score." She waved her hands dismissively. "No one ever gave women our rights, we had to fight for them. And we're going to keep on fighting." She sat back, arms crossed, shoulders tight, face like a bulldog.

I expected Paige to respond, but before she could, Gayle shrugged off Diana and turned the focus to Lark. "What about you, Lark?" she asked. "Sabrina says you violated your nursing oath. That sounds serious. Had she talked to you about it? Did she actually threaten to report you to the state board of nursing?"

Yikes. I wasn't prepared for Gayle pushing everyone to the wall this way. My throat was tight and my stomach rolled. I wanted to run away, but I sat tight, waiting to see what Lark would say.

Lark remained silent for a long minute, her face composed, looking intently at Gayle. Then she let her gaze roam around the room at each of us in turn, as if clinically assessing us. Her nursing experience no doubt had taught her to stay focused and avoid reacting defensively to an attack.

When she finally spoke, her voice was clear, firm and composed. "I don't know what you all think is going on here," she said, "but I have no intention of being part of it. Any disagreement I have with Sabrina is between her and me and is no business of anyone else. I don't know what happened to her and I don't think any of you do either. You can believe what you want to believe about talking to Sabrina's spirit, and you can cross-question and accuse each other all you want, but I'm done." She paused. "We've been friends and I care about all of you, but I don't have to answer to Moxie or continue to be part of it. I had decided to drop out even before Sabrina disappeared, but every time I was ready to tell the rest of you I was leaving, Sabrina talked me into staying one more week to see if things changed the way she hoped they would. Now that she's gone, I don't see Moxie in my future."

Lark stood up, walked over to the corner where the coats and bags were, and pulled on her coat. "I'm going now. If any of you want to get together to ski or snowshoe or hike, I'll be happy to hear from you. But I don't want to talk about Sabrina anymore until there's some real evidence of what happened to her. And I don't intend to come to any more Moxie meetings." Before anyone could reply, she walked to the door and left.

Paige burst into tears. "Sabrina trusted me. She told me to finish what she started, to have another circle ceremony, to return to the Moxie spirit, to fix our problems. And now look. It's all ruined."

"Get a grip, Paige," Diana said. "We all know Moxie is over. Even before Sabrina disappeared, we were split.

"You get a grip, Diana," Gayle said. "If you don't take down that website, we'll report it like Sabrina was going to do."

"Don't even think about it," Diana said. "If you make even one tiny move toward exposing our website, we'll implicate you and Cleo so deeply, you'll be up to your eyebrows in shit."

"How will you implicate us?"

"We have so many choices. We can put stolen money in your bank accounts so it looks like you stole it. Then we can simply deny everything. Neither of you has a sterling reputation. We found out that Cleo nearly lost her psychologist's license last summer for interfering where she wasn't wanted. And Brandi has a restraining order out on you, Gayle, for being so pushy about Ian. Neither of us has a smirch on our reputation. So when it's our word against yours, and we say you stole money and made up a big story to cover yourselves and blame us, who do you think they'll believe?"

Hana had quietly gotten up and gone over to the coats and bags and gotten her stuff and Diana's. "Enough, Diana," she said in a non-nonsense tone. "You know as well as I do that the authorities will never find our website. It's well hidden and protected by a series of strong passwords. And even if they did find it, they'd never be able to prove anything. We don't need to talk about this any more. Let's Go."

After they left, Gayle, Paige and I sat pondering our shredded expectations. Nothing had gone as we had hoped. What to do next?

"Paige, how about you go back into the apparition chamber and try to get more information from Sabrina." I said. "This time maybe she'll tell you what happened to her."

"Absolutely not," Paige said in an unusually firm voice for her. "I'm not going back in there to see Sabrina again. I can't face her. She asked me to fix Moxie and instead it all fell apart. How about you go, Cleo?"

"I can't do it," I said. "She's never even met me. Why would she contact me?"

"But if she's dead, doesn't she know everything that's going on? Wouldn't she know how you've been helping us?"

Now there was a question. One to which I had no answer. "I don't know what she knows," I said. "But I think someone she feels close to needs to be the one who tries to contact her."

Gayle had been sitting silently during this exchange, but getting increasingly restless. "Look," she said. "I know I lost a lot of credibility when I pretended I saw Sabrina. I'm so sorry that I did that, and I promise you it won't happen again if you let me try one more time. Please. Sabrina means so much to me. I have to find out what happened to her."

I heard her plea and decided to take Gayle at her word. I believe in second chances, especially when the person apologizes and appears to be sincerely remorseful. We set up her contact session for the next day.

But unfortunately that was not to be.

Chapter 31

When I turned on my phone after the Moxie meeting, I found six missed calls, all from Mary Ellen at Glenwood Gardens. Panic seized me like an icy claw. Something must be wrong with Gramma! I had three voicemails, which I knew I had to hear ASAP—even though I dreaded listening to them.

The first one had come in at 2:00 p.m. Mary Ellen said Gramma was listless, coughing, had a fever, wasn't eating or drinking. They were watching her and had talked with her physician. The next message came at 3:15. It said they think Gramma has pneumonia. They are sending her to the hospital by ambulance. The final message came at 4:05. Gramma is in the hospital ICU. Come as soon as you can.

Tears poured down my face. I could barely see to drive. Roads, still icy in places, slowed me down. Red lights seemed to last forever. How could this be happening? My dear sweet Gramma. She's everything to me. Even now that so much of her is gone, even though she's confused and disoriented most of the time, she's my rock. I need her. I can't lose her. I sobbed so hard I almost hit a car turning in front of me.

I screeched into hospital parking lot, parked crooked, and ran inside. "Where's the ICU?" I demanded from the first person I saw.

"To the right, down the hall."

I sped to the ICU where I found Gramma, looking tiny in the hospital bed. She lay unmoving amidst a web of intravenous lines and wires hooking her up to an assortment of machines whose dials showed wavy lines and rapidly changing blinking numbers. A tight-fitting clear plastic mask covered her nose. It was attached with bands around her head and connected to a machine by a plastic tube. Her skin was deathly white, her eyes were closed and the only sound in her little cubicle was the beeping of monitors and the whispery blowing of her facemask.

Chills shook my whole body. It was like I was caught in a blizzard with horrible freezing particles slamming into me from every direction. Nowhere to turn. I could hardly breathe. I struggled to remain upright. I wanted to run away to some place where none of this was happening, but I knew I had to get past my fear and be there for Gramma.

I closed my eyes and focused on my breathing until the shakiness stopped. Then I looked at Gramma's sweet face. I wanted to embrace her in a hug, to hold her close and keep her safe, but of course I couldn't. I leaned down and kissed her. "Gramma, it's Cleo. "I love you."

She didn't respond at all.

After quietly stroking her face for a few minutes, I stepped away from her bed and called Pablo. "Hang tight, Cleo," he said. "I'll leave Longmont right now and be there as fast as I can."

I knew it would be at least half an hour before he could get there. I went back to Gramma's bed, pulled up a chair and sat next to her, holding her limp hand and watching her every breath.

A nurse came in. I looked up and to my surprise saw that it was Lark Dove. "Cleo," she said. "I saw your name on the chart as next of kin. Martha is your grandmother?"

"Yes," I said, trying to hold in my tears.

Lark put her hand on my shoulder. "I'm sorry she's so sick," she said.

In the face of her sympathy, my emotions bubbled over. "She looks terrible," I sobbed. "Is she dying?"

"She's stable right now," Lark said. "We can talk more over at the main desk if you'd like."

I followed her out to the nurses' station at the center of the room. "We don't know what she can hear, so we don't want to talk about problems right next to her," Lark said.

"Does your grandmother have an advance directive—a living will?" she asked.

"No," I said. "She doesn't have a living will. By the time Grampa and I realized how confused she was, it was too late for her to consider what she might want."

"We should talk more about that," Lark said.

I didn't want to talk more about that, so I asked a different question. "What's that mask over her nose?"

"It's called a bipap machine. It helps push air in and out of her lungs. It improves her oxygen level and it's less invasive than putting a tube down her throat and having a ventilator breathe for her. Her doctor can tell you more when he comes," Lark said.

"Oh, here's Dr. Bremer, now," she said, turning toward a tall, skinny man who had just walked up.

I had only met Dr. Bremer a few times. Gramma's long-time physician had recently retired and Mary Ellen at Glenwood Gardens had recruited Dr. Bremer to take her on. He seemed capable and compassionate and I was grateful to have him, as it's not easy to find physicians to take new Medicare patients. But I didn't really know him.

He greeted me and I followed him over to Gramma's bedside. He listened to her heart and lungs, checked her chart and the numbers on the machines, then turned to me. "She has fluid in both lungs," he said. "We have her on some strong antibiotics. I'm hoping she'll respond well. We'll know more in a day or so."

"The nurse asked me about a living will," I said. "But Gramma never made one. When she got to where she couldn't make decisions, Grampa made them for her. But Grampa died eight years ago. Now it's all up to me. I'm her power of attorney." I dreaded the next question, but I had to ask it. "Are there decisions I need to make for her today?"

"Not right now," he said. "But that time may come. It will help if you tell us what you want us to do if she needs a breathing tube or if her heart stops, things like that. The nurses can go over the choices with you."

I didn't want to go over those choices. I didn't even want to think about those choices. I so wished Grampa were alive to help me. I didn't want Gramma to suffer, but I didn't want to be the one determining when she would die. I felt like I'd be signing her death warrant if I chose not to have everything possible done to save her. I sank back into my chair in alarm.

Finally Pablo came. I rushed into his arms, sobbing. He held me and stroked my back softly. Finally I pulled back, got a tissue to blow my nose and wipe my eyes. "She's so sick," I said.

"What does her doctor say?" Pablo asked.

Before I could answer, Lark came in to check Gramma's breathing and the numbers on the machines. "Cleo, can you come back out to the nurses' station for a few minutes? There are a few more questions I need to ask you."

I wanted to jump back into Pablo's arms and hide my face, but I got up like a grownup and followed her out.

I knew what was coming. I remembered Lark telling me that most nurses don't believe that someone in late-stage dementia who has no quality of life should be treated with antibiotics.

"Dr. Bremer suggested I go over your grandmother's healthcare decisions with you," Lark said. "You said she never made a living will or told you what she would want done in this situation?"

"What situation?"

Lark looked at me with kindness in her eyes. But her voice was firm. "A situation where she has advanced Alzheimer's Disease and pneumonia and can't understand why she's hooked up to all these machines. A situation where she might not be able to breathe without a tube down her throat attached to a ventilator. A situation where her heart might stop."

"No," I said. "We never talked about any of that before she got Alzheimer's. And after that, she was too confused."

Lark sighed. "That's the thing about Alzheimer's," she said. "By the time the patient might want to say she doesn't want aggressive treatment for pneumonia, given that she has Alzheimer's, it's too late. Now you have to make her decisions."

"I have to think about it," I said. "Right now I want everything done. Maybe I'll change my mind after I have some time to think."

"Look, Cleo, I'm saying this as a friend," Lark said. "Your grandmother is eighty-seven and frail and she has Alzheimer's. Her quality of life is very limited. Would she want to live more years with dementia? Sometimes the most unselfish thing we can do is to release those we love rather than make them stay to suffer longer."

Pablo was back in Gramma's cubicle, but he was looking over at me. He must have noticed that I looked distressed. He came over and put his arm around my shoulders. "Hey, babe, how about a short break to grab some food? I haven't eaten since this morning and I expect you can use a snack. We can come right back."

In the cafeteria, I got a grilled cheese sandwich—one of my go-to comfort foods. Pablo gobbled up a hamburger and fries.

"I feel like Lark has an agenda, and she's trying to pressure me," I said.

"Lark's the blonde nurse you were talking to?" he asked. "You looked devastated. What was that about?"

"About end-of-life decisions," I said. "She thinks people with Alzheimer's have no quality of life, so they shouldn't get treatment for pneumonia, that we should just let them go."

"Does Martha still have quality of life?" Pablo asked, gently, his eyes filled with love.

"I think some," I said. "She still recognizes me some of the time, she still enjoys music and art."

"So you want the treatment?" I heard sincere sympathy in his voice

Tears ran down my face. "Yes. She's still my sweet Gramma and I love her dearly. And I'm not ready for her to go."

He nodded emphatically. "Then that's it," he said. "It's your choice, not the nurse's choice. Just try to think it through and be clear about what you want."

Back at Gramma's bedside, I tried to clarify my thinking. But my mind kept slipping back to all those summers I had spent with Gramma and Grandpa as a teenager and how she had shared her artist's studio with me and taught me to paint. Gramma was an award-winning painter—so creative and productive. It's hard to accept that she's ended up like this. Was Lark right? Had Gramma lost so much of who she was that her life wasn't worth living?

It's agonizing to make life-and-death decisions for another person.

How could I know what she would want? Was I just trying to keep her here for myself?

Lark's shift ended at 7:00 p.m. and thankfully she left without bringing up the subject again. Pablo and I sat quietly with Gramma until about 9:00 p.m. when another nurse insisted we leave and get some sleep. We agreed to go with the nurse's promise to call us immediately if anything changed even the slightest bit.

When we got to my house, we both fell into bed exhausted and were asleep as soon as our heads hit the pillows. I set the alarm for 6:00 a.m. so Pablo could get to work and I could get back to the hospital.

But I awoke in a cold sweat at 3:00 a.m. thinking about Allie, whose mother had been at Glenwood Gardens with Gramma.. Her story kept running through my mind. When her mother had Alzheimer's and was in the ICU with pneumonia, the nurses there pushed Allie to consider withdrawing treatment. She didn't agree. She thought her mother was getting better with the antibiotics, but then her mom suddenly died in the middle of the night.

Omigod! What if that happens to Gramma? Why hadn't it occurred to me? There must be something to Allie's suspicions if the hospital offered to settle with her. Allie thought Sabrina might have been the nurse responsible. But Sabrina's gone so that would mean Gramma is safe.

But what if it wasn't Sabrina? I sat bolt upright in the bed, my heart racing. I almost screamed, but gulped down some quick breaths to stifle the cry. What if it was Lark? That's hard to believe when Lark is so kind and helpful. But she is very firm in her beliefs about not treating demented patients with antibiotics. Is Lark euthanizing demented patients in the ICU when their families choose to have treatment continued? What if that's what Sabrina meant about Lark violating her oath?

An image of Gramma lying there dead in her bed flashed before my eyes. I shook Pablo awake. "I have to get back to the hospital right now," I said, my voice shrill. "Gramma might not be safe with Lark there." I threw off the covers to climb out of bed.

Pablo grabbed my arm and shook his head sleepily. "What's going on, Cleo?"

I was way too jumpy to sit still and talk, so I pushed him away and stood up. "Lark thinks Gramma would be better off dead and I'm afraid she'll make that happen. I need to get over there to stay with Gramma and keep her safe." I headed for my closet to grab some clothes.

"Wait, Cleo," he said. "I'm not sure why you think that, but remember that Lark left at 7:00 p.m. last night. She won't be back until at least tomorrow morning. So you don't have to rush over there right now."

I grabbed my phone and called the ICU to check on Gramma. No change. I asked for Lark. They said she was off duty until Tuesday morning at 6:30.

"You're right," I said to Pablo. "She's actually off until Tuesday morning, so I have more than twenty-four hours. Oh—and they said Gramma's condition hasn't changed."

He held out his arms. "Come on back to bed," he said. "We can talk about this more in the morning."

I snuggled up next to him, listening to his even breathing as he went back to sleep. But my mind was active, running through what I could do to find out more about Lark before she could do anything to Gramma.

Chapter 32

Monday

The 6:00 a.m. alarm yanked us both out of a sound sleep. We were groggy from my middle-of-the-night panic, and I was kind of queasy. Pablo grabbed a shower and said he'd pick up breakfast on his way to work so he wouldn't make my upset stomach worse with the smell of brewing coffee. I would have liked to talk to him more about Lark, but I didn't feel up to it at the moment and I appreciated his thoughtfulness about the coffee.

He left, assuring me that he'd keep his phone on and be available to come any time I needed him. I called the hospital to check on Gramma and find out when her doctor would be coming. She was about the same. They expected Dr. Bremer to come by around 8:00 a.m.

I ate some soda crackers to settle my stomach and took a long hot shower. With all my focus on Gramma, I'd stopped thinking much about the baby, but my pregnancy symptoms were a strong reminder. Although I was on autopilot, I did what I needed to do. I knew my baby needed protein and by then my stomach was calm enough to eat, so I scrambled some eggs with cheese. Then I headed off to the hospital so I'd be there when Dr. Bremer came by.

Gramma opened her eyes briefly when I kissed her. "Hi Gramma," I said. "Are you feeling better?" She looked at me, but I saw no sign that she recognized me. "It's Cleo," I said tearfully. "I love you, Gramma." Of course she couldn't talk with the bipap mask on. What was I thinking? She closed her eyes again.

Dr. Bremer came and checked her. "She's not worse, but she's not better either," he said.

"Is she going to be okay?"

"It's hard to say," he said. "We'll know more in a day or so."

"She seems very sleepy. Is she sedated?" I said. "She does always sleep a lot, but now she can't seem to stay awake for even a couple of minutes."

"I have her mildly sedated," he said, "so she won't pull out her IVs or pull off her oxygen mask. We don't want to have to use restraints to keep her still."

"Can she move out of the ICU to a regular room?" I asked, thinking this would be one way to get her away from Lark. "I think she'd be more comfortable there."

"No," he said. "We have to keep monitoring her in here for now." His pager beeped. He looked at it. "We'll talk tomorrow," he said over his shoulder to me as he rushed off.

I leaned over Gramma's bed and spoke softly to her. "I love you so much, Gramma. "I want you to get well so you'll be around to meet my baby when it's born." I sat next to her quietly gazing at her and smoothing her hair.

Then worry crept in. I flashed back to a few days ago when Lark, sitting at my kitchen table, had said, " Most nurses don't believe a person in end-stage dementia who has no quality of life should be treated with antibiotics." I thought about Sabrina's thirty-day plan, which said Lark is violating her nursing oath. Would Lark somehow stop Gramma's antibiotics? Is that what she does? Is that what Sabina meant? Did Lark do that to Allie's mother?

I knew Lark would be back on duty in the ICU the next morning. I had to find out before then whether she was a suspect in the death of Allie's mother. I had to ask Allie about it right now. I jumped up and hurried outside to my car to call her so my conversation wouldn't be overheard.

When I told Allie about Gramma and my fears that something would happen to her in the ICU, she screamed. "Oh, no! Not again! Cleo, that's horrible! We have to keep your grandmother safe."

"I know," I said, tearfully. "I'm scared about the pneumonia, but

I'm even more scared that some nurse will stop the antibiotics or put something deadly in her IV. The hospital must think it happened if they offered you a settlement. I need to know what they know so I can keep Gramma safe. Do you know any more about what they found out?"

Allie sighed. "No, they never said anything specific," she said. "They didn't admit anything, just offered the settlement."

"Did you end up taking it?"

"I finally did." Allie sounded resigned. "What I really wanted was justice for Mom, but the settlement offer had a deadline and my lawyer convinced me that it would be way too expensive to go ahead with a suit against the hospital. My chances of winning weren't good. So I took the settlement. I'm going to take Mary Ellen's idea and use the money for a memorial to Mom, but I haven't decided what yet."

This wasn't getting me anywhere. Time was slipping away and I needed answers. Lark had made it very clear to me that she didn't approve of my choices for Gramma's treatment. "Do you think your lawyer knows anything more about what the hospital found out? Could I talk to him about it?"

"Oh, no, no, no. You can't do that." Allie said, her voice shrill. "Remember I told you the whole settlement thing is confidential. I had to sign a non-disclosure agreement that said I'd keep everything about the settlement secret. You can't tell my lawyer I told you about it."

"Well, could you ask him if he knows anything else?'

"I could but I'm pretty sure he doesn't know anything else. The hospital was very close-mouthed about the details."

"There's one nurse in particular that I'm worried about," I said. "Her name is Lark Dove. She keeps pushing me on whether I want all this treatment to keep Gramma alive, given that she has Alzheimer's. Was she one of the ICU nurses who took care of your mother?"

"Tall, blonde, athletic-looking, right?" Allie said. "Yes, she was in the ICU with Mom."

I felt my chest tighten. Bad news. "That's I was afraid of. I wish I could find out if the hospital suspects her. Maybe I'll talk to the Patient Advocate."

"Just don't mention me around the hospital, okay?" Allie's voice shook. "I could be in big trouble if they know I talked to you about this."

I assured Allie that I wouldn't betray her confidence. Then I hung up and went back to Gramma's bedside.

She looked the same. I sat with her for a while, then decided to go get lunch and afterward try to talk to the Patient Advocate. I found the Patient Advocate's office on the first floor and waited about fifteen minutes before I got in. Her name was Edith Wales. A sensible-looking woman in her sixties, with gray hair and shrewd blue eyes. "How can I help?" she asked.

"I'm worried about my grandmother in the ICU," I said. I told her about Gramma's pneumonia and that she had Alzheimer's, then got to the more delicate part. "Lark Dove, one of the nurses there is being very pushy about Gramma not having an advance directive," I said. "She wants me to make choices that I'm not ready to make."

"We do have to ask you about choices and we encourage all patients or their surrogates to complete an advance directive," she said. "We can help you understand the pros and cons of each possible decision. But it's up to you what decisions you make. Would you like me to go through the choices with you?"

"Not today," I said. "Maybe later. That's not why I came. It's about that nurse. She scares me."

"Can you tell me more about her and how she scares you?"

A neutral therapeutic question. This woman was sharp. "Okay," I said. "I'm assuming this is confidential."

"Of course."

I should have felt my way more carefully with her, but I was tired and scared, so I dove right in to the impact zone as Tyler would say. "Her name is Lark Dove and I know her outside of here," I said. "I know she doesn't believe that patients with Alzheimer's should be treated with antibiotics for pneumonia, and she keeps pushing me to make that choice. I'm starting to worry that if I decide to keep having my grandmother treated, Lark will make her own decision to do something to make Gramma die. I've heard of that happening in hospitals sometimes."

Edith Wales' face shut down like a post-office clerk's window at 5:00 p.m. "Not at our hospital," she said coldly. "I know it's worrisome to have your grandmother so ill, but you need to control your imagination. Do you have someone you can call to be here with you?"

"That's not the issue here. You're the patient advocate. Here's what I need. I need to have Lark Dove not be in the ICU while my grandmother is a patient there."

"I'm sure you realize we can't shift staff around at the request of patients or family members," Edith said. "Is there anything else I can do? I'm happy to go through that advance directive with you."

"Never mind," I said, standing up to go. What was I thinking? She's just a bureaucrat. I was so frustrated and angry that I really lost it with my parting shot. "You seem more like a hospital advocate than a patient advocate to me," I said, as I walked out the door.

I went back to Gramma's bedside and sat for a long time listening to the steady high-pitched beep-beep-beep of the machines she was connected to. Sometimes there would be a series of lower-pitched bongs or a louder scritchy ding. Then a nurse would come in, check the machines and touch the controls until the tones stopped. Gramma slept on and I dozed off too.

I woke up with a jolt from a dream where Lark as Gramma's nurse came in to check the machines and surreptitiously injected a deadly liquid into Gramma's IV drip bag. I shivered. If that happened, Gramma wouldn't have a chance. Her heart would stop and that would be it. My own heart pounded at the thought. My chest tightened so much I could hardly breathe. I knew this was a panic attack, but I also knew I had a sound reason for my terror.

I closed my eyes and focused on my breathing, taking slow deep breaths to get back in control. Then I walked out to the ICU waiting area for a little break. The room was empty and I stretched out on a plastic-covered couch to try to relax. About twenty minutes later, Pablo walked in. I flew into his arms. I told him about my talks with Allie and the Patient Advocate, and my horrible fears about what could happen to Gramma. "You have to help me," I sobbed. "Make them tell me what they know. Make them keep Lark away from Gramma."

Pablo held me and comforted me until my crying subsided. Then he pulled back and gave me a tissue to wipe my face. "You're exhausted, Cleo," he said. "And you're pregnant and you're not eating right. You need a rest, a good meal and some time way from this hospital."

I protested, but he was insistent, and I was too tired to object any further. Besides, Lark was off-duty for the night. We went back in and checked on Gramma and then he took me home, with a brief stop at nearby Ideal Market to pick up some groceries.

He made spaghetti and salad and we both stuffed ourselves. I felt better but I was still worried and I wanted his help. After we cleaned up, I pulled him over to the couch. "We still need to talk," I said, trying to sound calm. "I need to do something about Lark. I can't let her take Gramma from me. What right does she have? Like you said, it's not for her to decide."

In spite of my attempt to stay cool, I was fidgeting and my voice was rising. "She'll be back on duty at 6:30 in the morning. The hospital won't do anything. You're a cop. Can't you make them keep her away from Gramma?"

Pablo sat still, looking at me with gentle eyes. "No," he said patiently. "I have no jurisdiction there, and even if I did, I have no evidence that points to a crime or even a potential crime. What evidence do you have that this nurse, Lark, is planning to harm Martha?"

I went though the whole story again, about Allie and her mother, about how Lark had told me that nurses have issues with treating pneumonia in Alzheimer's patients, and about Lark pressuring me to discontinue Gramma's treatment. "Can't you see? I have to stop her."

Pablo wrapped his arms around me. "Cleo, you know that's not evidence," he said. "I know you're worried about Martha, and I know her condition is serious, but I really don't think she's in any danger from the ICU nurses. You just need sleep. Come on, let's go to bed. You'll feel better in the morning."

No point in pleading my case any further. I was tired and I did need sleep so I could get to the hospital early in the morning. It looked like it was going to be all up to me to stop Lark. I set the alarm and went to bed, but I tossed and turned a long time before I finally fell asleep. My thoughts tormented me. I couldn't lose Gramma yet. It was too soon. I needed to be able to hug her and hold her and spend time with her. I needed her to be able to see my baby and hold it when it was born. I couldn't let Lark cheat me out of all that.

Chapter 33

I got up at 5:00 a.m. Tuesday morning to make sure I'd be at Gramma's side before Lark came on duty. Pablo was still asleep. I got dressed quietly and left him a note.

Gramma looked the same—barely alive lying there so tiny and fragile in the hospital bed, eyes closed, still hooked up to machines, the IV dripping slowly into her arm.

Lark came on duty at 6:30 and checked all Gramma's beeping machines. I avoided making eye contact so as not to encourage conversation, and thankfully she didn't stop to talk to me about choices.

I was afraid to leave Gramma's side even for a minute. I needed to watch Lark—even though I didn't ever know what she was doing, what she was putting in the IV. Once I asked her what she was adding to it. "It's her antibiotic," Lark said. "Don't worry Cleo, we're doing everything we can for your grandmother."

Her comment didn't reassure me one bit. What did she mean by "everything"? And how could I know if she was telling the truth? I wanted to confront her with my suspicions, but I knew she'd deny it. And maybe she could get me thrown out of the ICU so I wouldn't be able to watch anymore. So I just sat and agonized.

Mid-morning a woman in a suit and high-heeled shoes, wearing a hospital ID badge stuck her head into Gramma's cubicle and asked Lark to come out for a minute so they could talk. Lark looked surprised and not particularly pleased, but she followed the woman out to the central desk. Their conversation quickly became intense with scowling faces and hands waving. But they kept their voices low enough that I couldn't hear what they were saying. Then they left the ICU together.

About ten minutes later, a tiny young dark-haired nurse appeared next to Gramma's bed and checked her chart and machines. "Hi, I'm Helen," she said. "I'll be taking care of Martha today." I introduced myself and asked her where Lark had gone.

"I don't know," she said. "She had to leave unexpectedly."

"When will she be back?"

"I don't know, but they asked me to finish her shift today."

I wondered whether my talk yesterday with the chilly Edith Wales had made some difference after all. But, whatever the reason, it was a relief to have Lark gone. Still, she might be back tomorrow, or even tonight. I needed to find out more about what she was actually up to.

It occurred to me that if Gayle could contact Sabrina, she might find out more about Lark from her. Maybe Sabrina would tell her what she meant in her thirty-day plan about Lark violating her nursing oath.

Gayle's contact session had been set to be our next step before Gramma got sick. But I had cancelled it. Now that Lark was gone for the day and I could leave Gramma for a while, I could re-schedule. I called Gayle and Paige and set it up for 1:00 p.m. at my office.

§§§

Gayle was eager to go into the chamber. I suggested she find out whatever else she could from Sabrina about the thirty-day plan and about what happened to her at the wilderness journey. I didn't want to prejudice the outcome by putting specific ideas in Gayle's mind, so I didn't mention my suspicions about Lark.

Paige and I sat quietly in the counseling room, listening to music while Gayle was in the chamber. When she came out, her face was tear-stained, but her body was relaxed. She walked slowly into the room, collapsed on the couch, and closed her eyes. I got her some water. She opened her eyes, sat up, took a big gulp, put the glass on the table in front of her, and smiled at us.

"I saw her, I really saw her," Gayle said. "It was amazing. I knew right away that it was her spirit, so that meant she was dead, but it was okay. She walked right out of the mirror and hugged me. She said, 'I'm fine and I love you and I know you've been trying to help Ian. I want Ian to be with you.' I told her that as long as there's no proof that she's dead, Brandi will keep insisting that she's only missing and Brandi will be able to keep Ian. I told her we need to know what happened to her so we can prove she's really gone. Then she said, 'A house in Nederland.' Gayle stopped and gave us a bewildered look.

Gayle's account of what happened and her reactions rang true to me, unlike the last time when she merely pretended she'd contacted Sabrina. This time I believed her. After a minute, I prompted her to tell us more. "What did she say about the house?" I asked.

Gayle slouched in her seat, like she was digging deep to dredge up a memory. "Not much," she said finally. "She's in a white room in a house in Nederland."

Paige twisted a lock of hair around her finger. "Did she say who put her there?" she asked. "Was it Erik and Brandi?"

"She didn't say," Gayle said, perking up a bit. "But we have to find that house."

"But how, if all we know about it is that it has a white room? Pretty much all houses have white rooms," I said.

Gayle shook her head and rubbed her eyes. "Wait, wait, wait—I just remembered—she said something else—I'm trying to remember. Oh, I know. She called it Busbee's house. We need to find Busbee's house."

"We should ask Lark," Paige said. "She lives in Nederland. Maybe she knows the Busbees."

Alarm bells rang for me. No way I wanted to involve Lark. But I couldn't tell them what I suspected about her. She was their friend, and I had no evidence, and even Pablo thought I was imagining the threat. So I tried a softball. "That's probably not a good idea," I said. "Remember on Sunday Lark said she was through with Moxie and she didn't want to talk about Sabrina anymore until there was real evidence of what happened to her?"

"I think she'd feel differently if we told her about Gayle's talk with Sabrina, and that we need her help to find the house," Paige said. "Let's at least give her the chance."

"Look," I said. "This may sound strange, but I don't feel comfortable with Lark right now. She's been my grandmother's nurse in the ICU and she's been pretty much telling me she thinks Gramma shouldn't be getting treatment for her pneumonia because she has Alzheimer's. It's really upsetting."

Paige was silent for a minute, looking inward. Then she spoke softly, "I know what you mean," she said. "My brother—the one I borrowed money from Sabrina to help—has Down's Syndrome. One time Lark told me I was wasting money on his education. I wanted to hit her. I can understand why you'd rather not be around her right now, but we can't just go around Nederland knocking on doors and asking if it's Busbee's house and if they're hiding Sabrina."

"Let's get the Nederland police or sheriff or whatever they have up there to check out that house," Gayle said.

"How?" I asked. "By telling them her spirit said that's where she is? They'd laugh at us."

"Wait," Gayle said, brightening. "I can probably find the house in my firm's real-estate database. Then we can get directions and go right to it."

"It could be risky to go to the house," I said. "Someone might be there."

"Who?"

"Who knows? The Busbees or someone they hired. We don't know anything about them. Maybe they're friends of Erik and Brandi."

Paige looked at me as if I'd lost my mind. "What can they do to three of us?" she said.

"Shoot us if they have a gun," I said. "And they probably have one. Most mountain people do. I've been surprised a couple of times in the past year when someone tried to shoot me. Maybe we should have a gun. Do either of you have one?"

"I do." Gayle said. "A group of us local real estate agents took a concealed-carry class last year and I have a gun and a concealed carry permit."

Paige's jaw dropped. "You carry a concealed gun, Gayle?" she said.

"It can be risky being a real estate agent," Gayle said. "We meet strangers at empty houses, sometimes in remote locations, sometimes at night. You never know what might happen."

"Do you have your gun with you?" I asked.

"It's in my car," Gayle said. "We'll take my car anyway and we'll have the gun with us. But first I need to find the house in our database. Let me sign on to it on your computer, Cleo."

I got her set up and she was into the database with a couple of clicks.

"While you're doing that, I'll call Diana and Hana and tell them what happened so they can come with us," Paige said.

Gayle jumped up from the computer and grabbed Paige's shoulder. "No you won't," she said. "Remember how hateful they were at your studio on Sunday? We don't need them with us and we don't want them with us."

"But they're part of Moxie," Paige said. "They deserve to know about Sabrina and they deserve a chance to join our search if they want to."

"No!" Gayle said. "Now look. I need to get back to my database and find that house. And as soon as I do, we need to get going with no more delays. Once we get there, if we find Sabrina, we can call them from there." She sat back down at the computer and returned to her search.

Paige frowned. "All right, Gayle, I'll wait until we're up there, but you have to promise I can call them if we find out anything at all."

"Cross my heart," Gayle said. "Oh, here it is. The address is 3420 Ridge Road. We just go up Canyon to Nederland and Ridge Road is off Hurricane Hill Drive.

"I'm going out to my car to get my water-proof boots and my hat," Paige said. "And I also need to call my kids and tell them I'm going to be home late. I'll let them order pizza. They'll be happy."

§§§

About an hour later the three of us were in Nederland. We easily found the Busbee's house—a wood and stone modern perched on a steep hillside, surrounded by evergreens and rock outcroppings. An unplowed driveway led off from the road to the garage. Gayle pulled off onto the side of the road into some icy tire tracks. The house looked empty, like it was closed up for the winter. "Must be summer people," Gayle said.

We waded through knee-deep snow in the driveway to the front door, where we rang the bell and knocked loudly. No response.

"Finding the house doesn't do us much good if we can't get in," Paige said.

"Luckily I came prepared to pick the lock," Gayle said, pulling out what looked like a pocketknife, but was actually a set of six tiny picks that folded into a handle. She inserted one into the lock, jiggled and twisted it, then took it out and stuck in a different one. We heard a click, Gayle grabbed the door handle, tried it, and opened the door.

I was impressed, but a little worried about the breaking and entering. I hung back. "We're breaking into private property," I said. "It's illegal and unethical. What if we get caught?"

"Not likely," Gayle said. "Look how remote this place is. And it's clearly closed for the season. "But if anyone shows up, I'll say I was checking on a potential listing and the door was unlocked. They can't prove I picked the lock." She stepped in. I followed.

Paige grimaced, but came along behind us. "It makes me nervous, too," she said. "Let's get this search over with before someone does show up."

Chapter 34

The house was dim, cold and silent. It felt like a tomb to me, probably because I feared we might find a body there. Even with my warm coat on, I shivered as I inched my way along in the dusk. Two pairs of boots sitting side by side in the entryway tripped me up. I gasped, pointing at them. "Someone's here."

"Shh," Paige whispered. "They'll hear us."

Gayle reached past me and touched the boots. "They're completely dry," she said, "And there are no cars outside and no lights are on. Nobody's here but us. She walked ahead of us and switched on the lights, revealing a huge great room with vaulted ceilings and a stone fireplace. Beyond it I could see an open kitchen with a breakfast area.

Paige and I stood rooted to our spots in the entryway. Even with the lights on, the place felt creepy. And those lights shouldn't be on.

"Shut the lights off," I shrieked, lunging for the switch. "People might see lights on in here and come after us." I hit the switch and plunged us back into the late-afternoon gloomy grayness. I could still see a couch and tables in the main room, but the kitchen and halls going off to other rooms remained ominous shadows.

"What people are you worried about?" Gayle asked..

"People driving by. People who might be watching this house. People we don't want to find us."

"Okay, you have a point. We'll use the flashlight," Gayle said. She pulled a flashlight out of her bag and shone it around the room. "But it will take longer that way. We'll have to stay together and go through each room, one at a time."

My heart raced as the beam of Gayle's flashlight swept slowly around the room. Following it, we bumped our way along the walls of the great room, opening the doors of large cabinets, looking for anything suspicious. Then we moved into the center of the room. I knelt and reached under the couch, running my arms back and forth. I felt something soft and furry. "Eww. " I squealed, jerking my arm out. "I think it's a dead cat."

"Let's see," Gayle said, shining the light under the couch. "Looks more like a hat than a cat to me." She laughed.

I laughed along with her, then took a deep breath, stood up and followed her into the adjoining kitchen. I opened the refrigerator, which contained a couple of bottles of wine, some organic juice, salad dressing, pickles and such. Definitely looked like leftover summer supplies rather than someone living there now.

After the kitchen, we began making our way down a dark hall, presumably to bedrooms and bathrooms. All the doors leading off the hall were closed. Gayle handed me the flashlight and got her gun out of her bag before she slowly opened the first door. I shone the light in. Gayle stood next to me with the gun.

It was a bedroom and it had white walls. Paige lifted the bed covers so I could shine the light under the bed. Nothing. Suddenly we heard a loud thump from the closet. We flinched, grabbed each other and stood silently, pressed against a wall.

Gayle pointed her gun at the closet doors. "Come out slowly," she said. "I have a gun and I will use it."

We waited. No one came out. The closet was silent.

"Okay. Let's open it," Gayle said finally. "Shine the light right where the door opens, Cleo. Then Paige can go around to the side and open the door. I'll stand right here with my gun pointed at the opening."

I held my breath as Paige pulled the door open. A suitcase fell out. "Phew!" I said with relief. "It must have fallen off the shelf and that was what we heard."

We moved on down the hall to a large dark bathroom. The stabbing scene from *Psycho* flashed through my head. My body tightened, ready to attack or run. But I kept it together and shone the light around. Just an empty bathroom.

The next door we opened showed stairs going down into darkness. "Yuck, a basement," I hissed.. "We have to look down there."

I took a deep breath, pointed the flashlight into the darkness and put my foot on the first step. We crept slowly down the stairs, me first with the flashlight, then Gayle with the gun, then Paige. A moldy smell made my stomach lurch. As I flicked the light around, dust motes floated in its yellow beam. The unfinished basement was cluttered with bulky shapes.

At the bottom of the stairs I turned left towards the furnace, slowly running the light over stacks of boxes. They all looked old and dusty and none of them looked big enough to have a person inside.

Suddenly Paige screamed. I heard her and Gayle both fall to the hard concrete floor, and Gayle's gun scuttle across the floor.

"Something grabbed me," Paige shrieked. "Get it off of me. What is it?"

I turned and shone the light back on them revealing a tangle of snowshoes, one of which was caught on Paige's foot. Paige was frantically flapping her leg. She and Gayle pulled themselves free and rubbed their bruises as they struggled back up.

"I dropped my gun," Gayle said. "Shine the light around the floor so I can find it." I flicked the light around but the gun was nowhere to be seen.

"It sounded like it went this way," I said walking behind the furnace over to the right. They followed. We dropped to our hands and knees, unsuccessfully brushing our hands around for the gun.

I stood up so I could shine the light farther out into the room. I saw a washer and dryer, and—uh-oh—a chest freezer. I forgot the gun search as my mind flashed back to a long-ago episode of *Picket Fences*, a quirky David Kelley TV series, in which the local sheriff finds a body hidden in a suspect's home freezer. My gut told me to run right back up the stairs, but my brain said we had to look inside that freezer.

I stood rooted to the spot, dizzy and weak. I tried to tell Gayle and Paige what I was thinking, but, just like in a nightmare, I couldn't speak. In my mind's eye, I could see myself walking over, opening the freezer and looking in. But my body refused to participate.

Finally my voice returned. "Hey," I said. "Do you see that?" I shone the light at the freezer. I had walked a few steps closer to it, but still wasn't within touching distance. I stopped. "We have to open that freezer and look in," I said.

Apparently Gayle hadn't watched *Picket Fences*. She stood up, grabbed the flashlight out of my hand, went over and opened the freezer. She shone the light in and peered down at its contents. She drew in a sharp breath of surprise, jerked her head up, then looked down again. "Omigod, I see a foot. It looks like there's a person in here, wrapped in a sheet. Omigod, do you think it's Sabrina?" She cringed and covered her face with her hands, her bravado finally cracked.

Paige jumped up, ran over and joined Gayle at the side of the open freezer. She looked in, moaned and turned away, hugging herself. She looked stricken. "Come look at this, Cleo," she said. Her voice sounded weak and small.

"No," I mumbled, staying right where I was. My skin crawled at the thought of looking down into that freezer.

Gayle walked over and put her arm around my shoulders. "You have to look," she said, pulling me toward the freezer. I steeled my-self, looked in, and saw a pale green striped sheet wrapped around something long and lumpy with a bare foot poking out the far end. My stomach heaved.

"I think we have to unwrap the sheet," Gayle said.

"No," I said, backing away. "We don't have to unwrap it. We can call the police and let them do it."

"No," Paige said firmly. "Sabrina was our friend. "We have to see if it's her, and if it is we need to see her and say goodbye before the police turn this into a crime scene."

My heart raced. I had to somehow convince them not to unwrap that body. I knew Pablo would be telling us to call 911 immediately. "If we unwrap this body, we're messing up a crime scene," I said. "And anyway, didn't you already say goodbye to Sabrina in the apparition chamber?"

"Never mind." said a voice from the stairs. "I'll save you the trouble of unwrapping it. It is Sabrina."

The lights blazed on, illuminating the entire room. Gayle, Paige and I blinked in the glare as we turned in unison to face the staircase. Lark stood halfway down the steps pointing a gun at us. "We won't be needing the police," she said, her voice hard. "Put your phones on the floor. Right now."

Gayle and Paige looked dumbfounded. They seemed momentarily paralyzed. Of course they were blindsided. Now I regretted not having shared my suspicions of Lark with them. But she was their friend. Would they have believed me?

"Didn't you hear me?" Lark demanded. "I said phones on the floor."

I cringed as I pulled my phone out of my pocket, bent down and placed it on the floor. As I bent over I looked around the lighted floor for Gayle's gun, but no luck.

Gayle's phone rang as she pulled it out of her bag. Lark grimaced. "Don't answer that," she said. "Just put it down." Gayle complied.

Paige stared down at our phones. "My phone is upstairs in my coat," she said warily. "Do you want me to go get it?"

Lark waved the gun at her. "No. Just hand me those two phones on the floor."

Paige picked up the phones, walked slowly over to the stairs and put them in Lark's outstretched hand.

"Now step back where you were," Lark said to Paige.

I was shaking so hard I could barely stand still. Did Gayle and Paige have any idea how dangerous Lark could be? Did we have any chance of finding Gayle's gun to save ourselves?

Gayle frowned, narrowing her eyes. "Lark, what is going on?" she said, sticking out her hands, palms up. "I can't believe this. You've been keeping this secret all this time? Did you kill Sabrina and put her in the freezer? Please tell me you didn't."

Lark squared her shoulders and gave Gayle a sharp look. "No. I didn't kill her. She died accidentally. But I did put her body in the freezer."

Paige's breath was rasping in and out. "Why?" she gasped. "Why would you do that to Sabrina?"

"It's a long story," Lark said. "You don't need to know the details." She sounded like we were unruly children questioning her authority.

Paige leaned toward her, eyes wide. "We have time," she said gently, her voice under control again. "And we'd like to hear what happened."

Lark shook her head. "No," she said. "You need to tell me something—how did you know to come here?"

Gayle took a step toward Lark, staring her down. "Sabrina's spirit in the apparition chamber told me to come to this house," she said, in a matter-of-fact tone. "So we came. And this is what we found. How did you know we were here?" Either Gayle wasn't nearly as nervous as I was or she was great at appearing unbothered in the face of fear.

"Stop right there, Gayle," Lark said sharply, motioning with her gun. "To answer your question, I didn't know you were here. Darby and I are leaving for Mexico tonight and I came over here to take Sabrina's body out to a remote area where I could bury her in the snow. But then I saw your car outside. It's hard to miss your car, Gayle, with that SELL2U vanity plate you have."

Watching Gayle and Paige confront Lark revived my courage. Burning questions bubbled up as my fear began to dissolve. "Does this have anything to do with the hospital's investigation into deaths in the ICU?" I asked. Then, before she could answer, the rest of my questions poured out. "Was that what Sabrina meant in her thirty-day plan about you? Were you euthanizing patients in the ICU? Did she know about it and threaten to report you?"

Lark scowled. "I know that's what you think, Cleo," she said. "The hospital told me that someone made a complaint about me, someone said I push so hard for advance directives, that they were afraid I might interfere with an elderly patient's treatment. I knew it was you, Cleo. You've been watching me like a hawk while I've been giving your grandmother excellent care."

"You did that, Cleo?" Paige sounded surprised. "You complained to the hospital about Lark?"

"Yes," I said. "But I had good reason to be suspicious."

"Really?" Lark said. "Really? If I wanted to kill your grandmother, why wouldn't I have done it by now?" She glared at me. "And what about you, Cleo. Are you the perfect granddaughter? Do you know how your grandmother is doing right now? Is she still alive?"

"*What?* What do you mean?" I tried to hide my fear, but my voice cracked.

"You left her. She may have died while you were on your way up here."

I felt a wave of horror. "What are you saying, Lark? Do you know something? Did you do something to Gramma? Give me my phone." I stepped toward her, hand outstretched.

Lark pointed her gun at my chest. She looked like she meant business. "Back up, Cleo," she barked.

"No. I need to call the hospital and check on her."

Lark raised her gun and shot into the wall behind us. Paige screamed as the blast echoed around the concrete room.

"Back up, Cleo or I'll shoot you next. Don't test me."

I stepped back. I could risk my life for Gramma, but I couldn't risk my baby's life.

Paige was crying now, hugging her arms around herself. "What has happened to you, Lark?" she sobbed. "Is Cleo right about you killing patients in the ICU?"

Lark stared silently, standing straight and strong, her eyes boring into us. Her brow was furrowed, her lips were tight, her chin jutted out. Finally she spoke. "You make it sound so evil and dirty," she said. "But it wasn't like that at all."

She stopped again, looking past us this time. Her face took on a superior glow. "I'm going to tell you the truth because I stand for principle over the law. And so did Sabrina. Sabrina and I had a cause—a cause we cared about as much as Hana and Diana care about their website that punishes abusive men. Sabrina and I were Angels of Mercy."

"Angels of Mercy? What's that?" Gayle asked skeptically. "That doesn't sound like Sabrina. She never said anything to me about it."

"She didn't tell you everything, Gayle." Lark smirked. "She knew you wouldn't understand. You haven't seen what we've seen. Sabrina and I have been ICU nurses for a long time. We've been caring nurses, but we knew it was time for our society to face the truth, to make choices, to set priorities. You know Sabrina believed in directing energy toward making things happen rather than letting things happen. We knew it was wrong to continue to waste resources on elderly patients with dementia who don't even know the difference." She gave me a knowing look.

I matched her glare for glare. "So you and Sabrina took it on yourselves to play God and decide who should live and who should die?" I asked.

"We had to do it," she said. "Doctors know who is ready to die, but family members like you are whiners who force them to go against what they know is right." She sounded like a politician giving a speech.

She continued her rant, eyes glazed, head nodding in rhythm with her words. "All the people Sabrina and I helped to pass on were demented and old and frail. They had no quality of life and they all had life-threatening illnesses that were being treated with antibiotics just so they could live on and get sick again. They were in the ICU and they were suffering. All we did was put some potassium chloride in their IVs to stop their hearts. It's painless. We did them a favor, putting them out of their misery. We liberated their souls."

My heart raced. If we didn't stop Lark, Gramma would be her next victim. Unless the hospital stops her. "Has the hospital figured it out?" I asked. "Is that what you were arguing about with that woman today?"

Lark shrugged. "They don't have any proof. They're just investigating. Potassium chloride leaves no chemical trace. Lots of people die in the ICU. Without actual cases to look at, to connect to times I was on duty, they're mostly guessing. It will take a long investigation before they can make a case."

Paige's eyes were wide. "But why did you kill Sabrina?" she asked in a shaky voice. "If she was doing it with you?"

"I told you, I didn't kill her," Lark said sharply. "It was an accident. And it was her fault. When that Allie started nosing around after her mother died, Sabrina got nervous. She decided we had to give up our cause and get out of nursing. I refused. I was willing to let her go off and do whatever she wanted to do for herself, but she wasn't willing to let me stay and keep on doing what I wanted to do. She said I had to leave nursing too or she'd report me. And she had the details of the cases, so she could give them all the incriminating information they needed."

"But wouldn't she be implicating herself also if she reported you?" I asked.

"No," Lark said. "She said she would report me and then if I tried to implicate her, they'd think I was lying to save myself."

Gayle was scowling. "You say Sabrina died in an accident," she broke in impatiently. "An accident? That's what Sabrina said too in the apparition chamber. How did the accident happen?"

"Fine. I'll tell you," Lark said. " Here's what happened. Sabrina and I had adjacent routes for the wilderness journey. Remember, Paige, you asked me to plan the routes since I know the area so well?"

Paige nodded.

Lark continued. "When I planned the routes, I set up hers and mine to be together. Ours were also the closest to the trailhead and the farthest from the main wilderness area where the other four of you would be going. That way you'd be unlikely to hear us or see us. I waited when Sabrina started off and then instead of going on my route, I went behind her on hers. I crept up behind her with a hypodermic needle with a sedative and plunged it into her neck."

I took a sharp breath and clutched my neck. "That doesn't sound like an accident," I said.

"That part wasn't an accident," Lark said. "But the sedative I gave her wasn't life-threatening."

"So what happened? How did she end up dead?" Gayle asked.

"I took her to my car—used a fireman's carry to throw her over my shoulder and get her to the trailhead," Lark said. "If anyone had seen us, I would have said she fell and hit her head and I was taking her to the hospital. But no one did. I take care of this house in the winter for the Busbees. They only live in it in the summer. I brought Sabrina here and I tied her to a chair so she couldn't get away. The house is isolated and no one besides me ever comes here in the winter, so I could keep her here without anyone finding her."

"But why? Why did you want to keep Sabrina here?" Paige asked.

"I needed to reason with her, but she refused to listen to me. I had to keep her where I could talk some sense into her. I couldn't afford to leave nursing and I needed to get her to see what would happen if she reported me to the hospital or the board of nursing. It would ruin my career, I might go to prison and I'd probably lose Darby. That would ruin his life, too. And for what? Because I had the courage to help some frail old people escape their suffering? The Victorians used to call death a blessed release for the weary, but now we try to avoid it no matter what."

A sudden coldness hit me. Lark was so committed to her crusade that she'd stop at nothing. "So when Sabrina didn't accept your reasoning, you killed her?" I asked.

Lark stamped her foot. Her eyes blazed with anger. "Aren't you listening to me?" she said, her voice shrill with impatience. "I told you I didn't kill Sabrina. She died accidentally. After I got her to the house, I had to get back to Indian Lakes so I could show up in the morning with the other Moxie members. I left her sedated and tied to a chair. Her arms were tied together behind her back and behind the back of the chair. Her legs were tied to the chair legs in front."

"Was she in a white room?" Paige asked.

Lark stopped, a confused look on her face. "A white room?" She thought for a minute. "Yes. It's the small bedroom upstairs and it is mostly white. Why?"

"Sabrina told us she was in a white room. Is that where she died?"

Lark rolled her eyes. "Yes. Apparently she woke up and was trying to escape and turned the chair over and hit her head on the edge of the bed frame. I got back here late the next day because I had to be with all of you pretending to look for her. She was lying in a pool of blood, no pulse, no respiration. She accidentally killed herself. I was sad for her, but it wasn't my fault. All I did was tie her up."

"Why didn't you tell the police then?" Gayle asked.

Lark's expression hardened. "I knew it would look very bad for me. I couldn't tell anyone. What I had to do was get rid of the body, but I needed time for the search to end so I could put her where she wouldn't be found. So I wrapped her in a sheet and put her in the freezer. The people who own this house won't be back until at least May, so there was no chance anyone would find her before then."

"So now you and Darby are running away to Mexico? Can you leave town in the middle of this hospital investigation?" I asked.

"Watch me."

"Lark, think about it," Paige said, leaning toward her a little bit. "Wouldn't it be better to stay and face the charges? If you run, leave the country, you'll never be able to come back. You won't be able to see your parents and your brothers. Darby will be cut off from his grandparents and uncles and aunts and cousins. Is that really the life you want for him?"

"If I stay here and tell the police what happened, I'll probably go to jail, and lose Darby," Lark said, her voice flat. "That would be a lot worse for him."

Paige took a deep breath and released it slowly with a deep sigh. "But like you say, Sabrina's death was an accident and the hospital has no proof of the euthanasia. You'd be guilty of something, but not murder. Maybe you could get a plea agreement and get a light sentence."

Lark made a sour face. "No thanks. I'm getting out of here while I can. But now I have the problem of all of you. You may not believe this, but I don't believe in killing unless the person is ready to go like the people I help in the hospital. I don't want to kill you. But I can't have you calling the police and telling them about Sabrina."

"How about we promise not to say anything until after you've been gone for a week?" Paige asked, running her hands through her hair. "That should give you enough time to disappear."

"Why would I trust you not to tell anyone?"

"We believe you about the accident because Sabina said it was an accident. And you know we care about you and Darby." Paige said.

Lark shook her head. "Sorry, I can't take that chance. What I'm going to do is tie you all up here and go home and get my nursing bag. When I get back, you'll all help me carry Sabrina to a remote wilderness area. Then I'll sedate all of you with a long-lasting benzodiazepine drug that should keep you under for twenty-four hours."

Omigod, sedation! What would that do to my baby? My pulse raced. First she wanted to hurt Gramma, now my baby. I had to stop her.

But before I could plead for my baby's life, Lark continued with an even bleaker picture of our future. "Once you're sedated, I'll leave you there in the wilderness. Whatever happens, happens. I'm not killing you. If you wake up and find your way out and live, then you're lucky. If not, no one will be likely to find you until summer. I'll drive Gayle's car back down to Boulder and leave it somewhere in town, so no one will know you were here."

"No!" I shouted. "If you do that, you will be killing us. What are you thinking? You're a nurse. You're supposed to save lives, not end them."

Lark repositioned her gun, pointing it right at me. "Enough, Cleo," she said. "I'm giving you the best chance I can."

I could tell from the set of her jaw that she was firm in her plan. Persuasion was a useless strategy at that point. We'd have to overpower her somehow. I thought about Gayle's gun. Where was it? How could we find it? We needed to be able to move around the room. "Lark, before you tie us up, could we stand around the freezer and say a few words of goodbye to Sabrina?" I asked. "I know I never met her, but I feel like I know her. And she was a good friend to you three for a long time."

"You can say your words from right where you are."

"But if we could unwrap her body and look at her face, it would feel more personal." Gayle said.

We heard a loud banging on the door upstairs.

"Be still," Lark said. "Don't say anything and don't make a sound."

"Gayle!" someone shouted. "I see your car here. "Now open up or we'll break in."

"Stay right here all of you. I'll shoot the first one who comes up after me." Lark went upstairs and locked the basement door behind her.

"Gayle, let's look for your gun?" I said in a stage whisper.

We all dropped to our hands and knees and crawled around the floor looking for the missing gun. "Hurry, we have to find it before she comes back down," I said, my voice hushed.

But Lark didn't come back down.

We heard a lot of shouting and banging coming from upstairs. "What the hell are you doing with that gun, Lark?"

"Get out of here," Lark yelled. "Or I'll shoot you both."

"You're not going to shoot anyone." A loud crash. Then a scream that sounded like Lark.

We jumped up and ran to the stairs. "That voice sounds like Diana," Gayle said. "What would she be doing here? Is she involved in this whole thing with Lark?"

Paige reached over to Gayle and put her hands on Gayle's arms. "No, no, Gayle," she said. "I called Diana and Hana before we left and told them about you seeing Sabrina in the chamber, and what she said to you, and where we were going. I know you didn't want to involve them, but it didn't seem right to exclude them."

Gayle grabbed Paige in a huge hug. "You did the right thing," she said. "Thanks for following your gut. You pretty much saved our lives."

More loud crashes from upstairs.

"I've got her down. Grab her gun," we heard Diana shout. "I'll sit on her until she settles down, or I'll knock her out if I have to. Now open the basement door and see what's happening down there."

The lock turned, the door opened, and Hana stepped down a few steps. "Gayle? Paige? Are you down here?"

Chapter 35

Ten days later - December 22

News about Sabrina had gradually dribbled out over the last ten days. First the discovery of her body, then the news of Lark's arrest, then a profile of Ian—champion snowboarder, Olympic hopeful and grieving son. Boulderites were shocked, saddened, and curious.

Elisa and I had arrived late enough to her memorial service that we had to look for parking, so we ended up seated at the back of the packed church. The service was called a "celebration of life," and I tried to think of it that way, but it was hard. Sabrina was too young, she had too much in front of her, and she left too much behind. I grieved for her and for Ian that she would never watch him graduate from high school or college, or see him compete in the Olympics if he achieved that dream.

Looking around, I saw Moxie, or what was left of it—Gayle, Paige, Hana and Diana sitting together near the front with several teenage kids. Ian was in the front row between Maria and Brandi. He hunched his shoulders, hung his head, and slumped towards Maria. She periodically rubbed his back. I was sure he was devastated now that he had finally had to face the fact that his mother was gone.

Brandi, however, looked calm and composed—at least from what I could see from behind. Despite all her rants about how precious Sabrina was to her, she showed no outward signs of distress. A hot-looking guy with big shoulder muscles and wavy dark hair sat on her left, his arm around her shoulders. She snuggled in to him.

While we waited for the ceremony to start, recent events played through my mind like a video on a continuous loop. The painful: Lark holding a gun on us; Sabrina in the freezer; police questioning us for hours. The joyful: Gramma improving so much she was able to go back to Glenwood Gardens where Pablo and I visited her yesterday.

A white-haired minister began the ceremony recalling that he had known Sabrina and her family since she was a young child. "She always opened her arms to the world," he said, "lovingly welcoming everyone she met. She gave much and asked for little in return. Her kind and generous nature led her to a career as a nurse, where she was loved and respected." He went on, describing Sabrina as a devoted mother, a loyal friend, and a joyful human being. He ended his eulogy with a short poem:

"A butterfly lights beside us like a sunbeam and for a brief moment its glory and beauty belong to the world. But then it flies on again and though we wish it could have stayed, we feel so lucky to have seen it."

A vocalist, with piano and flute accompaniment, sang "My Heart Will Go On." I was deeply touched by the poem, the music, and the strong feeling of love in the room. Even though I had never met Sabrina, I felt her loss in my heart.

Moxie members and many of Sabrina's other friends and co-workers shared fond memories, including humorous stories—many about her famous computer fiascos. But mostly they spoke about how much she meant to them. A young nurse from the hospital told about Sabrina going above and beyond the call of duty, coming in early and staying late to help her when she was new to the job. A physician complimented Sabrina's amazing rapport with patients, such that he and other doctors called her the hospital's chief empathizer.

Gayle spoke tearfully about how much Sabrina's friendship meant to her, how they had become like sisters over the years, and how she can still sometimes feel Sabrina hugging her. Paige gave thanks for Sabrina's love, which would always be part of her life. Diana said Sabrina lived life to the fullest and was always cheerful and enthusiastic. Hana talked about how much Sabrina treasured and cared for the people she loved.

Then Brandi stepped up to the front. "It warms my heart to hear how much you all loved and appreciated Sabrina," she said slowly.

"But someone has to talk about the elephant in the room." She leaned forward pointing at all of us. "You haven't heard the whole story."

My heart sank. Omigod. What whole story? I didn't think she knew about Lark's accusations that Sabrina was involved in euthanizing patients. But whatever dirt she was going to dish, this was no place for it.

She continued, bitterness and fury in her voice. "My sister was the victim of a vicious group of women who used her to further their malicious agendas." She paused and looked around, taking in the gasps and shocked faces.

"Yes, you heard me correctly," she said, her chin lifted and jutting forward. "And what I'm saying is the truth, not some bereaved sister craziness." Her voice was loud, shrill and spiteful. "They may think of themselves as her sisters, but I'm her only sister. Sabrina trusted these women with her life and they took it from her. And now they're going to profit from her death. This is wrong. They should all be held accountable."

"No! Stop, Aunt Brandi." Ian sprang to his feet, ran up and grabbed Brandi's shoulders. "Stop! You know Mom wouldn't want this. They were her friends."

Brandi pulled herself free and faced Ian. "You're too young to understand. You don't know what they're capable of. Everything they say is a lie."

Ian stood his ground. "No. You're the one who lies. You're the one who told me Mom had gone off with some man. I should have been looking for her, but I believed your lies." Ian buried his face in his hands. Sobs wracked his body.

"No, Ian…" Brandi began, but piano music drowned out her words as the pianist began playing "I Will Remember You." The music continued as the minister grabbed Brandi's arm and pulled her off to a side room. Ian and Maria followed slowly behind them. The rest of us emerged from our daze and stood up to begin filing out.

As we edged toward the front door, Elisa said, "I need to check on Maria before we go. Do you want to come with or wait?"

"I'll wait here," I said. "I don't want to get into it with Brandi one more time." I stepped to the side of the vestibule as Elisa headed off to the front of the room.

"How are you holding up, Cleo?" No mistaking that musical voice. Paige was standing next to me, her eyes red and puffy.

"I'm okay," I said. "But how about you after what Brandi just said?"

Paige shrugged. "It doesn't matter," she said. "Brandi is spiteful and destructive, but there's nothing left of Moxie for her to destroy. Moxie is finished. Sabrina is gone, Lark is in jail, and Diana and Hana refuse to take down their revengeful website. Gayle and I don't even want to try to resurrect Moxie."

I felt terrible for her. So much loss. "It's a shame that it ended this way," I said. "You all had so much together all those years."

"We did," Paige said quietly, looking inward. "And now we don't. Things change. People change. Life goes on."

"We did have one last Moxie meeting, though," she said. "The four of us talked a long time about Lark's accusations of Sabrina. What Lark said about Sabrina that day at Busbee's house was shocking. But bottom line, we don't believe her. We don't think Sabrina would have violated her nursing oath, or that she would do anything to help old people like your grandmother die before their time. Sabrina was a helper, a caregiver who would do anything for someone in trouble."

"So you think Lark lied about her and Sabrina having a cause, being angels of mercy?"

"Yes. We can imagine Lark having that cause, but not Sabrina. As Hana says, Sabrina's destiny number is six. Sixes are responsible nurturers who like to give help and comfort to those in need. Lark's number is one. Ones are independent, individualistic and determined, and can be overly aggressive and egotistic."

"Do you think Lark killed Sabrina because Sabrina found out what she was doing and threatened to report her?"

"We do. But we'll leave it to the police to find out the truth. Our concern is for Ian and for Sabrina's reputation. We decided not to tell Ian, or anyone, what Lark said As far as we know, there's no way anyone but us would have heard about it. We were the only ones Lark told and she's been in jail ever since."

"But we told the police what Lark said. They may have told Ian."

"I doubt it. None of us believed her then and we told the police that too. We told them Lark was saying that about Sabrina to make herself look better."

I thought to myself that these Moxie women may have their problems, but they're all good mothers and they care about Ian. "I agree," I said. "Why make it worse for him."

"Thank you," she said. Then she put her hand on my shoulder and looked deeply into my eyes. "I also want to thank you for all you did to help us find Sabrina, Cleo. And especially for the contact I had with her spirit in your apparition chamber. That will always be with me. Come to my studio some time. I'd love to give you some free yoga classes."

"Thanks," I said. "I just might do that."

After she walked off, I mulled over Moxie's strengths and weaknesses. All strong women who cared deeply about others, but some of whom went too far trying to remake the world to fit their image. I admired and wanted to emulate their strength and support, but also wanted to take a lesson to act consciously, thinking carefully about the consequences of my behavior.

An arm around my shoulders interrupted my reverie. Elisa.

"You ready to get out of here?" she asked, tugging at me.

"Absolutely," I said. "How's Maria?"

"She's okay. I'll tell you in the car. Come on."

We headed out into the cold. The sidewalks were icy where snow had melted and refrozen, so we picked our way carefully over to the parking lot. It wasn't the best place for a serious conversation, so I kept my curiosity in check until we were in the car pulling out of the lot. Then I asked again. "Tell me about Maria."

"She's doing a great job of supporting Ian and helping him let go of his anger toward Brandi." Elisa said. "And—get this—he's not just angry at what Brandi did today. There's more. That hunk sitting next to Brandi is her new boyfriend. He's an Elvis tribute artist."

"He's what?"

"You know—he does Elvis improvisations. Puts on shows. Anyway

Brandi is moving to Las Vegas with him. She's planning to get a gig as an exotic dancer." Elisa laughed.

"You mean one of those girls who dances topless and gives lap dances?"

"That's it. Ian hates the new boyfriend, hates that Brandi is moving to Vegas, and really hates the exotic dancer plan. Even worse, he feels like she was using him and now that she can't use Sabrina's money anymore, she's dumping him."

"Phew. That's intense on top of grieving his mother's death. Maria has a huge challenge helping him deal with all that. Please tell her I'm there for her if she needs any help."

"I will. But fortunately Ian isn't just leaning on Maria. Gayle and her daughter Nicole were back there too. Gayle was really there for Ian and Nicole was talking about sadness in a way that seemed to be reaching him. Apparently he's staying with them now."

Elisa pulled up in front of my office to let me out. "You need to get some rest and enjoy the holidays, Cleo," she said. "Build up your energy for our New Year's Eve party."

"Rest, relaxation, and holiday parties," I said. "Sounds perfect."

§ § §

Two days later - Dec 24

I've always loved the night before Christmas. Anticipation hangs in the air as the frenzy of holiday preparation recedes and the celebration begins.

Pablo and I were curled up on my couch, with a fire crackling, Christmas carols playing in the background, and pine-scented candles burning on the coffee table. Lights twinkled on my Christmas tree decorated with Gramma's antique ornament collection. My gift to Pablo, a top-of-the-line digital camera, sat under the tree wrapped in glittery paper.

We'd visited Gramma that afternoon for a special Christmas Eve lunch at Glenwood Gardens. Tomorrow we'd be at his parents' house for Christmas dinner with his sister and brothers, nieces and nephews. Tonight was our special time.

After a romantic candlelight dinner of shrimp scampi and Caesar salad, we moved over to the couch, where we snuggled and fed each other bites of a decadent black forest cake. I felt soft, warm and cozy. But I sensed some impatience or excitement in Pablo. Maybe he was eager to open his gift.

I was ready to move on to the gifts. I'd spent a lot of time researching and picking out the very best camera for Pablo and I couldn't wait to see how he liked it. "Are you ready to open your present?" I asked, pulling my arm free to point at the box under the tree.

He unwrapped himself from my arms and turned to face me, taking my hands in his. "I want to give you my gift first," he said with a huge grin. I can't stand to wait another minute."

"Great," I said, looking around the room. "Where is it?"

"You'll see in a minute," he said. "But I have to tell you about it first." He looked lovingly into my eyes and spoke softly. "The Boulder Police Department had a couple of openings. I applied and they've offered me a job, starting next month. It will mean I can live in Boulder." He reached into his pocket and pulled out a tiny box, which he popped open. A gold ring with a huge sparkly diamond in the center. "Cleo, I can't imagine the rest of my life without you by my side. Will you please marry me? I want to live here with you in your grandparents' house and raise our baby together."

My heart overflowed with love for him. He cared enough to take a big risk, changing jobs so we could live where I wanted to live. He trusted that we could build a happy life together here with our baby. Could I match his trust with my own? Could I put aside my fear that he would not always be there for me? Did I want to take the chance?

Suddenly it felt right. Us together for the rest of our lives. Us raising our baby here in my grandparents' house. Us helping and supporting each other through life's ups and downs. Us loving each other for years and years and years.

"Oh, Pablo," I said. "It means the world to me that you would move to Boulder so that we can be together. I love you so much, and yes, I want to marry you."

As he slipped the ring on my finger, we fell back onto the couch in a hungry kiss. My head spun into a dreamy place where visions of our fabulous future floated before my eyes. At the same time, my ears tuned in to a distant voice, "Yo, Cleo. Awesome re-entry. Surfing those big waves. Outrageous!"

Acknowledgements

Again I acknowledge Raymond Moody, M.D.'s *Reunions* (Villard Books, 1993), which was the inspiration for Cleo's Contact Project. Also, *Afterlife Encounters* by Dianne Arcangel (Hampton Roads Publishing, 2005), and *Without Conscience* by Robert D. Hare, Ph.D. (The Guilford Press, 1999) were helpful references as I wrote this book.

Many thanks to those who read and edited drafts of this book, especially Marian, Janet and Andrea from my Boulder Media Women's critique group.

As always my husband, Allan, and my daughter, Laurel, were my go-to readers who went through draft after draft, giving me useful notes and unwavering support. I couldn't have done it without them.

About the author

Lynn Osterkamp, Ph.D., MSW, is the author of three mystery novels, Too Near the Edge, Too Far Under; and Too Many Secrets; as well as two nonfiction books, numerous articles, manuals and national newsletters. Her professional experience includes hospital and hospice social work, university teaching and research, special education, and long-term-care ombudsman. She lives in Boulder Colorado, where she works for Boulder County Aging Services.

For information about Lynn Osterkamp's other books, visit her website at:

www.lynnosterkamp.com

PMI Books
Boulder, CO
www.pmibooks.com